Fourth Reich: Phoenix Rising

Sara LeMay

A Mad Tiger Ink Publication

Fourth Reich: Phoenix Rising is a work of fiction. Names, characters, places, and incidents are the products of the author's imagination or used fictitiously.

A Mad Tiger Ink Publication

Copyright © 2018 Rachael Wilson

Illustrator: gb wilson SDG

www.madtigerink.com

Dedication

For my mother-

Your unwavering devotion to me and this book made it possible for my dream to come to life. Thanks for being my biggest fan and best friend. Let va en France. Tonitrus equurn forever.

Acknowledgments

A big thank you to those who believed in my dream. First, my husband who brought my company to life and is always there to rescue me. Thank you for your support in my dream.

To Amelia Lackey, Nard, C.L. Roman, Huyen Le, and Barbara Eubanks, thank you for your dedication to my book. Without you, this would not have been possible.

For my friend who wears the necklace, thank you. I will always be inspired by your "Spirit" and "Determination." I know you are forever pointing the way forward for me.

For a Phoenix to rise from the ashes, it must first feel the flames of destruction.

Prologue

Berlin, Germany
Experimental Hospital A
May 29, 1940

"I can do this. I can do this." She mumbled to herself as the glare of the overhead florescent lights and the heavy smell of antiseptic cleaner added to her anxiety as she sat on the small bed in the all-white room. Edda could hear the bustle of the nurses and the doctor as they prepared for her procedure. Her heart beat thumped hard against her chest. The best doctor in Germany repeatedly told her this operation was safe and had been completed on over a hundred women with success. She would be a hero for Italy and Germany and she would finally make her father, Benito Mussolini, proud.

A group of doctors and nurses with her father and a priest entered the space. Edda took a big gulp of air and tried to appear composed. The priest stepped forward and gave a blessing and a prayer for a successful outcome. As if on cue, the occupants left and were replaced with men in brown Nazi uniforms with the red, black, and white arm patch. These were high ranking Nazi officers. They were here to be with the Fuhrer on this momentous day and to ensure the operation was completed as scheduled.

Edda's breath caught when she realized that Adolf Hitler had entered her room. He motioned for everyone to leave except her father. He placed a bouquet of red daisies on the table beside her bed. Taking her hand, he kissed it gently and said, "Today, you will give the world the greatest gift ever. I will be in your debt and you will always have a home in Germany with me. You are now the mother to our people."

Not knowing how to respond, she whispered, "Thank you."

Kissing her hand again and leaning over kissing her head, he left the area. Edda didn't realize it till he was gone, but she was shaking. She glanced over at her father and could see the look of pride in his eyes. His look of joy is why she had agreed, she wanted her father's love.

Her father then took her hand and said, "Make me proud today. Do this for Italy and the Mussolini name."

Her throat constricted and she was barely able to squeak out, "I will Father." He kissed her cheek and left the room. The nurses and doctors flooded back around her. They put her on a gurney and rolled her into a stark white, freezing room filled with terrifying medical equipment. Turning her head, she could see one wall had been made of windows so the operations in the room could be watched by others. Edda had heard of the horrible experiments conducted here and the tortured deaths of the victims. Praying silently to God to save her, she looked over and could see her father behind the glass. He gave her a nod of encouragement.

The nurses in masks helped her onto the surgical table. They placed her legs in cold metal rests that stuck out from the bed exposing her lower half. The bright lights above made her eyes squint. Closing her eyes to block out the terrifying images, she could feel the hospital gown being lifted and now she was exposed from the waist down. They had prepped her for this moment, this was expected. The nurses were murmuring how brave she was and how she was helping Hitler and Germany. As they talked, they lowered her back and gave her reassurances.

The doctors came over and spoke to her briefly then moved down to work between her legs. She tried to close her legs to stop them, but the nurses held her open. They started shoving instruments inside of her without tenderness or caution. The pain was intense and she started to scream as the instruments tore into her body. The nurse closest to her put her hand over Edda's mouth to muffle the sound. They didn't stop when she cried and begged, they just held her down and continued their probing and cutting.

Her life blood was freely pouring out of her body and down her legs. The blood was dripping on the floor making a sound as it splashed against the white tile floor. The metallic smell was only adding to the sick feeling building inside of Edda. It was too much, they were killing her slowly. She began to pass in and out of consciousness due to the pain and blood loss. The surgeons continued with the procedure without care for her well-being. Finally, she heard one doctor say they had an embryo. The instruments were pulled from her body roughly and she felt the sting of a needle in her arm. The medicine stung as it entered but she immediately felt the effects. The pain medicine circulated her body and she closed her eyes and mercifully passed out.

The doctors worked on the embryo. Celebrations were held throughout the room as the procedure closed. The specimen was stored in a freezer to keep it safe.

The doctors stopped working on her when the room filled with German soldiers. A pathway was made and Hitler stepped into the room. He walked over and kissed Edda's head to show respect. He then bent down and bowed to her. Everyone in the room bowed also. Hitler rose and walked over to the freezer. The doctors walked over and explained the process. Stepping back, Hitler gave the Nazi salute to the freezer. Everyone repeated the salute and shouted, "Heil Hitler." Hitler seemed satisfied and left the room with a smile on his face. He knew a child would mean he would live on. This child would be the next uprising for Germany. This was his goal, a future for Germany.

Germany

May 1, 1945

The Village of Oberammergau

Morning broke to a new day in war torn Germany. "We must go now. My contact has guaranteed they will not shoot on sight. I have traded everything we own to get us a truck to take us. We go now or we stay here and die." The voice was strained as it came from a dirty, dark-haired man in his early forties. The war had aged him. Gone was the brilliant scientist with the world eating out of his palm. Here stood a shell of a great man. Malnourishment and lack of clean water only added to the desperate scene. The only choice now was between starvation and death if they didn't leave today.

The war had broken Germany. The government had turned on their own people and death was guaranteed. This was their only chance to live. In the smoke filled dimly lit room, a group of men were talking in rapid fire German. This small house was now their refuge. The murmur of voices was electric in the small room as the men gathered in a circle trying to hatch plan to escape. The excitement and tension was palpable and was reaching a fevered pitch. This group of Germans knew that the Americans were close now and Hitler was dead. His death meant they had a chance to be safe and to live. Now was the time to make their move to get to the Americans and beg for their lives.

In this dark room was a group of scientists who had arrest warrants for crimes against Germany. They were led by a fiercely loyal Nazi who was the front runner in the development of rockets and weapons. His team of scientists had developed the advanced weapons and rocketry that had propelled Germany into a great war machine. In his heyday for the Nazi party, he was considered a god among men. As the war continued the tides had turned. The German empire turned against him when he was unable to stop the Americans with his weapons, and they realized that Germany would fall. They blamed him and his team for their failure.

Now, he was forced into isolation with his team in this village in a cramped house to stay alive. The threat of capture was constant as the Germans were killing anyone who was an enemy of the state. He wanted to get his team to America so they would be safe and they could use American resources to build their rockets. Building rockets and science was all he had left in his life. He was going to put a man on the moon, so the United States was the only option for him and his team.

The leader decided it was time to find the Americans. It was a risky plan, but so was staying here in this small village. He and his team loaded up three trucks and left the village to seek asylum in the United States. If the team was spotted by the German military, he would be shot and killed, but he had to reach the Americans. This was life or death for him and his men. The leader checked his bag and held it tight against his body because inside was his ticket to freedom. It was all he had left of his motherland. The road was bumpy and the landscape was sparse. The war had taken its toll on Germany. The leader watched the road anxiously as he feared an attack at any moment. The threat was constant in this area with the military still patrolling. Nothing was safe, especially not him or his team.

Hours later, after traversing over harsh terrain, rattled by the threat of bombs and bullets, the leader and his team entered the American encampment. Relief poured over the leader as he saw the American forces. The enemy had become his friend. A sense of relief was strong in the truck full of scientists. Some smiles crossed the faces of his men. As they neared the camp, they were met by First Lieutenant Charles Stawart, who curtly greeted them and asked, "What business do you have with the United States?"

It was the secret in the bag that the leader of the group had filled him with courage and a new sense of purpose. It was time to let the contents of the bag and the secrets it carried save him and his team. The only thing stopping him from freedom and building his beautiful rockets was this American soldier. The leader answered with a newfound determination.

"We are here to seek asylum and to go to America and work on your rockets." The leader squeezed the bag tightly. Hope was all he had.

First Lieutenant Stawart laughed out loud when the German spoke. He said in a snarky tone as looked at the ragged group, "Sure pal, and I am going to be a brain surgeon. We don't need a Nazi working on rockets. If you haven't noticed, we are over here fighting a war against you. Take your men and leave." Stawart started walking away.

The leader, in an act of desperation, walked over and grabbed First Lieutenant Stawart, halting him in his steps. He opened his bag so that Stawart could see inside. The bag held a simple metal canister. The leader whispered in his ear, "I have something you want. This is an experiment by the Na…"

Lieutenant Charles Stawart raised his eyebrows and then pointed to one of the American soldiers, "Get me headquarters now!" He waved the trucks through the gates of the camp. The leader held tightly to his bag. The contents were doing their job. It was then the leader smiled an evil smile. All was not lost. His team would be great rocket scientists and would have a chance at a new life. Where the Third Reich had failed, the Fourth Reich would be a Phoenix rising from the ashes.

Chapter 1

Red Bay, Alabama
Present Day

The early spring storms of the morning set the background for a devastating moment for one unlucky soul. For her, it was the moment in life when everything slows down and you know, down deep in your soul, the life you knew was over. Everything you knew was going to be corrupted. Nothing, not even time itself, would be the same. Looking back, you will always remember it- that moment. That singular moment, everything reshapes itself and a new life begins and sometimes not for the better. That moment for Fallon Whitten happened in her math class.

Mr. Jeffers, her boring teacher, was prattling on about algebraic equations. "You must follow the steps on the board to finish the problem." His voice was irritating and was grinding on her nerves. She wasn't listening to some stupid math problem. Fallon was thinking about her family. Not so long ago, she had a complete family who cared about her. In the memories, everything was right. There was no horror, no loss, just love and family. Outside of the dreams of the past, the feeling of loss and pain were constant. She could lose herself in the happy memories of her family together.

Tragedy was her new best friend. In the past few months, Fallon had lost both of her parents in two separate car crashes. First, her father, three months ago, then her mother, last month. All that was left was Fallon and her sister Eva. Although they were sisters, they looked nothing alike. Fallon was short with dark hair, brown eyes and pale porcelain skin. Eva was a tall blonde, with big blue eyes. Together the sisters were striking, forming a picture of complete opposites, yet one incomplete without the other.

Eva Whitten had her Ph.D. in American History, with an emphasis in the Civil War. Really, she was a freak of nature, one of those people who could read a page and recite word-by-word all its content. Eva was off working on a post doctorate fellowship for the National Park Service who allowed her to touch all the cool artifacts, so she was in heaven.

Fallon had stayed at home in Alabama with her friend Rebecca and her parents after her parent's death. It had been weird moving into Rebecca's house with her Jewish family, but Fallon felt welcomed and cared for there. It was the only option available for Eva to complete her work and for Fallon to complete high school.

Fallon and Eva had planned to live together after Fallon got out of high school. Fallon was going to go to an Ivy League college and Eva was going to work for the government. They wouldn't have to worry about money as their parents had left them a small fortune. Everything was set to go, the future before them was perfect; all that was left was a piece of paper and a small graduation ceremony for Fallon.

Without Eva, Fallon was truly alone in the world with nothing. She was constantly worrying Eva would leave her also. There was no one else left of her family. The sisters were orphans. All of grandparents were dead and she didn't have any aunts or uncles. It was just Eva and Fallon together facing the world.

Fallon snapped out of her memories when Mr. Entrekin, the principal, walked into the math classroom followed by the Guidance Counselor, Mrs. Brinson. The talking in the room subsided, and the class watched as the principal walked to the front of the room. He went over and whispered to Mr. Jeffers. Mr. Jeffers quieted and then the room fell completely silent.

Something was not right.

Class was never disrupted at her school. The silence was deafening. They both turned and looked at Fallon. The realization they were looking in her direction made Fallon sick. Her stomach cramped and she felt like she was going to vomit all over the floor. She knew that look of sympathy. The reality of losing her parents had taught her to sense when things were bad. Mr. Entrekin frowned and walked over and stopped in front of Fallon's desk. Fallon was silently praying that they were not there for her. "Ms. Whitten, please come with me."

Forcing herself to move, Fallon looked up at him and said, "Am I in trouble"? Fallon saw the look in his eyes; it was pity.

He shook his head and motioned for the counselor to come over. Mrs. Brinson, looked down and said gently, "Come with us, we need to talk. Grab your things."

Fallon got her backpack and followed them out of the room. Her legs felt like they weighed 1000 pounds each. She could barely move and was envisioning the worst-case scenario. Was it Eva? That was the longest walk of Fallon's life, even though Mr. Entrekin's office was just down the hallway. She knew something terrible had happened. The world started to narrow as everything filtered out. All she could concentrate on was one foot in front of the other. To focus on anything else would allow the nightmare to catch up to her and the possibility that she was alone in the world to become real.

As Fallon and her escorts entered the front office, the room got quiet. The normal hustle and bustle of the office stopped. People were staring. Fallon wanted to scream at the people to stop. There were two police officers standing inside the principal's office door. They looked away as they saw her. Fallon knew why they were here. The police had shown up twice before to deliver the news of the death of her parents. Fallon felt her already shaky knees give out. Mrs. Brinson caught her as she was stumbling. She started whispering in Fallon's ear, "It's okay, I've got you."

The officers came over and helped Fallon get into a chair. The tallest of the police officers spoke. The police officer seemed to be struggling to get the words out. He cleared his throat. "Ms. Whitten, I am terribly sorry to tell you that your sister was killed in a car accident this morning in Missouri." They continued to drone on, maybe offering words of sympathy but to Fallon it was just white noise to the pain crawling up her chest.

She felt that familiar sickness in her stomach. That vile sickness that is only associated with grief. They were gone and she was left alone in the world. Her greatest fear had come true. What would she do, where would she go? The people in the room kept talking to her, but she didn't hear them. The thoughts in her head drowned out the talking in the room. Panic set in and Fallon was desperate to free herself from this cage of pain-fueled despair.

The room grew quiet as the adults realized that Fallon was overwhelmed. All of a sudden, the door flew open and there stood Rebecca's mother, Leah. She came over and dropped to her knees and grabbed Fallon in a bear hug. Leah started sobbing. Fallon couldn't help herself, she started crying uncontrollably, while Leah kept her wrapped in her arms. The school staff tried to console her without any luck. Everything began to fade out and her grip on reality faltered. Suddenly, all that was left was darkness and pain. Fallon accepted the darkness and numbness that filled her. The police officer called an ambulance and Fallon was taken to the hospital. She didn't remember much because as soon as the ambulance arrived as she was given a shot. The paramedic injected the needle into her arm and the room darkened. Fallon felt herself slipping into a sleep as the emotional pain was mowed down by the sweet relief of the medication.

The coldness crept in and Fallon awoke to a strange room. Her body involuntarily trembled. She was in the hospital, curled up in a ball. As she looked around, she realized there were bars on the window and her mind began to race. Did they put her in the psychiatric ward? Could they do that over just crying?

Fallon slowly got out of bed feeling the effects of the medication. She wasn't steady on her feet and had to close her eyes to maintain her balance. She stumbled over and looked out through the bars on the window. Sluggishly, she walked to the door that was the access point to the hallway. Fallon tried the door, but it was locked and it only added to her panic. She was a prisoner. The fear of being locked in caused Fallon to bang loudly on the door and yell for help. She didn't belong here. She wasn't crazy; she was just upset over terrible news. There was no answer to her attempts to gain attention. Fallon banged and yelled until she had no energy left. Finally exhausted, she slumped at the base of the door, and brought her knees up to her chest, and rested her head on her arms.

The sudden realization of what brought her to the hospital hit her full force. The feeling of being abandoned by the death of your whole family was indescribable. Fallon didn't get to say goodbye to any of them; they were just taken. How does a person continue to live when the life they have known is over? For a brief moment, the urge to end it all flashed in

Fallon's mind. *I can make this stop. If my heart stops beating, I will feel no more pain.* The dark thoughts entered her mind where heinous and it almost took hold in her soul. The pain needed to stop.

Fallon was looking for an escape from this life and the sorrow ever present. In her thoughts, Fallon knew the truth. *There was no cure, no getting better when death takes your family. You only learn to live without them, always looking for them and wanting to be with them with no resolve. It is a dark, soul splitting bitter struggle reserved for a few unlucky people who walk this earth. Only those who have faced such great loss would understand.* Looking for anything she could use, Fallon spent a couple moments running over the options in her mind.

With a heavy sigh and a broken heart, Fallon finally got off the floor and crawled back into the bed. As she lay there, she realized she didn't want to die. The fight of the human spirit took hold and Fallon knew at that moment that suicide wasn't an option for her. As much as it hurt now, the pain was almost unbearable; she still wanted to go to college and maybe find love and have a family. In her heart, she knew wouldn't be alone for the rest of her life if she could just hang on and not give into the dark side of grief. A lump formed in her throat as she thought about Eva and her parents. In that moment, Fallon decided to fight, pushing the thought of death from her mind. Her family would want her to go on living, they would expect her to get up and to stop feeling sorry for herself. Never stop, push forward.

Fallon's determination to fight through this crisis came from her parents. Her father, James, was a former Army Ranger. He got out of the Army and worked in telecommunications for a local German firm based in Alabama. Her mother Vivian, was a nurse and was tough as nails. She worked at the local ER as a trauma nurse. Fallon's parents had little sympathy for those who wouldn't help themselves. They always said, "If there is a will, there is a way." Fallon got so sick of hearing those words. Just the mention of them was enough to make Fallon have a temper tantrum. Fallon continued to lay in bed and thought about what she wouldn't give to hear them preach to her.

The door opening brought Fallon out of her musings. A short, stocky nurse walked in and went over to the bed and hovered over Fallon. "How are you feeling?"

Fallon sat up looking at the woman curiously and responded to the nurse and said, "Fine". The nurse took her pulse and blood pressure. She sighed and headed towards the door.

"Please tell me why I am locked up in here."

Coldly the nurse responded, "I will get the doctor for you." The nurse didn't address the reasons why Fallon was here; she just turned and left the room.

It was several minutes before door opened again. The door creaked open and a doctor walked into the room. Catching a full view of him, Fallon blushed. He was extremely handsome. The doctor was a tall, well-built black man. He had beautiful dark eyes and flawless mahogany skin. He was in scrubs, a white lab coat and sneakers. Fallon observed he was athletic from his build. "Fallon, I presume? I'm Dr. Smith."

Fallon sat up in the bed. She was wary of new company. What did he want with her? He walked over and pulled a chair next to the bed. "How are you doing?" Dr. Smith watched as she answered.

Finding her voice, she replied, "I'm okay, I would like to go home tonight."

Dr. Smith sat quietly and continued to look at Fallon closely. "I don't think that is possible right now. I can't send you home." Dr. Smith got quiet again.

Following his lead, Fallon stayed quiet and waited to hear what he had to say. She was expecting an examination and questions.

After some time had passed, Dr. Smith looked at Fallon and said, "You look nothing like your sister."

Eyes wide, Fallon looked closer at him. She thought that she had heard wrong. "What did you say?"

Dr. Smith stood up and walked over to the window and stared outside. Fallon could tell he was sad. "When she came to me, I thought she was crazy. You know how Eva is sometimes. She was specific about you and what she wanted to happen. Eva wanted you to have an out, an escape. She couldn't have known this was going to happen."

Fallon stared at the young doctor in disbelief. It took a second for her to formulate her words. "How did you know Eva? What did you mean by instructions?"

Dr. Smith looked at Fallon and said, "Eva was my tutor in medical school. I wouldn't have made it without her, and she was my good friend. She wanted me to tell you this: <u>Surrender means that the history of this heroic struggle will be written by the enemy."</u>

Fallon half cried, half laughed out loud. Dr. Smith frowned and asked, "Does that mean something to you?"

She stared at Dr. Smith with a look of disbelief. She was uncomfortable having to address this with a black man; she didn't want to offend. Fallon laughed again and then started to cry. Big tears ran down her cheeks. "Eva did her dissertation on Patrick Cleburne. My family has a thing for the Civil War. My middle name is Ronanye after Cleburne and my parents said we were related. That quote is from him."

"Great, a highly inappropriate civil war general who supported slavery. Well, that doesn't surprise me. Eva had mentioned to me once that Cleburne was misunderstood and she was going to prove it." Dr. Smith winked at Fallon. "It's okay, I get it."

Before he could say more, there was some movement in the hallway. Dr. Smith moved over and grabbed Fallon's hand. "We don't have time. Listen, you must leave tonight. You are not safe here. I think your parents and your sister were murdered. Before she died, I made a promise to your sister and I will fulfill it today."

Fallon looked him with big eyes. Wanting to ask questions without being able to say the words, she shifted on the bed. She was uncomfortable with Dr. Smith talking about her family. Her mind wasn't able to process this information.

"When the nurse comes in, she will have a shot filled with medicine. You will take the shot and inject her with it and then take her clothes and get out of here. There is a grey sedan in the parking lot with the keys under the floor board on the passenger side."

Fallon stared at him in wonder. "Wait, what, where am I going to go? What nurse, why?" Her words ran together as she tried to speak.

Dr. Smith replied in a stern voice, "Eva said for you to go Johnny Hearts."

Fallon was stunned into silence. Johnny Hearts? Her pseudo God Father? Fallon shook her head. "I can't, that's so far away. Eva was crazy. I'm going home to Rebecca's house. I will be safe there."

"No, you will not. You will listen to your sister's directions. She was trying to protect you." Dr. Smith reached and took out his wallet and said before Fallon could react, "Here is $2000 dollars. That should get you as far as you need to go. Don't stop. Get there as fast as you can. Be ready when the nurse comes in. She is a friend, so don't hurt her." Doctor Smith stared at Fallon and then directed her eyes to his eyes with two fingers to have her attention, "Where are you to go?"

Hesitantly, Fallon responded. "I'm to go to New Jersey and find Johnny Hearts." She wanted to argue to stay, but felt the threat was real and she was scared. Dr. Smith was right, she needed protection and Johnny Hearts would keep her safe till she could figure this mess out.

To her surprise, Dr. Smith leaned down and gave Fallon a hug. "Best of luck, my friend. When this is over, come back and let me know how you are doing. Be ready."

As if on cue, the nurse from earlier walked in. "Let's get this over with." She handed Fallon a syringe with a needle. Still in a cold voice the nurse said, "Doctor, it's time for you to go. I got this."

Dr. Smith gave Fallon a wink and headed out the door.

Fallon got up off the bed. "Why are you doing this?" She asked the nurse. She didn't have time to question Dr. Smith as he quickly disappeared out the door.

The nurse frowned at her question. "Money of course. Plus, I knew your momma. She was a good person. I hope that if my children ever need help, someone will help them." Fallon thought this was an odd response. The nurse was so cold in her tone, but was willing to help her escape.

Fallon took the needle and plunged it into to the nurse's arm squeezing the medicine into her body. The nurse started to melt and sink to the floor. Fallon arranged her on the floor and began the task of removing her clothes. Fallon draped her hospital gown over the nurse. Thankfully, the scrubs were easy to get off. Fallon pulled on the scrubs and attached her name tag. She walked over and checked her appearance in the mirror. She looked bad. Fallon's hair was a tangled mess and she had dark circles under her eyes.

Fallon took the keys off the nurse and headed to the door, which was easy enough to open. Fallon peeked her head out the door to the hallway to find it was clear. She then gathered her courage and walked out. She tried to act like she belonged in the hospital as a nurse. Her walking was purposeful with a nurse's stride. She walked past the nurse's desk without disturbing the group of nurses that were working. Before she got to the end of the hallway she realized that the door there was locked and monitored.

Fallon looked around and realized that she was still alone. She quickly found the intercom button and pressed it hard. Her heart pounding in her chest was so loud, Fallon was worried that someone would hear it beating. After a few seconds, the door unlocked. Feeling a sense of relief, she walked over to the door for the parking lot.

Freedom was close. Fallon walked out of the hospital without incident and easily found the car Dr. Smith had told her about in the room. After retrieving the keys, Fallon found a bag containing some items for her trip in the back seat. There was a change of clothes, a wig, her favorite Tammy Wynette CD, and a map. She was shocked to find the clothing was in her size. *Did Eva do this?* Fallon cranked the car and exited the parking lot.

Suddenly, Police cars screeched into the hospital and she could hear them approaching fast. Fallon knew that she had to get out of town quickly because for all she knew, they could be after her. She slipped on the wig and slowly made her way out of the parking lot. Fallon drove around town for a couple of minutes to make up her mind. Slipping the CD in the player, Fallon waited for the comforting sounds of the First Lady of Country Music to soothe her mind. While the music played, she passed the beautiful city park and the local main street area. Could she do what her sister asked?

Fallon knew where she had to go. Johnny Hearts was a nickname for her father's best friend, John Valentino, Italian mob boss in New Jersey. According to her dad, Johnny Hearts was a compassionate man with a big heart when it came to those he loved. Cross him and he had no qualms about killing people to get what he wanted. The Valentino family ran the New Jersey mob. Fallon wasn't sure what he did; it was likely that is was something in the import/export business. Probably all illegal and probably all bad.

None of that seemed to matter to Fallon's dad. James Whitten had served with Johnny Hearts in the military. They were both in some ridiculously exclusive and crazy Army Ranger unit. Their unit had worked on dangerous, secret missions and Fallon didn't know what they had gone through together, but it must have been rough. After they both left the Army, the men remained close, as they were forever warrior brothers.

It wasn't that Fallon didn't like Mr. Valentino; it was his son Jack that bothered her. Jack was a few years older than she was. He was gorgeous with his dark black hair and green eyes. He stood at 6'4 and did it so beautifully it was hard not to stare at him. A square jaw line and a straight nose completed his good looks. He couldn't stand Fallon, and he had gone out of his way to let her know that the last time he had seen her.

Fallon had seen Jack was several years ago at his house in New Jersey. He was a total jerk to Fallon. Jack and Eva hung out together all weekend, going to the movies and out to eat. Fallon tried to join them, but Jack made it clear that he wasn't hanging out with a young teenager, telling her things like, "Go away little girl." He had been rude with his comments. He was so brutal with his words to Fallon that she stayed at home with the parents to avoid him while he took Eva out and showed her a good time. Fallon felt embarrassed and awkward for being so young and she had hated Jack since that moment.

Fallon's dad however, loved Jack. He was the all American, perfect son. Jack was the starting quarterback at an Ivy League school in Cambridge, Massachusetts. He had plans to play professional football after this season. It was all but guaranteed. Fallon's dad talked about Jack like he was the son he never had, being that Jack was a scholar and an athlete. Those were things that her father respected above all else. Jack this, Jack that. It was enough to drive a person crazy.

The problem was that the Valentino family lived in Jersey City, outside of New York City and Fallon was in Red Bay,

Alabama. Jersey City was well over a thousand miles away. The thought of driving that far was terrifying to Fallon.

Chapter 2

The decision was made. There was no other option. Fallon turned her car towards Alabama Highway 24, the road out of town. Tears rolled silently down her face as she left the city limits. This was goodbye to her life. This was goodbye to her family and her friends. This was goodbye to her high school and her education. The road was empty and Fallon felt so utterly alone with only the music to keep her company. Still, Eve wanted her to do this, so Fallon hit the accelerator and took off. She had to make it to Johnny Hearts. He would know what to do to help protect her.

Many mile markers passed and the road began to blur. The night was dark and the stars seemed too dim for her. The road was silent, it just left her with thoughts of the people she had loved. Hours passed and the road seemed never-ending. The knowledge that her sister was looking out for her drove Fallon onward. Fallon drove all night before the miles started to wear on her. It was early morning and things were starting to get blurry. It was hard to concentrate and to keep her eyes open. She was in the upper edge of Maryland when Fallon saw the signs of the Pennsylvania Welcome Center in Greencastle. She decided to pull in a take a quick nap.

The rest stop was deserted. It was scary and poorly lit. The lights did little to help as the new day was starting to break through the darkness. Although she was afraid, her stomach demanded that she find some sort of food. Reluctantly, she got out, used the restroom, and bought some water and snacks. The fear subsided as she sat outside on the bench and ate her terrible dinner. After she finished her vending machine dinner, she threw away her trash and headed back to the car.

The car seats were comfortable enough, just hard to sleep on. Eventually, exhaustion took over and she was finally able to doze off. It was only a couple of minutes before Fallon was being rudely awakened with a tapping sound on the window. A light shined in her face.

"Ma'am, you can't sleep in your car here." It was a uniformed security guard. Fallon's hands started trembling.

Had she been found? She wasn't even sure if she was in danger or who it was she was running from now. The monsters were out there.

Fallon rolled down the window. "My apologies. I'm on my way out." Fallon tried to sound calm and convincing.

"Be careful out there. Traffic will start to pick up soon." Fallon nodded in agreement. She started the car and pulled out of the parking lot before he could ask any more questions. The early morning sunlight was peeking through the clouds.

Fallon felt a new sense of hope. If she could make it through Pennsylvania, she would be in New Jersey. It was easy for her to start fantasizing about a warm bath, a comfortable bed, and delicious food. She needed to focus on these comforting things to keep her going as she was in survival mode. The road was long, dark, and quiet so she kept telling herself that she could make it. She needed to drive into the sunrise. There was hope in the new day. There were five hours or more left of driving depending on traffic. New Jersey would be safe.

The traffic was light and Fallon made good time pulling into Jersey City. Her problem now was how to find Johnny Hearts. Fallon couldn't advertise herself so where would one of his "businesses" be? Fallon drove around Jersey City trying to remember where he lived but she had no luck. It was time to take control of the situation. She knew Johnny had ties to the criminal underworld. She just needed to find him.

Fallon found the nearest gas station that looked safe. She hopped out and walked inside while constantly checking over her shoulder. There were no other options for her other than to ask around till she found someone who knew Johnny. Fallon wasn't sure how to ask for Johnny so she started with an easy question. An older white gentleman with greasy grey hair and bad teeth was behind the counter. "Excuse me sir, I am looking for the local bar."

"Aren't you too young to be drinking this early in the day?" He asked, laughing at her.

Fallon pursed her lip and replied, "That sir, is none of your business. Can you help me or not?" Fallon didn't have time to waste on this old man. Either he could help or not, she was mentally exhausted, irritated, and physically too tired to play games.

The older man chuckled, "Where are you from? Your accent doesn't belong here."

Fallon straighten her shoulders and said, "I'm here for work. I just need to know where I can start."

The man replied, "Try the gentleman's club on 4th Street. They are always looking for girls to hire. You sure that's what you want to do? A pretty girl like you shouldn't have to do that kind of work."

Fallon smiled, feeling creeped out. "Thanks for your help." Fallon turned to leave but stopped before opening the door. "Will I be safe there?"

The old man smiled again. "You will be as safe there as anywhere. I just wouldn't drink anything if it's offered to you. You'll be fine."

Fallon waved at him as she left the store. Finding the Gentlemen's Club on 4th Street was easy. Fallon drove around the block a few times to see the activity around the club. It was deserted. She parked a few streets over and got out. Fallon felt weary as she walked the short distance to the entrance of the club.

The building was not as large as Fallon thought it was from the street. Fallon pushed open the heavy oak door. As soon as she entered, a large, black man came over. "You don't belong here, leave." He grabbed her arm and started pulling her out of the building.

"Wait! Wait, please!" Fallon started dragging her feet. "I'm just looking for someone. I'm looking for Johnny Hearts." The man immediately dropped Fallon, she sprawled out on the pavement.

Looking down at her with menacing eyes, the man growled, "Listen girl, I don't know who you are or where you come from, but don't ever say that name again. Next time, I will slit your throat."

Fallon stood up on shaky legs. Her breathing was labored. "Please sir, I need your help finding John, I mean, umm... Mr. Valentino. He is a friend of my family and I am desperate to find him."

The man stood for a moment. "What is he to you?" he asked with a snarl on his face.

Fallon stumbled over words. "As I said, he is a family friend and it is important I find him today. He will want to see me."

"I can't imagine what he would want with you. Go away." The man barked as he turned and started back to the club door. "Don't ever come here again. Next time, I won't be so understanding." He put his hand on the door to walk back inside.

"Wait! I have money, I'll pay you." The man stopped.

"How much?" He asked.

"How much will it take? I need to see Mr. Valentino personally today."

"I can't guarantee he will want to see you. I can get in touch with his men. That's all I can offer. It'll cost $500 for my trouble."

Fallon quickly thought about her options and extended her hand. "We have a deal."

The man took her small hand in his big one. "Name is Bull. Come inside and I will be needing the money upfront."

Fallon shook her head. "No way, I want to see Mr. Valentino and you will get your money when you make it happen. Half now, half at the end."

Bull shook his head and laughed. "You have no idea what you are doing, do you? I could kill you and nobody would care. Full payment or no deal."

Fallon shifted her weight and put on a serious face. She couldn't show fear. "You should know my family will in return kill you and everyone in your path. I'm not one to threaten. I will pay, just don't mistake my desperation for fear."

Bull stared at her and chuckled. Fallon wondered if he was about to hurt her. Maybe this wasn't the best time to be smart mouthed. "I like your spirit and the way you talk."

Fallon sighed in relief. She was safe for the moment.

Fallon reluctantly agreed to the conditions. She was afraid he would just take her money, but she had no choice if she was going to find Johnny Hearts.

"Come in and let's make some calls. Who should I say is here seeking the assistance of the great Mr. Valentino?" Bull asked.

"Tell him James Whitten's daughter is here and needs help." Fallon followed Bull into the bar.

"Have a seat. Do you want a drink?"

Fallon snorted remembering the warning from the gas station attendant. "I think I'll pass." Fallon pulled the bills out of her pocket and handed them to Bull. He made a huge production of counting the bills, then Bull left the room with the money in hand. He was gone a long time.

The room was dark and empty with the smell of stale beer and cigarettes. Fallon laid her head on the table. It wasn't long before she was fast asleep, dreaming of Eva.

Chapter 3

Fallon awoke to someone touching her hair. It was Johnny Valentino. He didn't speak, he gathered her in a hug and held her tight.

"Thank God you made it to me." He said a prayer of thanks that Fallon couldn't make out.

Johnny Hearts was a middle aged, handsome man. He was tall, olive skinned with black hair peppered with gray. He was just an older version of Jack. Johnny released Fallon and held her at arm's length. "Baby girl, you're here now. Johnny Hearts will take care of you." He grabbed her into a hug again. "I can't believe it's you. Come, let's get you out of here." Fallon allowed Johnny to take her hand.

Fallon felt a sense of relief now that she had made it to Jersey City like Eva had planned. Trusting her sister in this situation was not easy, but it was all she had now. Fallon knew she would be safe with Johnny Hearts. In her exhaustion, his face was enough to make her cry, but she reined in the tears. The relief of being with him kept her from totally coming apart.

"Wait!" Fallon exclaimed, "I've got to get my car."

Johnny looked confused but didn't question Fallon. He signaled and a man appeared. "Where is your car?"

Fallon responded, "It's parked on the street, a couple of blocks over. It's a grey small car with an Alabama plate." She handed the keys over to one of the men with Johnny.

The man with the keys nodded to Johnny. "Where you do want it to be taken?" He asked. Johnny looked at Fallon.

"I need my bag out of the car. It's the only clothes I have."

Johnny told the man, "Bring the bag to the house then take the car to the warehouse."

On the way out of the club, Johnny stopped in front of Bull. "You have served me greatly today. I will return the favor." Bull seemed at a loss for words. Gone was the tough man from earlier. Fallon could tell that he feared Johnny and his power.

Bull tried to hand Fallon back the money she had given him as part of their deal. He seemed panicked that Mr. Valentino would be angry with him. "Please take this back, I had no idea. I would never take cash from Mr. Valentino or his family."

Fallon smiled and hugged Bull. "Thank you, you probably saved my life. The cash is a gift." Bull didn't seem to know how to react to her kindness.

Fallon hadn't noticed the group of men in suits who were lined up in the bar. Johnny took Fallon's hand and led her out the door where there was a shiny black limousine awaiting them. One of the men in a suit opened the car door for Fallon. "Thank you," Fallon said as she climbed in the car.

As Fallon slid in on the leather seat and got in the car, Johnny settled in beside her. "Tell me, how are you?" he asked.

Fallon considered how she would answer, but found herself trying not to cry. All she could do was shake her head. The thought of all that had happened was too much to handle. To even open her mouth to speak the words would open a floodgate. It was best that she locked that inside and work to figure out what was driving the chaos around her life. Johnny reached over and patted her hand. "I am grieving with you. Your father was one of my best friends and brother. Your mother was a sister to me. I can't believe they are both gone."

Fallon nodded and said in a trembling voice, "They loved you and Jack."

Fallon looked out the window and asked, "Do you know about Eva?"

Johnny shook his head no. "I realized something must be terribly wrong if you are here in a strip club trying to track me down. What happened?"

Fallon sighed and tried to control the tremble in her voice. The words rushed out jumbled together. Fallon couldn't get them out quick enough. "I don't know. I was at school when the police showed up and told me that Eva had been killed in a car crash. They put me in the hospital yesterday, but I escaped with some help. Dr. Smith gave me a car and some money to get here and he said I'm in some kind of trouble and they have killed my whole family." Fallon's voice broke as she was talking.

Johnny didn't respond. He seemed to be processing the information. He clenched his jaw and Fallon could see the storm raging behind his eyes.

Fallon grabbed his hand. "I'm sorry to drag you in this. Eva arranged for me to come here if something bad happened to her."

Johnny took a closer look at Fallon. She wasn't making sense. "How long has it been since you slept and had a decent meal?"

Fallon replied, "This all went down yesterday. Once I left the hospital, I drove all night. I tried to sleep at a rest stop with no luck."

Johnny pulled her into a hug and kissed the top her head. "You are under my protection now and you are safe. Let's get you home where you can get some food and rest. Then we will talk about yesterday. Do you remember Maria, my housekeeper? She heard you were here and started cooking for you."

Fallon allowed herself to relax in his embrace.

The car ride to the Valentino's house seemed to take forever. Fallon was desperate to go to sleep. When the mansion finally came into view, Fallon felt a tremendous relief. The house was sprawling over a beautiful piece of land. The mansion was in the style of an Italian villa with multiple floors and balconies. The house shined with white stonewashed walls, a deep red clay tile roof and ornate fixtures that screamed money. The wrought iron gates opened and Maria rushed out of the house.

Johnny stepped out first and held out his hand for Fallon. Maria stepped forward. "My child, my child, Maria is here now. You don't need to worry. Come in and eat."

Fallon was hustled into the house and directed to the kitchen. Maria promptly sat her on a stool and put a huge steaming bowl of spaghetti in front of her.

Maria kept a constant stream of conversation going while Fallon tried to eat. Bless Maria's heart, she tried to avoid any topic that would upset Fallon. Fallon ate the whole bowl of spaghetti. As she finished, Fallon rose to clean up her mess. Maria's hand shot out and stopped her.

"Don't even think about touching those dishes. Maria is here to take care of you. Let's get you showered and in bed." Maria led Fallon down the familiar hallway. Dark wood and beautiful dark floors with white walls and furniture that was in the best taste enfolded them as they walked down the hallway. Maria led Fallon into the bedroom, the same beautiful room that Fallon had stayed in the last time she visited with her family. A large bed with silver and white bedding greeted her as she walked through the room. Fallon felt like she could close her eyes and pretend her parents were in the room down the hall from her. This felt right as if she belonged here with the Valentino family.

Maria's voice snapped her out of her thoughts. "This will be your room while you are here. Through here is the shower. There are towels under the sink. I'll give you some privacy to enjoy it."

"Thank you, Maria, you have no idea how much you have helped me today." Fallon couldn't help it. She started to cry. Big tears rolled down her cheeks.

Maria came over and hugged Fallon. "You are so young to have experienced such tragedies. You need not to worry now; you are with family. We take care of our own."

Fallon nodded as she talked.

"Get a shower and a nap, you will feel better."

Fallon followed her advice and took a hot shower. When she got out, she dried her hair and stepped in the room to find a nightgown laid out on the bed. Fallon barely got it on before Maria appeared.

"To bed with you." Maria pulled back the cover and Fallon climbed in. "Goodnight my girl, sweet dreams." Maria leaned down and gave Fallon a kiss on the head. Fallon was asleep as soon as her head hit the pillow.

While Fallon slept, a meeting was being held in office of the house. Johnny, Maria, and important members of the family were in the room. As head of the family, Johnny spoke first. "We know what must be done. I will not break my contract with James." The members nodded in agreement. Johnny continued, "The arrangement was made at birth. I will bring Jack home in a couple of days. Fallon is eighteen. The marriage will happen and she will be under our protection."

Maria chimed in, "Do we know what is going on with her parents and Eva?"

Johnny shook his head no. "I have sent a team to Alabama to find out more information. That's why I want to give this some time. In the meantime, let's keep the marriage secret from Fallon. She doesn't need any more stress."

After the meeting ended, Maria pulled Johnny aside. "How do you think Jack is going to respond to this?"

Johnny seemed angry with the question.

"It's time Jack takes his responsibility to this family seriously. I had an arranged marriage and it turned out to be the best thing of my life. Jack will do this or I will disown him."

"What happens if Fallon doesn't want this?" Maria asked, timidly.

Johnny responded, "Fallon is a smart girl. It might take some time and persuasion, but this is what her parents wanted. Fallon will be Jack's wife." Johnny paused briefly and then said, "I will not take no for an answer." Johnny's voice had a tone of finality.

Maria nodded and said, "I just want Jack to be happy. He might resent being told to marry her, I don't think they have gotten along in the past."

"The past is over. Jack has grown up and Fallon will also. This is the right move for the family."

Maria sighed and said, "Jack is hard headed. I worry about his reaction to this."

"Let me worry about my son. Your job is to care for her."

Maria smiled and tried to change the tone of the conversation, "It's good to have a young person back in the house."

Johnny snorted and walked off without responding.

Fallon woke to the sounds of the early morning. The light was dim in the room and it took a moment for her eyes to focus. She had been asleep for a long time and would probably still be asleep if her stomach had not woken her. She got out of bed and saw that Maria had laid out a robe and a pair of slippers. She slipped quietly from the room and headed to the kitchen to grab some breakfast. Fallon glanced at the clock in the hallway it read 6:00 am. Instead of being here, she should be at home getting ready for school with her family. Her old life was gone. This was her new reality.

Fallon got to the kitchen to find both Johnny and Maria enjoying their breakfast. Fallon spoke first, "Good morning".

Johnny and Maria responded, "Good morning" at the same time.

Johnny asked, "Did you sleep well?"

Fallon nodded and smiled, "I don't think I moved all night."

Maria got up and headed over to the stove. "What would you like for breakfast? If we don't have what you want, we can send the boys out to get it."

Fallon shrugged, "I'm fine with what you're having."

Maria smiled. "Such a sweet girl. Let me make you some eggs, toast, and bacon."

Fallon started to argue but Johnny stopped her. "This is what Maria lives for. Let her fatten you up."

Fallon smiled and then frowned and shook her head slightly. "I don't know how I can ever repay your kindness."

Johnny got up and grabbed her in a hug, "You are our family. Learn this, we take care of our own."

Fallon hugged him back, and mumbling, "Thank you," into his chest trying not to cry again.

As Johnny finished his breakfast, he announced to Fallon, "I have some business to attend to this morning. After I'm done, I would like to meet with you and talk about what happened. Until we figure out what is going on, you will need to stay here in the house. It would be better if your location was kept secret for now."

Fallon nodded her head in agreement. She was too afraid to leave the house. "I will do what you say. I'm too scared to leave."

Johnny continued, "I know that you need some clothes and beauty supplies. I'm going to send my niece, Christine, to you. She will go out and buy you whatever you need and bring it back to the house. Don't be shy, get what you need because you may be here for a while."

Fallon thought for a moment. "Do you think it is possible to make contact with my friend Rebecca and her parents? They must be worried sick by now."

Johnny shook his head, "For now, we need your trail to fall silent. I'm sorry, but I feel I need to protect you." He gave her a quick kiss on the head. "Maria will be with you today. Make use of this big house."

As he was leaving, Fallon couldn't help but say, "Love you, Johnny Hearts."

Johnny stopped and turned with a big smile on his face and said, "Love you too, daughter."

Fallon thought it weird that he had called her daughter. It must be a mob thing. At this moment, it was what she needed; feeling loved and not alone.

The time flew until lunch. Fallon was anxious to talk to Johnny, eager to figure out why her whole family had been killed and to find out if she was next. She was so out of sorts she was unable to grieve. Fallon felt like it was all a lie and that someone had been joking when they said her sister was gone. It was unimaginable that her fireball of a sister was dead and she had suddenly been left to walk through life alone.

While Fallon was waiting to meet with Johnny, she explored the mansion with Maria. The dwelling was huge with multiple bedrooms and baths. It was clear that Johnny Hearts was extremely rich. While they walked around the abode, Maria questioned Fallon about food and other things that she would like to have in the kitchen during her stay.

Fallon was surprised at lunch to find everything she had mentioned to Maria was present in the kitchen. When Fallon realized that Maria had arranged for the groceries and supplies to be there, Fallon couldn't help but tear up.

While Maria was cooking, Fallon tried to hide her sobs. Maria put down her utensils and pulled Fallon into a hug. No words were spoken or needed, and Fallon was able to compose herself quickly. "Sorry, I don't know what came over me."

Maria patted her on the back. "You are doing great. You wouldn't be human if you didn't show some emotion about what has happened to you in the past few months."

Fallon walked over and took a seat at the table. "What time does Johnny show up for lunch?"

Maria laughed, "Johnny runs his own schedule, I just try to have everything ready around noon. Don't be surprised if there are a group of men with him; I usually feed about 20 for lunch."

Fallon looked surprised. "You do this every day?"

Maria said with pride in her voice, "This is my life. This is what I do."

"Do you get paid for all that hard work?"

Maria really laughed aloud this time. "Fallon, this is my life. I want for nothing. I enjoy being with my family."

Before they could speak further, the room was filled with a group of men. Johnny stepped forward, "Fallon, this is my family." Fallon listened as Johnny rolled through the list of names. Each man came over and gave her a kiss on the check, and she wondered whether or not she would be able to remember their names.

The men sat down and Maria started serving them. Fallon got up and tried to help Maria but was quickly told to sit down and enjoy lunch. Fallon was amazed that Maria had time to cook all this wondrous food. Johnny pulled out a seat and motioned for Fallon to sit by him. As she walked over to take her seat, all the men around the table stood up. Johnny held out her chair and the men sat when she was seated.

The men at the table shared lively and funny conversation. It was nice to forget, for the moment, the horrors of her life. Fallon found herself laughing out loud at some of the funny stories. As lunch wound down, Johnny asked to meet with her in his study. Reality was back and a sense of doom filled Fallon.

Fallon followed Johnny and another man into the study. "Fallon, this is my brother Marcos."

Marcos stepped forward and kissed Fallon on the cheek. "It's nice to meet you. I knew your father and share Johnny's feelings that he was our brother."

Fallon was surprised at how much Marcos resembled Johnny. They could be twins, both extremely good looking.

Fallon replied, "It's nice to meet you." Fallon was shown to a seat; she started shivering having to think about the horrific events of yesterday and the past few months.

Johnny went and sat down behind his desk. "Fallon, we need to know every detail of what happened over the past few months."

Fallon sighed and slumped down in the chair near Johnny's desk. It was tough to talk about the torture she had endured with the death of her parents and her only sister. Fallon spent the next hour reliving the horrific details of the past few months up to the moment that she showed up in a New Jersey strip bar.

Johnny and Marcos exchanged a look. Marco spoke first, "Did anyone threaten you or your family?"

Fallon shook her head no. She wanted to help and add some information, but she didn't know anything. "There was never any mention of anything going on or any problems. My parents died so suddenly that there was no time to talk. Eva left a few weeks after the last funeral. We talked every day on the phone, but she didn't say anything to me about any troubles."

Johnny walked around and sat on the edge of his desk. "Do you think it's possible they were hiding something from you?"

Fallon shrugged her shoulders. "I don't know. Do you know anything?"

Johnny looked at Fallon and said, "I have sent a team to Alabama to find out any information they can. So far, they haven't turned up anything. Not to concern you, but there is no record of your being in the hospital, and there is no record of a Dr. Smith."

Fallon stood up. "What? That makes me look crazy. Eva contacted Dr. Smith and he told me where to go on her orders. He said she helped him get through Medical School and he owed her."

Johnny looked at Fallon. "I'll tell you what I think. I think it is possible, that Eva worked for the CIA or the FBI as a spook. They have a history of making things like this disappear. While you are here, try to remember any details that you can."

Fallon stared at Johnny in disbelief. "You really think it is possible that Eva was in the CIA or FBI? I find that hard to believe."

Marcos spoke up, "I really believe Eva knew something was going down and took precautions to get you some help. The problem is we just don't know what she, or your parents, were involved with at the time of their deaths."

Cutting Marcos off, Johnny said, "I think this enough to go on for right now. You need to focus on getting rested up."

Fallon asked in small voice. "I wasn't able to bury Eva. Is there a way to find out where she is?"

The men exchanged looks at each other. Johnny replied quickly, "That is part of the problem, we haven't been able to find a body. If we locate her, I will let you know as soon as I do. You have my word that she will have a proper burial." Fallon could hear the regret in his voice that he wasn't able to help her give Eva a proper burial.

Fallon looked at Marco with tears in her eyes, "It was nice to meet you and thank you for your help."

Marco walked over and gave her a hug and wiped a tear from her face. "Welcome to the family."

The next days for Fallon were terrible. The impact of her situation hit her with full force. Fallon fell into a deep depression and barely got out of bed. Maria became worried when she stopped eating. Johnny would come and sit by her on the bed. He didn't speak, he just stroked her hair as she blankly stared off into space. It was on the third day of the depression, when Fallon fell into a deep sleep.

In her dream, Fallon found herself walking with her mother and father. Her dad was in his military uniform and her mother was in her nursing uniform and they were gently reminding her of Eva. It was so clear to Fallon they were trying to tell her something she couldn't make out. She became frustrated; it was like the information was there, but she couldn't understand.

Her dad said, "If there is a will, there is a way." Fallon watched her parents fade and she tried to run after her parents with no luck.

She woke up breathless and with wet cheeks from crying. Fallon lay in bed and tried to make sense of the dream, replaying her dad saying, "If there is a will, there is a way." What were they trying to tell her about Eva? Was she missing something important?

It took Fallon some time to remember the purpose of the dream - her sister. Fallon replayed the conversations and events of the past few days. Something was nagging in the back of Fallon's mind. She just couldn't make the connection.

Fallon decided to face the day, as lying in bed was doing her no good. She quickly showered and got ready and headed toward the kitchen. Maria, Johnny, and some of the men were sitting down for dinner. Maria smiled and Johnny stood up to hold out a chair. All the men around the table stood until Fallon took her seat.

"I'm glad you decided to join us tonight," Johnny said with a smile.

Fallon smiled a weakly and nodded her head. In true Maria fashion, she put a huge plate of food in front of Fallon.

"Sorry about the past couple of days." Fallon said as she stared at her plate of food. She felt embarrassed that she hadn't been able to get out of bed. They must think that she was weak.

Johnny responded, "You needed some time to grieve. We understand."

Dinner was finished and Fallon approached Johnny concerning a topic she was concerned about. "Do you think there is way for me to finish school? I was so close to finishing."

Johnny ran his fingers through his hair. "I know you want to finish and get your diploma. I just don't know how to accomplish that without giving away your location. Worst case scenario, you'll get your GED."

"Okay," Fallon replied out of respect. Inside she was dying. A GED? After all the International Baccalaureate and Advanced Placement classes she had taken? She was close to having her IB diploma. That would never happen if she missed the end of the year tests.

Back home in Alabama, she was on track to receive a full academic scholarship. Fallon was a dedicated student who was serious about her education. She had been waiting for the Ivy League schools to post acceptance. It was going to be close, but she felt she had a chance to get accepted to one of the Ivy League school based on her academic merits. Fallon felt a strong surge of anger. This was just another thing in her life that had been taken from her. Why was this happening to her? In her anger, Fallon made a commitment to finish her diploma.

Chapter 4

The next morning Fallon was sitting at the table enjoying breakfast when she heard the front door close. Both Maria and Johnny smiled at each other. Jack walked into the kitchen looking as beautiful as ever, just like a model that had stepped off the pages of a magazine. Jack was so tall and well-built that Fallon could not help but stare at him. Jack had his dad's olive skin, dark green eyes and jet black hair that was cut and styled short that made him look like royalty. He immediately went over and hugged Maria before he pulled his father into a bear hug. However, when he saw Fallon, his face turned into a mocking sneer. "What's the brat doing here?"

Jack walked over and messed up Fallon's hair, "Just joking kiddo. Where's your crazy sister?" The room fell silent.

Johnny spoke first and broke the sudden quiet of the room. "Jack, could I see you in my office?"

"It's okay," Fallon looked at Johnny.

Jack's eyes bounced from Fallon to Johnny. "Is she okay?"

"Eva was killed a few days ago in car wreck." Johnny stated with no emotion on his face.

Jack looked at Fallon in disbelief and began fumbling over his words.

"Fallon, I had no idea. I'm so sorry. I…"

Fallon nodded, "It's alright, you didn't know." She was stinging from the brat comment earlier.

"Jack, let's go to my office." Jack looked back at Fallon and followed Johnny.

Johnny's office sat at the front of the house. It was well-appointed with pictures of Jack and his accomplishments throughout high school and college. As soon as the door closed Jack started peppering his dad with questions.

"What happened? Is Fallon living with us now?"

Johnny discussed what he knew while Jack sat in disbelief. "I just don't know what to say. When I saw Eva a few weeks ago, she didn't let on that anything was wrong."

Johnny stopped him, "You saw Eva recently?"

Jack responded, "She stopped by while guest lecturing at school. We had coffee."

"What did you talk about?"

"Nothing of importance. She just wanted to know my plans and if you were in good health. Just small talk," Jack said.

Johnny grunted. "That wasn't small talk, she was gleaning information about us."

"Why would she need information?"

Johnny came around and sat on the edge of his desk. "Eva is very smart. She knew what she was doing. She was checking on us."

"That doesn't make sense to me," Jack scratched his head.

"I need you to keep an open mind," Johnny said.

Jack nodded in agreement.

"You know that Fallon's dad and I served in the military together. We ran some black ops, completing secret missions that were never discussed. James and I were a two-man team and we were inseparable. On one mission in Africa, James took a bullet for me and was hurt pretty bad, but he saved my life anyway. My father considered it a blood debt."

"What did grandfather mean by a blood debt?"

"A blood debt is a favor that is repaid at all costs. When Fallon was born, James came to me and asked for protection for his girls, especially Fallon. Your grandfather felt it was not enough, so to ensure protection for the girls, specifically Fallon, he proposed an arranged marriage between you and her."

Jack's mouth fell open. "You can't mean me?"

"Jack, your mother and I had an arranged marriage and we were extremely happy together. I know this is a lot of information to take in, but I need you to understand this is your responsibility to the family."

Jack turned red in the face and stood up. He started yelling, "I will not do this, you can't make me. I'm an adult. I will choose whom I will marry."

Johnny got up in his face. "You forget your place son. Have you forgotten who I am? I'm not asking you, I'm telling you. Don't cross me on this."

Jack sat down. As tough as he was, he feared his father. Jack had witnessed his father dealing with people who did not obey his commands. Johnny was head of the family because he was ruthless.

"Does Fallon know?" asked Jack.

"No, Fallon has no idea. She will be told in a few days when the time is right. The wedding will happen after she knows and has some time to adjust to the idea. Take some time and get to know her. You may end up thanking me when it is all said and done."

Jack snorted, "You just sentenced me to my own personal form of a prison. You'll force me to marry a girl that I don't even like. I don't think I'll be thanking you anytime soon."

"Fallon will need to time to adjust. She is a good girl and you are a lucky man."

Jack walked out of the room not acknowledging his father.

Later that night, Jack headed toward the kitchen and found Fallon eating ice cream at the counter. "Still love the sweets, I see."

Fallon turned around and looked at Jack. He was leaning in the doorway in a tight football shirt and khaki's. Fallon was momentarily struck speechless. Her heart rate took off and she had to look away. Jack was too handsome for his own good.

Fallon cleared her throat, "Would you like some?"

"I don't eat sweets." Jack smiled at her reaction and her southern voice.

Fallon screwed up her face. "Really?"

Jack came over and tussled her hair. "It's not part of my training program."

Fallon licked her spoon. "Oh, how could I forget? The great Jack Valentino, part football player, part god. I'm shocked you would humble yourself to speak to me."

Jack laughed out loud. "I see you've grown a backbone since I saw you last." He took the moment and really looked at Fallon and found himself surprised to see that she was beautiful. Gone was the little girl who used to drive him crazy.

Jack replied, "I missed you kiddo."

"You missed me?" Fallon asked. "I'm pretty sure I have always gotten on your nerves. You and ..." Fallon couldn't say her name.

Jack took Fallon's hand. "I'm sorry about your sister and about earlier. I didn't know."

Fallon pulled her hand away from his. "Don't worry about it. Thanks for the concern."

Jack decided not to push it tonight. He ruffled her hair again. "Goodnight, brat."

"Goodnight, football Neanderthal."

Jack smiled and left.

Later that night, Jack lay in bed and thought about Fallon. Could he really marry her? He had no romantic feelings for her. Of the two, Jack would have chosen Eva because she was his equal. Fallon was just a kid. Jack had a sinking sick feeling that he was trapped. He couldn't take her to school with him, it would be embarrassing to have to tell his friends that he had a wife.

Chapter 5

The sun welcomed in a new day in New Jersey as Jack woke up with a plan the next morning. He would try to buy some time before marrying Fallon. There was no way to get out of the marriage when his father had made up his mind. Besides, he understood his obligation to his family and to agreements that had been made. Maybe there was a way around this happening now. He was going to try to sell his father on waiting and giving Fallon time to heal from the losses in her life. It felt wrong to use her tragedies to try to buy some time, but he had to try.

Jack found his father working at his desk when he walked into his study. "Son, how are you this morning?"

Wasting no time in telling his dad his plan, Jack said, "Dad, I'll marry Fallon. But, I would like to respectfully ask for some time, not just for me, but for Fallon also. It would be better if she had some time to process what has happened. She is just a kid and needs some time to mature." Jack continued, "I could finish college and possibly play football before we marry."

There was no response. Johnny's face changed, gone was the man who raised him. In his place was a fearsome crime lord. Jack knew at that moment he had made a mistake. "No" was not a word in his father's vocabulary, especially when it came to those under his protection. Johnny walked over to the cabinet and pressed a button. A drawer emerged with a loaded hand gun.

Johnny calmly picked it up and walked over to Jack and put it to his right temple. Jack backed up until his back was flush with the wall. Johnny said in the coldest voice, "I didn't raise you to run away from your responsibilities. Let me make this clear to you son, you will marry her in the next week or so, or I will put a bullet in your brain. Time for play is over now. You will do what is required of you for the family. Do you understand me?"

Shaking, Jack nodded. He could feel the cold of the metal still pressed at his temple.

Johnny continued, "I will never have this conversation with you again. Are we clear?"

"Yes, sir."

Johnny lowered the gun, walked over, and put it back in the drawer from which it came. Jack was still standing against the wall, shocked at what had just happened. Johnny motioned for him to take a seat. Not wanting a repeat of another threat, he followed his father's directive.

In a controlled voice, Johnny said, "Jack, listen to me. Fallon is now under our protection. To fulfill the debt owed to her family, one of us must marry her. I couldn't betray your mother so the responsibility falls to you. If she is under our protection, no one would dare touch her. Do you understand the importance of this?"

Jack wanted to argue, but didn't. "I did not fully appreciate the situation. Whatever you want, I will do."

Johnny nodded, pleased as he sat down behind his desk. "I realize you need some time to adjust. It's early spring. I will give you time to finish the semester. You will come back as soon as your semester is out. I will make all the arrangements."

Jack sat quietly. His father seemed to have it all planned out, whether Jack liked it or not. "She will be returning with me to school in the fall?"

Johnny answered quickly. "I have been thinking this through. I am going to buy you and Fallon a place in Cambridge close to campus. She will enroll in your school once she completes high school. I have made some inquiries and it is all but set. They are willing to overlook her completing with just a GED. Fallon got waitlisted based on her high school performance, but will be moved up the list. The athletic department is anxious to keep you happy."

The question that Jack needed to ask felt stuck in his throat. Jack desperately wanted to play professional football. He even had agents begging him to sign with them, telling him he could go number one in the draft pick. Working up the nerve and he finally asked, "Do you have any thoughts on my trying to play professional football?"

Johnny smiled. "My gift to you is to allow you to play for a couple of years. This is a reward for you doing the bidding of the family. If something should happen to me though, the family will look to you to take over. Do you understand?"

Jack was not surprised at his father's proclamation about taking over the family's business. He had heard it his whole life. He had been groomed from a small child to run the business. Jack just wanted an opportunity to explore football before becoming his dad, but his dad just didn't get it. Football was everything to him. Relief poured over him as the answer sunk in deep. He would get his chance.

Abruptly changing the topic, Johnny spoke. "I want you to take Fallon out of the house. Take her to dinner or a movie. She has been cooped up here, and it would do her good to get out of here."

"Will it be safe?"

"I have made arrangements for you to have your own security team when she is out of the house. You will need to be careful, but I think it'll be fine."

"I will go talk to her and see if she wants to go out tonight." Jack got up and shook his father's hand before leaving the room. They both needed their relationship to be solid.

Jack found Fallon in her room lying on her bed. "Time to get up, lazy bones. I'm freeing you from this prison of a house."

Fallon sat up in bed. "What? Can I leave and go home?" Before Jack could answer, Fallon jumped out of bed and put on her robe. Jack couldn't deny that Fallon was beautiful, but she definitely looked young.

"Whoa, Fallon. I should have stated that differently. Let's go to a movie or out to lunch. Nothing has changed, but dad feels like it's safe enough for us to go to town. That's the benefit of being under the protection of the mighty Valentino family."

Fallon snorted and sat back down on the edge of the bed, "You want to go out? I appreciate your concern, but I'm fine."

Jack walked over, sat on the bed and put his arm around Fallon. Jack felt a spark when he made contact with her skin but acted like nothing happened. "It's not good for you to be stuck here in the house. Dad has arranged for security, so it'll be fine. Why don't we go out to this pizza place nearby? It's a safe place for my family to eat."

She considered his offer. "Do you really think it would be safe? What if being with me puts you in danger?"

Jack laughed out loud, "Fallon, do you have any idea about my family business?"

Fallon pulled away from his embrace. Shyly she responded, "My father told us you were the mob."

She looked so cute when she answered in her southern voice, Jack laughed again. "Do you even know what that means?"

Fallon shook her head, agitated that he continued to laugh at her. "I have some idea, but dad never gave us any details. I only know what I have seen on the movies. Should I be afraid of you?"

Jack smiled and pulled her close to him again before he realized what he was doing. He snuggled her and smiled into her hair. "Baby, don't ever be afraid of me or my family."

Fallon pushed him away and stood up. "Gross, Jack. Don't ever call me baby. I'm not another one of your rich college girls that you can smooth talk."

Jack had no idea why he was acting this way, but Fallon's reaction shocked him. He had never had his touch rejected by a girl. He dropped his arms to the side and tried to play it cool as he could. "Sorry kid, I forgot who I was talking to for a moment." Jack got up to leave, hoping that he seemed unaffected. "Be ready at 7:00. I promise to be on my best behavior."

"Thanks, Jack. I really appreciate what you and your family are doing for me," she said.

He smiled at her as he left the room.

Fallon fell back on the bed. Did Jack just make a move on her? Fallon was confused. One minute he was calling her "kiddo," and the next he has her snuggled in his embrace. Fallon had never considered Jack boyfriend material, mostly because she felt he was rotten to the core: Rich boy, athlete, and generally not a nice person. Though he was so handsome it hurt, Fallon thought it would be easy to fall for a guy like Jack. He was dangerous, unpredictable, and capable of taking your heart without you ever knowing you lost it. He was after all, the son of Johnny Hearts.

Jack left the room in a state of confusion also. For a moment, Fallon felt right in his arms, like she was supposed to be there. Jack had to keep his mind straight. He didn't need the distraction of a woman to get in the way of his plans. It seemed he would have to keep Fallon at a distance. It would be easier that way.

Walking down to her room, Jack realized he was nervous. This was new to him to be anxious for a date. Opening the door to her room, he saw her checking her outfit in the mirror. Leaning the doorway watching, the sight that greeted him left him speechless. Fallon looked stunningly beautiful. Her hair was in loose curls around her shoulders framed her glowing face. Her makeup was light, but effective. Jack couldn't stop himself. "I'm glad to know I will be eating with the most beautiful girl in the room." The compliment rolled off his tongue before he could stop it from happening.

Fallon blushed and rolled her eyes at him. "Thanks. I'm ready to go."

Giving her a smile, Jack motioned for Fallon to leave the room and as she passed, he put his hand at her lower back. Fallon didn't know how to respond. Jack guided her through the house. Fallon was struck with how easy Jack was around women. She guessed that he had plenty of experience in dating and being around females.

At the door to the driveway, Jack and Fallon passed Johnny. Johnny said, "Don't worry, Fallon, we have this outing covered."

"Thanks Johnny Hearts."

Jack continued to lead Fallon out the door. There was an army of men in suits and three black SUVs parked waiting to escort the couple. Jack led Fallon to the middle one and helped her inside. Two men got in the front while the others filed into the other two vehicles.

Sensing her anxiety, Jack reached over and grabbed Fallon's hand, and said, "Don't panic, we are just going for dinner. You are safe with me."

Jack didn't release Fallon's hand all the way to the restaurant. He continually caressed her thumb and hand as they rode in the SUV on the short ride. As they pulled to a stop, the men surrounded the SUV and opened the door for Fallon and Jack to get out. Fallon was quickly escorted into the restaurant. Jack reached over and grabbed her hand again. "I know this is uncomfortable, but this will establish that you are with me. You will be safe in this town, there is no one crazy enough to mess with my father."

"Thank you." Although it was awkward to be holding Jack's hand, Fallon understood what he meant when they were escorted into the restaurant. The establishment went silent as they entered.

Jack leaned in and whispered in Fallon's ear, "See what I mean?"

Fallon smiled and nodded even though she was still uncomfortable holding Jack's hand.

The owner, Vinny, walked over and grabbed Jack in a hug. "Our son has returned home with a beautiful woman!" Vinny turned to Fallon and kissed her on both cheeks. "Welcome, welcome."

Jack pulled Fallon close to him, "Vinny, Fallon needs a good pizza."

Vinny pulled back, "What kind of pizza would you like?"

Fallon smiled and said, "I'd love a vegetable pizza."

Vinny clapped his hands together. "I will make you a pizza you will never forget." He signaled and a server showed Fallon and Jack to their seat.

Fallon looked around the restaurant and then at Jack and said, "It's like you are some kind of superstar here. Everyone is staring at you."

Jack took a moment, turned, and looked around. Fallon was right. People were openly staring. In a complete surprise, Jack stood up and said, "Vinny, drinks for everyone on me!" The restaurant exploded in applause. People came over and introduced themselves to Fallon and paid their respects to Jack. Jack was kind and introduced Fallon as his girlfriend, holding her hand and smiling.

Fallon was shocked when he called her his girlfriend. Jack squeezed her hand offering some reassurance and leaned over, "Remember what I said earlier. This is for your protection."

Fallon's shock disappeared, replaced with disappointment. It was all part of his act. He still saw her as a bratty kid. Did she want more from Jack? She had only been with him a short while, yet she found herself falling under his spell.

After the crowd left, the waitress came and took their order. Fallon stayed with the pizza and Jack ordered pasta and drinks. Two of the security guards stood close by the table. It was awkward at first, but Fallon understood that they were necessary.

The food came and Jack and Fallon fell into easy conversation. Jack found he was pleasantly surprised by Fallon. She was intelligent and witty. He even found himself purposefully arguing with her to see her react and to try to prove him wrong. Time flew by and before they knew it, it was time to close the restaurant.

Jack looked at Fallon, "Come on beautiful, we have to leave so that Vinny and his family can go home."

"We should probably help them clean up since we have stayed so long."

Jack shrugged his shoulders. "How about I give them an outrageous tip and we call it a night?"

Taking out a credit card, Jack handed it to one of his men. He whispered something into the man's ear, which caused the man to go to the counter and pay. Vinny came over, gave Jack a hug, and said, "Don't be gone so long the next time."

Jack agreed and ushered Fallon out the door into the waiting SUV.

As the cars rolled up to the mansion Fallon said, "Thank you for tonight. I didn't realize how much I needed to get out of the house."

"Are you saying in your own way I was right?"

Fallon realized that Jack had painted her into a corner. She didn't want to admit he was right. "Maybe this time you were slightly right."

Jack looked pleased.

As they entered the house, Jack asked Fallon, "Would you like to go to the movies tomorrow?"

Fallon was surprised that he asked so quickly. "I would love to go to the movies. Just nothing that that is too sappy. Maybe a man drama."

"A man drama?" asked Jack.

"I just don't want to watch anything sad," Fallon said.

Jack pulled Fallon into his arms and gave her a hug. "I got you, pretty girl, no sadness. I will try to find the best drama or comedy for us to watch."

Fallon stepped out of his embrace. "Until tomorrow then," she said.

Jack leaned in to kiss her goodnight. It was a natural move for him as this had been a date. He sensed Fallon tense up and stopped himself. He was so close to her face. One slight move and his lips would be touching her. It was torture for him. She was his to kiss, but she rejected him again.

Fallon moved quickly and escaped to her room. Her stomach was in a twisted knot. Jack was giving off some strange vibes tonight. He was acting as if they were in a relationship. She wondered to herself if he acted like this with all women. It had been so easy to be with him tonight; Fallon had to remind herself it was not a date. She didn't want to fall for Jack and be another one of his girls.

Confused, Jack returned to his room and climbed into bed. He was surprised at himself. Fallon sparked something inside of him. Was it that she was so vulnerable, or was it he was crushing on her? Jack felt protective of her. After all, she was his.

His thoughts churned throughout the night wavering between wanting her and the reality of his situation. Tossing and turning in bed, he wrestled with the idea of taking Fallon back to school with him. She wouldn't fit it in with his schedule or his friends. Would it be right to remove her from here and make her adjust to his lifestyle? Also, what would he do about security? Would there be security everywhere they went? These thoughts kept him from sleep.

Jack got up very early. The sun hadn't peeked through the clouds yet. He couldn't sleep with all the thoughts rolling around in his mind. Something possessed him to go into Fallon's room. The door creaked slightly as he opened it up. The sight of her sleeping took his breath away. She looked like an angel in her sleep. The angel in the bed was his forever. Jack stood there for a moment staring and lost in thought. Giving up the fight, he went over and slipped into the bed. The warmth of the bed felt comforting against the cold. Fallon opened her eyes and found Jack lying on the bed beside her.

"Is everything okay?"

Jack turned and faced her. "You kept me up all night. I thought maybe I could get some sleep if I was in here. Is that okay?"

Fallon reached out and touched his faced smiled and said, "Of course, but stay on your side." In her state of sleepiness, Fallon didn't put up much resistance because she still thought of Jack like a brother. She had dismissed any earlier romantic thoughts about him as a mistake. There was no way Jack was interested in her. Fallon turned on her side and fell back to sleep.

When her breathing evened out, Jack snuggled close and wrapped his arm around her. Surprisingly, Jack went to sleep quickly.

A few hours later, Maria and Johnny were in the kitchen. Maria asked, "Where is Jack? He's not in his room."

"What do you mean he is not in his room?" Johnny barked angrily.

Maria responded in a timid voice, "I walked by and his door was open, the room was empty."

Johnny got up before Maria could finish talking. He started walking down the hall to Fallon's room. If he was with her, Jack would make this right today.

Chapter 6

The door to Fallon's room slammed open. Both Fallon and Jack quickly sat up in bed. Johnny never looked at Fallon. He was only focused on Jack. "You know what this means."

"I understand. Nothing happened in here; we would not disrespect you."

Johnny looked between Jack and Fallon. "I will see you in my office in an hour." Jack nodded at Johnny.

When Johnny left the room, Jack collapsed back on the bed and turned toward Fallon. "I need to go and get ready. You need to get ready too, and please dress like you are going to church. My dad likes our appearance to be perfect. A reflection of our family status."

Fallon responded, "What is going on Jack? Is he mad?"

"Mad is not what dad is today. He is determined."

"What does that mean, determined?" Fallon was frustrated. It was as if she was being left out of the conversation. She grabbed Jack's arm as he got out of bed. "Tell me the truth, Jack. What's going on?"

Jack sat back down on the bed. "Don't freak out, okay."

Fallon nodded.

Jack looked at Fallon and said, "Before I tell you, I want you to know that I'm alright with this."

"Alright with what?"

"Fallon, my family believes in repaying debts. My father owed your father a great debt." Jack went on to explain the blood debt.

Fallon responded, "What is payment for the debt?"

Jack took her hand, "An arranged marriage."

Fallon was speechless. It took her a moment to find her voice. "You must be joking. I can't marry you. I'm barely eighteen."

"Well, I'm hurt," Jack said playfully. Fallon was sitting in a state of shock.

Jack tried to make her understand. "Listen Fallon, I know this is a shock. It was shock to me, but I see the wisdom of this plan. You would always be safe. My family will always protect you."

"But shouldn't we marry for love, not protection? I don't want to be your wife. I'm too young, and we don't really get along with each other. This is crazy, I'm not getting married."

"I know that you are upset, but this deal was done long ago. My father will ensure that we are married today. There is nothing to do now but face reality. This is what your father wanted." Jack took Fallon's hand. "Get ready and be in dad's office in an hour. Please don't make me come and get you."

"Jack, please stop and talk to me."

Jack ignored her and walked out. Fallon stood in shock for a couple of minutes. None of this made sense. Why would her father seek protection for her? Why was her family dead? Fallon decided to get ready and meet Jack in Johnny's office to argue her reasons for not wanting to get married. They had to understand that she didn't want this.

Fallon walked down the hallway like she was going to the guillotine. Married? She was too young. It took all her strength to push open the door. When she walked in, she found Johnny, Jack, and some other men in the room. Maria came in followed by a priest. Jack walked over and took Fallon's hand.

Johnny spoke first. "Fallon, Jack has explained the situation?" Fallon nodded trying to find the courage to speak. Before she could utter a word, Johnny spoke again, "Fallon, I think this is a good thing for our families. Your dad wanted this, and I want this. After today, you don't need to worry any longer. You and Jack will be happy together."

Fallon started to speak but Jack pulled on her hand and shook his head no. Fallon didn't have a chance to protest. The priest stepped forward and the ceremony started. They got to the part when they had to say, "I Do." Jack repeated the line with a firm voice. When it was Fallon's turn, she couldn't say it. She wasn't ready to be a wife. The priest asked again.

Johnny stepped forward and said, "As Fallon's guardian, and on behalf of my brother James and his wife Vivian, she accepts Jack as her husband." The moment was awkward. The Priest stopped and waited for her verbal consent. Fallon couldn't find the words. Johnny grunted and the Priest continued the ceremony. Fallon couldn't believe that the Priest would continue without her consent. Jack squeezed her hand to reassure her, but Fallon could not believe she was getting married at this moment. She wanted to run from the room.

The rest of the ceremony passed in a blur. It was quick and to the point. Both Fallon and Jack signed the marriage certificate. When it was over, each person in the room came over and gave the couple a hug and best wishes. Fallon teared up. Her family should be here with her. They would have stopped this madness. She shouldn't be forced into marriage with a guy, who up until a few days ago, hated her guts. A small tear escaped and ran down her cheek.

Jack reached up and wiped it away. "I'm sorry that your family isn't here. I know you miss them terribly right now." Jack pointed to the people in the room. "Look around the room, Mrs. Valentino. You now have more family that you can possibly imagine."

Johnny heard what Jack was saying to Fallon. He asked everyone to leave the room so that he could speak to the couple.

When everyone cleared the room, Johnny asked Fallon and Jack to sit down. "I wanted to take a moment to congratulate you. Fallon, when the time comes, Jack will explain the family business to you. There is no hurry for that to happen. You both need to decide where you are going to live and how Fallon is going to finish school."

Fallon looked at Jack. Jack answered his father. "I think it best if Fallon and I take a vacation and try to figure some of this out."

Johnny thought for a moment and said, "Sounds like a good idea. Come up with some places and I will make the arrangements. How about Italy? It would be easy to arrange security with the family."

"Dad, let me talk to Fallon. We need a moment to process."

Fallon looked at Johnny and Jack. "I don't know if this is the proper time, but I wanted to offer some money to help with the expenses."

Jack clenched his lips together. Fallon could tell that this made him angry. Jack turned and stared at Fallon. She felt small sitting in her chair.

Johnny interceded on Fallon's behalf. "Jack, she doesn't know." He continued, "Fallon, in our family the men take care of everything. Your offer was nice, but we will take care of everything, including all of the costs."

"I'm sorry, I meant no offense." Fallon felt small sitting in the chair next to Jack. They had been married just a few minutes and he was already angry with her.

"None taken. In fact, you should know that today you became a very wealthy woman."

Fallon didn't know how to respond other than to say, "You have worked hard to provide for all of us. Thank you."

Johnny looked pleased. "I will leave you two alone. Make plans and meet us in the kitchen in a few minutes. Maria has a special breakfast planned."

After Johnny left the room, Jack and Fallon stared at each other. Fallon spoke first, "I didn't mean to offend you. I thought I was being polite."

Jack still looked aggravated, "You will learn the ways of our family." After a pause, he continued, "This is awkward. I really don't know how to have a wife." He gave Fallon a killer smile that melted her insides.

"Well, I don't really know how to have a husband. I guess we'll have to figure it out together. We could agree to be friends first and finish school before we try to have a real relationship."

Fallon watched Jack visibly relax. She knew that he was not ready for this commitment. Frankly, it made her sick to her stomach to realize she was married. She wasn't ready and she was sure that he wasn't ready either.

"I like your idea. What did you have in mind?" Jack quizzed Fallon.

"I want to finish high school. I can't quit now, I'm so close to finishing. It just seems it would be easier if I did that here." Fallon added, "I feel like I could be protected here and you could finish your last year in Cambridge."

"If we did that, we would have to offer dad a plan to be together after you finished school. Maybe during the summer or early fall we could move you to Cambridge. How does that sound to you?"

"Cambridge? Where would I go to school?"

"Fallon, you've been accepted to my Ivy League. Dad called and made some inquiries."

Fallon sat back in her seat. "Was I accepted because of you?"

"Don't look at it that way. You were on the waitlist and you got moved up." Jack added, "Congratulations, it's an accomplishment."

Jack got up and pulled Fallon out of her seat. "Let's not focus on this today. Let's go celebrate with our family. Where would you like to go on a short trip?"

"I don't know. Can I have some time to think?"

"Of course, let's go party." Jack took Fallon's hand and headed to the kitchen.

Fallon was shocked when they entered the room. There were people everywhere. Johnny raised his hand and everyone in the room got quiet.

"Today is a special day for our family. We welcome Fallon to our fold. Jack, your mother would be so proud of the man you have become. You have brought great honor to the Valentino name."

Johnny then addressed Fallon. "Fallon, you were the light of your family. Your parents wanted this to ensure your happiness. We miss them today. It is important to know that you are no longer alone. We are your family. We all love you and Jack, and wish you the best of luck."

Johnny motioned and a man in the group brought forward a box and handed it to Jack. "This was my wife's ring. Fallon wear this with pride." Jack stepped forward and took the box. He opened it with care. Nestled inside was a huge diamond.

Fallon's hand shook as Jack slipped the ring on her finger. It fit perfectly. "It was meant for you," Jack whispered as he took Fallon's hand and kissed the ring. "Mine forever." Jack tipped Fallon's chin up and gently kissed her on lips. The room exploded in applause.

Johnny walked up and took Fallon's ring hand. He raised her hand and kissed her ring. "This is where it belongs."

As soon as Johnny dropped Fallon's hand, people started gathering around her giving her hugs and well wishes. The party went on for the entire day and Fallon started to tire from the activities. As night began to fall, Fallon excused herself to her room.

Even though she was surrounded by people, Fallon felt alone. It was as though she was a stranger in a strange land. This was all new to her. The life that she had known and loved was over. Fallon went and looked out the window at the beautiful spring night. If she was at home, she would have been sitting at the dinner table working on school work while her family went about their normal daily activities. Nothing was normal now. Everything was wrapped in a thick veil of crazy and secrets.

Fallon was so lost in her thoughts she did not hear the door open. Jack came into the room and wrapped his arms around her. Fallon stiffened at his touch. He pulled her so her back was flush with his chest. Fallon leaned back and relaxed against Jack. He pulled her tighter against him.

"Are you okay? I saw you leave the room."

"I'm fine. I just wanted a moment to myself."

"My family can be overwhelming at times. They mean no harm."

"I know. I just miss my family." Both stood in silence, their breaths turning rhythmic. Fallon asked, "How long can you stay before you head back to campus?"

"I can stay for a few days then I have to get back. Have you thought about where you would like to go?"

Thinking about her dream about her parents and Eva, Fallon responded, "I think I would like to go to Missouri." Fallon had thought a lot about her dream of her parents. She concluded they wanted her to go find out about her sister. She couldn't just walk away from her family and their deaths.

"Missouri?"

"Eva was working at Wilson Creek Battlefield. She sent a message by Dr. Smith, the guy that helped me at the hospital. It was a quote from Patrick Cleburne. She was working on a project there for the Patrick Cleburne display. Eva had some crazy theory that Cleburne had changed during the war and was trying to end slavery in the South. The people that she worked with might have some information about what happened to her. I have to know."

"If it's important to you, then we will go. I'll make the arrangements. Let me go find dad and tell him and we can leave tomorrow." Jack tightened his arms around her before backing out of the room. "Come back to the party." Jack left the room.

Fallon felt hopeful for the first time since she had lost her sister. Maybe Missouri would hold some answers. She took a moment to collect herself and then returned to the party.

It was getting late, but the party was still going strong. As the night went on, Fallon got nervous. She was worried about her wedding night. Although she cared for Jack, she wasn't ready for the next step. Jack had been holed up in his dad's office for hours, drinking with the boys.

When she saw him again, Fallon had been in the bed for some time. Sleep would not come easy for her. The door to the room opened and in walked Jack. "Fallon, are you asleep?"

"No. There was too much running through my mind about today." She responded in a nervous voice.

Jack entered the room. He looked gorgeous, of course. He went straight to the bathroom and came out in just a t-shirt and underwear. Fallon was embarrassed, but couldn't help but stare. His body was beautiful. Jack had muscles in all the right places. He pulled back the covers and climbed into bed. "We have to talk," he said. Fallon could smell the alcohol on his breath.

It was time for Jack to face his responsibilities. He had no choice. Jack reached out and caressed Fallon's face. "You are so incredibly beautiful, it hurts."

Fallon smiled and placed her hand over Jack's on her face. Jack shifted in the bed, pulling Fallon under him. He propped his arms around her head so that his full body weight was not on her and Fallon didn't protest. Jack leaned down slowly and kissed her on the lips. He gently kissed her gently a few times before he really started kissing her. Jack was unprepared for his response to Fallon. She was a siren song to him. He felt like he could never kiss her enough and he wanted more.

"Fallon, my family has expectations. One of them is that you are my wife in every way possible. My family would expect you to be my true wife. Do you understand what I mean?"

Fallon turned a bright shade of red. She was glad Jack couldn't see her complexion in the dark. It was hard to tell him no. Part of her wanted to be his wife in that way, but her senses quickly snapped her out of it.

"I appreciate what you're saying, but I'm not ready for that type of relationship. I need some time to adjust."

"Listen to me, I know this is a lot to take in, but I have to make you mine." Jack said confidently. "My family, especially my father, would not understand. This is greater than just us. I promise you baby, it won't be bad."

Fallon reached up and touched Jack's face. "I'm sorry, but I'm not ready. I don't feel that way about you."

Jack was stunned. He had never been rejected in his entire life. His alcohol bolstered anger kicked in. "Do you think I relish the thought of making love to you? You're like my sister."

Fallon felt her temper rising. She was hurt by his words and lashed out with her own. "Do what you have to do to make your family happy without touching me."

Jack shook his head. "I can tell you are going to make me miserable for my entire life." Jack groaned in the dark. "Do you have any idea how many girls are desperate to get in my bed?" Fallon glared at him as he continued. "I get married to a beautiful woman and my wife doesn't even want me. This is great." Jack moved off Fallon and left the bed. Mumbling to himself about marriage as he walked to the bathroom.

Fallon could hear him fussing in the bathroom. He came out of the bathroom holding a pocketknife.

"Jack, what are you doing?" Fallon asked in a concerned tone.

"As old fashioned as it seems, my father will want proof that we consummated the marriage."

"You must be kidding me." Fallon's eyes got big. Was she living a nightmare?

"No, my dad will be in here bright and early looking for proof on the sheets and I plan to give it to him without touching you, as requested. My dad is not the man you want to disappoint."

"What do you mean proof?" Fallon asked in disbelief. "Are you serious?" she exclaimed when she realized what Jack was about to do.

"I wish I was kidding. Get up." Jack took the top layers of covers off the bed exposing the fitted sheet. He took the knife and pierced his pinky finger with the blade before spreading his blood on the sheet. After he was done, he walked back in to the bathroom. Fallon was left dumbstruck staring at the blood on the sheet.

When Jack walked back into the room. Fallon couldn't help herself. She walked over and gave him a hug. "I'm so sorry. I'm sorry you had to marry me. I'm sorry that your finger is bleeding, that ..." Jack caught her face in his hands and kissed her. As the kiss deepened Fallon, almost began to regret her decision. Jack was delicious. They both kissed hard as Jack backed Fallon up till she was against the wall. Jack ran his hands down her body while Fallon tangled her hands in Jack's hair. The kiss erupted. Fallon moaned slightly as Jack pulled her even closer.

Jack broke the kiss. "Baby, this might not be so bad after all. If you change your mind, I'm available."

Fallon laughed. "You are too much, Jack." She left the embrace. "Can we change the sheets?"

"No, we will have to make do tonight. Grab a towel out of the bathroom and cover it up." Fallon went in the bathroom and got a large towel to cover up the bloodstain on the sheet and tried to pretend that was not reality.

In the sexiest move Fallon had ever seen, Jack reached up and pulled off his shirt with one hand. Fallon openly stared at him. "You are in really good shape."

"Football baby. I have to be in top shape to be ready for the next season. You probably didn't know this, but I plan on playing professional football after next year."

Fallon didn't respond. She distracted herself with arranging the towel and covers before she climbed in. Jack was disappointed that she didn't comment on his plans.

Fallon scooted over near the edge of the bed as Jack got under the covers. "Really, Fallon? Scoot over here. I want to sleep with you in my arms. You can give me this."

Fallon hesitated, but scooted over. Jack pulled her next to him and wrapped his arms around her. "Night, Mrs. Valentino."

Fallon responded, "Night." She could barely process the day's events. She was married to a gorgeous man who just announced that he planned to play football professionally. It was some time before she settled enough to sleep. Jack fell asleep immediately.

Early morning came quickly. Jack woke first, knowing his father would be in shortly. He didn't want to move. Fallon was sleeping with her head on his chest. It was nice to wake up with her in his bed. Jack gently shook Fallon to wake her, but with little result. She moaned as he tried whispering to her. In response, she moved off him and laid back on her pillow, completely ignoring his request. The morning light was enough for Jack to see her face and was astonished to find she looked like an angel.

"Fallon, you need to wake up. Dad will be in here at any moment."

"Shut up Jack, I don't care." She groaned in reply, swatting him away sleepily. Fallon had never been a morning person. She particularly hated to be awakened early in the morning. "Let me sleep."

"Do you want Dad to find us in bed together?"

"I don't care, just please be quiet."

"Fallon, wake up. I don't want you to be embarrassed."

Fallon suddenly reached up and put her hand over Jack's mouth. "Shut up old man."

"Old man? I'll show you an old man." Jack pulled on Fallon until she rolled over. In one swoop, he had her under him. Jack took her arms and pinned them over her head with one hand. "Now tell me my grumpy wife, about me being an old man." Fallon struggled to get loose with no success. Jack took the opportunity to find out where Fallon was ticklish. He was delighted to hear her cackle with laughter. She begged him to stop.

"Not fair, you have man strength!" Jack started raining kisses down her face and onto her neck and collar bone. Fallon moaned. "Really not fair, old man."

"Kiss me properly and I will let you up." Jack released her arms. She waited for him to make the first move.

"Waiting, Fallon."

Fallon reached up timidly and caressed Jack's face. Gently she pulled his face down to hers. She saw him close his eyes. He moved forward and pressed his lips to hers and Fallon couldn't help but close her eyes. Jack reached down and pulled her legs up, linking around his body. He groaned in her mouth.

Neither noticed that the door had open until they heard Johnny Hearts clear his throat. Jack reached down and pulled the sheets to cover Fallon. "Dad, couldn't you knock?"

Johnny responded in kind, "Tradition holds. I'll give you a moment to get decent."

Jack kissed Fallon on the head. "Go to the bathroom. I'll come get you when we're done." Fallon got up and scampered to the bathroom.

When she was gone, Johnny said nothing. He walked over and pulled back the covers to see the proof he wanted. Without a word, he turned to leave the room. He stopped when he reached the door. "Thank you. My debt to her father is paid." He continued, "I have your travel plans ready. The jet is fueled and ready to go."

Jack didn't know what to say. His dad had never thanked him before. He stood in silence as his father left the room. Jack walked over and stripped the bed. He balled up the sheets and put them in the trash can. Fallon came out of the bathroom in a robe with her hair pulled up. Jack was struck by how cute she looked.

"Dad was pleased. He said the jet was ready to leave whenever we are."

"Jet?" Fallon inquired with surprise in her voice.

"We are rich, baby. Please understand. We don't travel by commercial air."

Fallon simply answered, "Oh. Well, I'm glad I married a rich man. Commercial flights can be tedious." She smiled.

"I wish I could warn you properly, but I have no idea who'll be waiting for us when we go into the kitchen. Let's get packed so we can make a quick exit. Missouri, here we come!" Fallon nodded in response.

Getting ready was hard. Fallon couldn't keep her attention on packing. It was weird to think she would be traveling with Jack, especially as his wife. She couldn't help but wonder what had brought the Valentino family its riches. She wanted to ask, but didn't want to upset Jack.

Jack came into the bathroom as she was getting ready and turned on the shower. He didn't act embarrassed that she was there in the slightest as he dropped his underwear and stepped into the shower. Fallon turned bright red. He was so comfortable with his nudity, but Fallon was not.

Fallon collected her makeup and went into the other room to finish getting ready. She chose a mini-skirt and short sleeve top for the day. Jack came out of the bathroom. He looked yummy fresh from his shower. He had a towel wrapped around his waist. On display was a chest sculpted with muscles. As he grabbed a shaving kit from the counter he remarked, "You know, at some point, you're not going to be embarrassed around me."

Fallon turned red again. "I doubt that," she replied.

Jack walked back into the bathroom to shave while she finished her makeup. Her hair dryer was in the bathroom. She walked in as Jack had his faced lathered up. She gathered the cord and turned to leave. Jack grabbed her wrist. "Stay here and dry your hair." He released her hand and picked up his razor.

Fallon followed his command. She wanted to watch him shave. It was an intimate act. She dried her hair and she caught Jack watching her several times. She couldn't decide what she saw in his eyes. Was it lust or humor?

Jack finished and cleaned up his mess. Fallon finished with her hair. She turned and left the bathroom. Jack came in the room and said, "I need to pack my stuff. Wait here until I get back. We'll go face the crowd together."

Fallon was getting her clothes together when a knock on the door startled her. Johnny came in wheeling a new set of overly expensive luggage. "A small gift for your trip."

Fallon was stunned. "Thank you. They're beautiful, I'll be afraid they will get harmed on our trip."

Johnny walked over and gave her a kiss on the cheek. "Don't worry, if there is any damage, I will replace it with two."

Fallon smiled and said, "This is really nice. Thanks again."

Johnny looked at Fallon, "You make a beautiful bride. Seeing you this morning reminds me of my wife. She would have been happy with this match. Jack is not an easy person to deal with sometimes and you will need a lot of patience. Make him happy, is all that I ask of you."

Fallon choked up, "Jack has been nothing but wonderful to me. I will do my best to make him happy."

Johnny walked over and gave her hug. "I've always wanted a daughter to spoil. You're going to have to get used to my gifts."

"I'll do my best," Fallon responded through a tense voice.

"You know, I leave her happy and when I return and she is crying. Dad, what did you do?"

Fallon wiped a tear from her cheek. "We were just talking. Your dad gave me this beautiful luggage."

Jack smiled. "You know, he will spoil you rotten. He's always wanted a girl."

Fallon laughed, "I've heard."

Johnny gave Fallon a quick hug and turned to Jack, reaching his hand out to shake. "Morning, Son."

Jack took his hand, "Morning, Dad."

"Come, let's eat breakfast so we can send you on a proper honeymoon."

There was a crowd waiting in the kitchen. Some of the guys decided to give Jack a hard time and thankfully Jack played along. Breakfast was quick and painless. Everyone was in a joyful mood; even Maria sat down and enjoyed the meal.

When it was time to leave, Johnny called Fallon and Jack into his office. He handed Jack an envelope. "Open this after you leave." To Fallon, he handed a black American Express Card with her name on it. "Buy whatever you want. There is no limit on this card." He went over behind his desk and pulled out a box. In it was a 9mm handgun. He handed the weapon to Jack. "Keep this on you at all times," was the only instruction he gave.

Fallon was shocked as Jack took the gun and loaded the clip. "Love you, Dad." Jack walked over and briefly hugged his dad. Fallon followed the lead and gave Johnny a quick hug, still reeling from his parting gift to his son.

Johnny followed Jack and Fallon out to the SUV. There were three again. Jack and Fallon climbed in and waved goodbye to Johnny. She felt sad to leave, but excited to go to Missouri. She needed some answers about her family.

Chapter 7

The drive to the airport was quick. Jack held her hand the whole way. The three SUV's pulled into the airport where they were waved to a small road that led to a tarmac. There sat a sleek, beautiful jet. It was bigger than Fallon expected. When the truck stopped, a man in a suit opened the door.

"Mrs. Valentino, this way." He helped her out of the vehicle. Fallon couldn't help but stop and stare.

"She's a beauty." Jack whispered in her ear. "This is dad's latest toy." Jack took her hand and led her up the stairs to the plane. Fallon was awed when she stepped inside and saw the luxurious interior. The inside of the jet was made of up of dark Brazilian Cherry wood and cream leather seats. Three rows of chairs led to a private area in the rear of the plane. Jack took her on the tour. The plane came equipped with a bedroom and a bathroom.

"Wow," was all Fallon could say.

"Dad has great taste." Jack said as they toured the plane. "Do you want a nap?" Fallon nodded yes.

"Let's get the plane in the air. I could use some sleep also." Jack picked up a phone and gave the command to take off. Fallon was awed by Jack, watching him be in control. It was a side of him she hadn't seen before. They both buckled in. The take-off was smooth and quick.

After the plane was a safe cruising altitude, Fallon crawled into the bed and Jack followed. He pulled Fallon into his arms. They were both asleep quickly as they only had a few hours of sleep the night before. The knock on the door woke both of them. "Sir, we are making our descent into Springfield."

"Thanks," Jack replied.

"Fallon, wake up. We are here." Fallon sat up in bed. "Really? That was super quick."

They unloaded from the plane to find a security team and more SUV's on the tarmac. Jack went over and met the team. Fallon stayed back until he motioned her over.

"Do you want to go to the hotel or to Wilson's Creek?"

"I would love to go to Wilson's Creek first." Fallon looked at Jack. He nodded to the men and they started up the

SUV's. One of the men opened the door and they both crawled into the vehicle.

Fallon felt sad to think that her sister was here recently. She tried not to dwell on that fact as they traveled. Jack sensed her mood change. "Are you alright?"

"I'm fine. Just a little sad but I'll be alright. I just want some answers so that I can move on."

"Come over here and sit on my lap." Jack opened his arms in invitation.

"I don't think that would be very safe," Fallon teased back. Jack made her feel better by his invitation. She didn't feel alone.

Jack reached over and hit the button to unbuckle her seat belt. He took her hand and pulled her over so he could wrap his arms around her middle while she sat on his lap. She leaned back against him. Jack was security for her. Fallon was trying to remember all that Dr. Smith had told her in the hospital about Eva. They sat in silence, lost in thought until they arrived at Wilson's Creek Battlefield.

The Battlefield was not what Fallon was expecting. She envisioned it being bigger. They pulled up in front of the museum that sat off to the side of a long pathway up a hill. Fallon crawled off Jack's lap. She sat and stared out the window.

"We don't have to go in. We can turn around and leave. You don't need this. You have us now." Jack kissed her hand as he talked.

"Thanks Jack, but I want to go in and see."

Jack tapped on the roof of the truck. The door was opened by one of the men in suits. Fallon got out and waited for Jack. On cue, Jack came around and reached for Fallon's hand. He led her up the stairs to the small building. The security detail went in first and gave the all clear for them to enter.

Jack led Fallon in the building. The room was quiet and empty aside from two park rangers at the welcome desk. Fallon let go of Jack's hand and walked around. There was a small shop in the room so Fallon looked around at the merchandise. She saw the museum opening and walked in. The building was small. A few exhibits and photographs adorned the wall. Nothing jumped out at her as she scanned the room.

Fallon walked to the back of the building where the exhibit was located. There it was, the display that Eva had been here working on, Patrick Cleburne's sash. Fallon stood in front of the display. Jack stayed back and let her have some alone time.

Fallon shook her head as tears threatened. There was nothing here. There were displays and great photographs, but she didn't know where else to look. She stood there for a moment longer waiting for a sign. She finally started to turn and leave as a female park ranger came and stood by Fallon.

"Fallon, I presume?"

Fallon turned and looked at her with suspicious eyes.

"I'm Karen. I worked with your sister here. I know you from your photograph."

Fallon was stunned. Jack read her expression. He started over to where she was standing but stopped when Fallon held up her hand.

"Can you give me any information about my sister? No one will tell me anything."

Karen looked around as if she was afraid someone was watching. "Things regarding your sister are weird. I don't know what's going on, but she was acting strange before her death."

"What do you mean, weird?"

Karen looked around again. She reached out and held a brochure out for Fallon. "This is all I know. I told her I would give this to you. Take it and go. You need to leave."

Fallon stuffed the brochure in her pocket. "Thank you, Karen."

Fallon turned and started towards an anxious looking Jack. He immediately quizzed her, but sensing her mood, focused on the basic facts first. "Everything okay?"

"I'm ready to go."

Jack nodded at the security staff. As they were leaving, a group of men walked in and surrounded the door. It seemed for a moment they were not going to let Fallon and Jack out. Jack pulled Fallon behind him and checked to make sure his gun was ready. The security team went to the door and made a path for them. No words were spoken. The group of men moved aside and let them out, staring at them as they walked by.

Jack had been in enough bad situations to realize having her out in the open was dangerous. He hustled Fallon to the car but she wasn't moving fast enough for him. He picked her up and ran for the vehicle. Jack threw Fallon in the car and jumped in. "Go!"

The vehicles took off and started heading back to the airport. Jack helped Fallon fasten her seat belt. He made sure she was secure. Jack got on his phone and started barking orders. "Get us in the air. I don't care. We will be there shortly. I want wheels up as soon as we get there. Make it happen!"

Jack hung up his phone. He stared at Fallon. "I don't know who they were. That was suspicious and dangerous. We're headed home. I can't protect you here."

"You overreacted. For all you know they were just there to visit the battlefield."

"Really? Trust me, they were there for us. I'm surprised they let us leave with no problems."

Fallon sat quiet. She remembered the brochure in her pocket. She took the brochure out and opened it up. A necklace with a Celtic knot dropped out of the paper. She dropped the brochure and held on to the necklace. Fallon made a sad yelping sound. Jack reached down and picked up the brochure. "What's this?"

Fallon was shaking and the tears were already forming. She tried to talk but it sounded like a garbled mess.

"Slow down, just tell me what it is." Fallon snatched the brochure of his hands. Inside was a message: "Fallon, your name is not inscribed on Fames Immortal Scroll. Go to the Hornet's Nest and where we bought this necklace. You will find what you are looking for. Love you."

"What is it? Tell me." Fallon handed Jack the brochure. He read it and handed it back to her. "What does this mean?"

Fallon shook her head and said, "Don't you get it? The Hornet's nest, Fames Immortal Scroll? Eva left me clues. I can't believe it. Why would she go to all of this trouble?" Fallon's voice trembled as she went on talking. "I just don't understand why they had to die. Were they protecting me from something? Will I ever know?"

Jack shook his head. "Fallon, I don't know what you are talking about when you say the Hornet's Nest and Fames whatever."

"It's Shiloh and Gettysburg, Civil War Battlefields."

"There is no way I'm taking you anywhere but home."

"What? Jack wait, I have to go! She is trying to tell me something. Don't do this. I have to go see."

"No." Jack was adamant. He clenched his jaw. "We are going home tonight. I know this is important, but we can't go right now. We will let whatever this is calm down, and I will take you."

"Please Jack, please."

"No way."

"Let me out of the car then. I'm not going to New Jersey. I'm going to Tennessee."

"No you are not."

"You're not the boss of me." Fallon gave him an evil look.

Jack didn't respond. The SUVs pulled up to the tarmac and Fallon's door was opened. She ignored the man waiting to help her out and instead continued to sit in the car. Jack got out and came around to lean into the open door where she was sitting. "Fallon Whitten Valentino, please get out of the car. We need to go."

Fallon responded, "I'm going to Shiloh." She continued to sit in the car.

"I'm giving you about three seconds to get out of the car and load the plane. Please don't make a scene. You won't like the outcome."

Fallon hesitantly got out of the car. She grabbed Jack's arm. "Please, take me to Tennessee." Jack stopped walking.

"You know I can't, so stop asking." He tried to pull her along. "Let's go."

Fallon stomped her foot down and started yelling at Jack. "I'm going to Tennessee. You don't control me. I have my own money, I don't need you or your permission." Before she could get another word out, Jack bent down and grabbed her legs and lifted her up over his shoulder.

Fallon started screaming and hitting his back with her fists. "Put me down!" She started crying hysterically, "I have to go! Please Jack!"

Jack carried her up the stairs to the plane entrance. He gently put her in a seat. Fallon was openly crying. One of the men in a suit brought Jack a glass of water to give to her. "Drink up, you're going to make yourself sick."

Fallon sat, steadily crying. She took a gulp of the water but Jack tipped the glass up as she was drinking before she could stop. The water poured down her throat.

Fallon heard Jack saying, "I'm sorry, baby. It has to be this way." Fallon suddenly felt woozy and the room began to sway. She couldn't focus on Jack. She knew he was talking, but she couldn't make out what he was saying. Fallon could barely hold her eyes open. She could feel herself swaying in the seat before Jack lifted her and carried her into the plane's bedroom. She remembered him removing her shoes and putting her on the bed. He whispered to her, but she didn't know what he was saying. Fallon blacked out.

Jack looked at Fallon in the bed. He felt terrible. He had no choice. He had to get her home to keep her safe. Jack felt the plane taxiing down the runway. The plane roared to life and was quickly in the air.

Jack made a phone call to his father to inform him what had happened and they were on their way home. Jack put down the phone after finishing his call and crawled in the bed beside Fallon. She would hate him for this and he hated her for making him this way. He just wanted to go back to his old life. He didn't need a wife. She was too much drama. Jack sat beside her watching her sleep, feeling guilty, as the plane made its way back to New Jersey.

The jet landed back in New Jersey where they were met with the usual security detail. Jack gathered Fallon in his arms and walked down the stairs to the waiting SUV. Fallon was still passed out and was limp in his arms. One of the men stepped forward to take Fallon but Jack refused. He lifted her into the seat and buckled her seat belt. Jack dreaded the inquisition that faced him when he got to the house.

They arrived at the house to find Johnny waiting for them at the door. He didn't question Jack as he carried Fallon to their

room. Maria came and helped get Fallon into bed. Jack walked
back to his dad's office.

Jack went and took a seat. Johnny sat on the side of his
desk. "Well, what do you think?" He asked.

Johnny shook his head. "I'm not sure. We don't know
who they were."

Johnny responded, "I think Fallon needs to stay here for a
while until we get this sorted. The question is, what are you
going to do?"

Jack took a deep breath. "I don't want to shirk my
responsibilities, but I feel Fallon needs some time to deal with
this. She was out of control tonight, and I think she is
overwhelmed. It would do her some good to get in school and
graduate."

Johnny thought for a moment before speaking. "I agree. I
made some calls today, and I can get her into the Academy to
finish her year and graduate."

"I want to return to school and finish the semester. Spring
practice has started but I'll come home as much as possible. Are
you okay with Fallon staying here?"

"I think it's for the best." Johnny replied. "She needs
some time to adjust. When are you leaving?"

"Tomorrow, after we talk. She needs to agree to let me
take her to Tennessee after everything has cooled down. It is too
dangerous for her right now when we just don't know the threat."

Johnny agreed to the plan. Jack left his office and walked
into the bedroom. Fallon was fast asleep. He felt badly for her
and couldn't imagine what she had been through in the past
couple of months. He reached over and brushed a piece of hair
from her face. She was undeniably beautiful. Jack stared at her
for a moment and wondered if she would be okay with him
leaving. He felt guilty for wanting to live his life. Jack leaned
over and kissed her on the head and left the room.

Chapter 8

Fallon woke confused. Her head was cloudy. She couldn't remember what happened. It took her some time to realize that she was back at Jack's house in New Jersey. Her mouth was terribly dry. She got out of bed, put on a robe, and headed to the kitchen.

Jack sat at the table with his father and Maria. Fallon walked over, got a glass, and filled it with water and drank it all down. "What did you give me yesterday?" There was an accusation in her voice.

"Fallon, please." Jack answered.

Fallon gave him a look that pierced his soul. She felt betrayed, he saw it in her eyes.

Johnny spoke up, "Please come and eat. You'll feel better." Maria got up and fixed Fallon a plate.

Johnny addressed Maria, "Please give us a moment alone."

Maria nodded and left the room. Johnny continued, "Jack is leaving today to head back to Cambridge. I've arranged for you to start school here next Monday."

"What about Tennessee?"

Johnny responded, "We have talked and we feel it is best you finish school. Jack has agreed to take you as soon as school is out. We need some time to find out who that was in Missouri and if you are in danger."

A tear fell down Fallon's cheek. She had her chin held high in defiance. Jack reached over and wiped it away. "I give you my word that you will go to Tennessee when it is safe. Do you trust me?"

Fallon nodded. She was unable to speak.

Jack didn't speak, he just sat there. It was awkward. Fallon looked at Jack, "What time are you leaving?"

"I have my bags packed. I just wanted to say goodbye and that I will be back soon." He looked at Fallon and nodded his head in the direction of their room. "Can I speak to you privately?"

Fallon got up to leave and Jack followed her back to the room. "I'm sorry to leave, but I have responsibilities at school. Will you be alright here?"

Fallon lifted her chin stubbornly. "I will be fine."

"I spoke to dad. They are taking you shopping later today. Get whatever you need. I assume you need a computer, a tablet, and other things for school."

"Thanks. I do need those things." Fallon was cold with her responses.

"Please don't be mad at me. I'm sorry about yesterday. I just wanted you to be safe."

Fallon didn't respond. She just looked away and said, "Bye Jack."

Jack had never been dismissed by a woman in his life. He started towards her to give her a hug. She stepped away. He could see that she was visibly angry with him. "Bye, Fallon." With those words, he turned and left the room.

Fallon waited till he left to let the tears fall. She climbed back into bed and cried herself to sleep. It was dark when she woke up. She was time confused again.

Fallon got out of bed, and put the robe back on, and headed to the kitchen. Maria was cooking. Johnny was not around.

Maria addressed Fallon, "Are you okay?"

"I think it was the medication. I still feel sleepy."

Maria gave her a quick hug. "Sit down and let me feed you. Oh, by the way, those arrived for you as you slept."

Fallon looked at the table where there was a new phone, computer, and tablet laid on the table. Fallon walked over and touched them. There was a note: Enjoy these Mrs. Valentino. Signed, Jack.

Fallon ran her fingers over the note and smiled.

Fallon picked up the phone. It had been so long since she had a phone. She opened it to find that it had been set up for her. She checked the messages to find there was one from Jack: "Call me when you get this."

Fallon was still upset with Jack. She didn't want to talk to him tonight. She picked up the tablet, happy to find that she had video streaming. She quickly ate dinner and took her treasures to her room.

Her phone rang showing a picture of Jack. She hit the end button. A few moments later, the voicemail dinged and Fallon ignored it. She needed a break from him. Fallon enjoyed browsing the shows on her tablet. Finally, something that felt normal to her. She lost herself in her favorite show.

Later that night, a knock sounded at her door. Johnny walked in her room. She was lying on top of the bed in her robe. "Hello, Love. How are you feeling?"

"I'm fine. I just feel a little sluggish."

"That's normal. Can I give you some advice?"

"What's that?" Fallon asked.

"Jack called me to check on you. He said you're not responding to his calls or texts."

Fallon looked away.

"The Valentino men are proud. We don't really chase after women. A word of warning: Jack is loyal, but he is young. Don't push him away."

Fallon looked at Johnny, "I'm not really mad at him. I just really wanted to go to Tennessee. The logical side of me knows that you're right, but my heart wants me to go."

"I understand, but know Jack is sensitive. Call him please."

"I will call him."

"Good girl. Do you want to go see the school tomorrow and do some shopping?"

"Sure."

Johnny leaned over and gave her kiss on the check. "Love you."

"Love you too, Johnny Hearts."

Fallon crawled back on the bed for a moment before working up the courage to video call Jack. When she finally dialed him, he answered on the second ring. "Hello, Wife."

"Hello Jack. Thank you for all the technology."

"My pleasure. How are you feeling today?"

"Good considering you drugged me yesterday." Fallon smiled.

"Ouch!" Jack replied. "Do you forgive me?"

"Maybe. But only if you promise to take me to Tennessee."

Jack sighed, "I have already given you my word. I meant it."

"Okay."

Fallon tried to determine where Jack was in the background. It looked he was at a construction site. "Where are you?"

Jack laughed. "Well my new bride, I am standing in our new living room."

"What?"

"Do you remember when we were leaving that dad handed me an envelope?"

"I remember."

"Dad bought us a place in Cambridge near campus. It has three bedrooms and two baths. Do you want the tour?"

Fallon was flabbergasted. The place was beautiful and it was empty. Jack took his time explaining every detail. All Fallon could respond was, "Wow". It must have cost a fortune.

Jack sensed her wonderment. "I was thinking you and dad could come to the spring game and see the apartment. I would love to have you at my football game."

Fallon smiled, "I don't know how I would feel about watching you getting hit in a game."

"Baby, you know it doesn't hurt. I love to play. If I get hurt, you can nurse me back to health."

Fallon giggled. "I don't think you want to trust your health to me. I'm not the super protector you are."

Jack got serious. "I know what you are, Fallon. You're the best."

Fallon turned a bright shade of red. "Well this is awkward."

"Don't be embarrassed. You are my wife. You need to be able to take a compliment."

Fallon shrugged her shoulders "I've got to go. Talk to you tomorrow?"

"Sure baby, answer your phone when I call. "

"I will. Goodnight."

Fallon ended the call and leaned back in bed. Jack was confusing. He was so beautiful to look at it was hard to stay mad at him. Fallon spent some time wondering what it would be like to live with him in Massachusetts. Could she be his wife? Would college get in the way of their relationship?

As always, Fallon cried herself to sleep hurting over her family. She needed to know why they had died. Why was she allowed to live and they weren't? She had no doubt that her parents had been killed, as well as Eva.

Fallon awoke from a restless sleep. She had dreamed of her sister again. It was always as if Eva was trying to tell her something, but Fallon couldn't understand what she was saying. She missed having Jack in her bed. How could she become attached to having him with her so quickly?

Fallon got dressed. She was excited to go shopping and to go to the school. She desperately needed some friends to make her feel less alone. She walked to the kitchen to find Johnny and Maria having breakfast. Johnny looked at her outfit and frowned. "I've arranged for Jack's cousin Ellie to take you shopping. She should be here any moment. Give her your credit card. She will know what to do."

"Thank you for setting this up today. I'm excited to get back to school."

It wasn't long before there was a commotion in the hallway. Maria announced, "Ellie's here." Ellie walked in the room. She was barely five feet tall and had long blond hair and blue eyes. She was beautiful. She walked over to Fallon and gave her a quick hug. "Hello! Are you ready to go spend this old man's money?" Fallon stepped back. She had not heard anyone speak so to Johnny.

Johnny laughed, "Fallon, Ellie will be with you at school. Don't learn her habits, she has no respect for her elders." Ellie walked over and gave both Johnny and Maria a kiss.

Ellie held out her hand to Fallon, "Cough it up."

Fallon looked at Johnny, who nodded. Fallon went to her room and brought her purse. She took the credit card and handed it over. Ellie looked at her and said, "Are you ready to go?"

"I'm so ready."

The girls walked out of the house. They were escorted by more security. Ellie scrutinized Fallon. "I can tell you like a preppy look. Let's go find our friend who makes those lovely polo shirts."

Fallon smiled, "Thanks for helping me out today. It will be nice to know someone at school."

Before Ellie could answer, Fallon was video called by Jack. She answered, "Hello."

"Good morning, beautiful wife. What are you doing?"

Ellie took the phone. "I'm about to spend all of your money!"

Jack laughed. "Poor Fallon, take it easy on her, Ellie."

Fallon snatched her phone back. "What are you up to?"

"I'm headed to class in a couple minutes. I'm working out with the team today, so it'll be late before I can call again."

Fallon felt shy having a conversation with Jack around Ellie. She quickly hung up the phone.

"You are one lucky girl. Everyone at school will be jealous of you. I can't wait to rub it in their faces."

"Rub what in their faces?

"Girl, you married the hottest ticket in town. Everyone wanted Jack. FYI, they all think you're pregnant."

"Well, I'm not. I don't appreciate people making assumptions about me."

"Chill lady. I've got your back."

The girls spent the next few hours on a shopping spree. They hit up the local mall and some exclusive shops. It was weird at first with the security, but they adjusted. After they bought a truck full of stuff, they headed back to the house.

"I'm going with you to school today. I'll give you the grand tour. Hopefully, they will have your schedule ready."

"Thanks, you are a life-saver."

After lunch, Johnny, Fallon and Ellie went to the Academy. Fallon was shocked at how beautiful the grounds were kept. It must cost a fortune to attend this school. The group was greeted at the door by Mr. Williams, the Headmaster. Mr. Williams fell all over himself to kiss up to Johnny. "Welcome! How exciting to have another Valentino at our school." He exclaimed as they entered the school.

Mr. Williams addressed Fallon. "Welcome to the Academy. I hope you find your remaining months enjoyable here. I understand from Mr. Valentino you have already been accepted to the Ivy League for fall admission. Well done."

"Thank you, Mr. Williams."

"Per your request, Mr. Valentino, I have spoken with the staff regarding the security detail. There should be no problems."

Johnny nodded his approval.

Mr. Williams slid a piece of paper over to Fallon. "Here is your schedule. Ellie, will you take her on a tour?"

Ellie got up and led Fallon down the hallway. "Old Mr. Williams. He is probably fleecing some money out of Johnny as we speak."

Ellie led Fallon through the tour. The school was huge. People openly gawked as they walked down the halls. Fallon felt overwhelmed but happy, she discovered that she had several classes with Ellie. Everywhere they went people openly stared at Fallon.

"Why is everyone staring at me?"

Ellie chuckled. "They want to see the child bride of the great Jack Valentino. Ignore them. They're stupid and jealous."

The girls finished the tour and headed back to the office. They found that Johnny had left. Ellie escorted Fallon back to the house. "Will you see Jack this weekend?"

"I don't know. He starts spring training soon."

"If he doesn't show, call me. I'll show you a good time. We can sneak into the local club and get our drink on."

"Ellie, you are awesome! I'll let you know."

Fallon spent the next few days at home trying to catch up with the classes at school. Friday arrived and there was no sign of Jack. He called daily, but made no mention of returning home.

Late Friday, Fallon decided that she was sick of staying at home. She called Ellie and made plans to go out for the night. She cleared her plans with Johnny, who trusted Ellie.

Ellie arrived looking beautiful as usual. She had on her clubbing clothes. Fallon looked at her clothes and pulled Ellie into her room.

"Pick out something good for me to wear. I want to look like you."

Ellie spent the next hour getting Fallon ready. When Fallon checked her appearance, she couldn't believe it her staring back in the mirror. She had on a tight short black sequin dress. Ellie had arranged her hair and applied her makeup. She looked dressed to kill.

Ellie and Fallon left the house. They picked up some girls from school. The girls were friendly. They were all ready to be out.

They pulled up to Club Falcon. It was the hottest club in town. Ellie looked at Fallon. "Ok country girl, be cool." Ellie handed her a fake ID. "They won't check. They know who you are." Ellie took Fallon's hand and worked her way through the crowd.

The bouncers at the door nodded to Ellie. The girls flashed their IDs. The doorman removed the rope at the entrance and just like that, their party was admitted without incident. The club was hopping. The music was loud and blaring. Ellie held on to Fallon's hand and led her to table at the back of the club.

"What do you want to drink?"

Fallon had never had a drink. "I don't know, surprise me."

Ellie smiled and left her at the table. The other girls made their way over to the table. They were loud and obnoxious, but funny. They included Fallon in the conversation. Ellie returned with a round of drinks. "Drink up ladies, we have all night."

Fallon took a sip of her drink and found that it was gross. She pretended to drink it with the group. Ellie pulled her out on the dance floor. It was awkward at first, but Fallon got into the music. The group of girls attracted the attention of the men in the club. The girls took turns dancing with different men that meshed into their group on the dance floor.

Chapter 9

Fallon was having a great time. It felt good to be out with people her age. A cute boy was even dancing with her. She turned her back to him and suddenly she noticed the people around her stopped dancing. Fallon looked around. Jack was staring at her. He walked over and grabbed her and pulled her close. He started swaying to the music with Fallon pulled tight against him. He turned her and she put her arms around his neck. Jack leaned in close.

"You should know I am the jealous type." He leaned in and kissed her. It was a possessive kiss. A kiss to let everyone on the club know she was his. Jack broke their kiss and led her off the dance floor to the table. He sat down and pulled Fallon on his lap.

A waitress came around and Jack ordered whiskey shots for everyone. The drinks arrived. Jack ordered everyone to take the shot. Fallon was hesitant. "Take the shot." Jack showed Fallon how to drink a shot.

Fallon wasn't sure of Jack's mood. She took the whiskey shot and poured it down her throat. It burned all the way down to her stomach. Jack kissed her. He tasted of whiskey and wickedness. Fallon ran her hands through his hair. Jack pulled her closer and kissed her harder. Then he pulled back and stared at Fallon.

Jack pulled Fallon off his lap and motioned for the bill. He opened up his wallet and pulled out five 100 dollar bills that he threw them on the table. He took Fallon's hand and led her through the club to the waiting vehicles outside.

When they got in the truck Fallon asked, "Are you mad?"

"Yes," was Jack's curt response.

"Why? We were just having fun. I wasn't doing anything wrong."

"Really, Fallon? My wife is dancing in a club with a random guy, and I should be fine with this?" He took Fallon's left hand and held it up. "Where is your ring?"

Fallon snatched her hand out of his. "I didn't wear it because I was afraid it would get stolen."

Jack took the ring out of his pocket and placed it back on her finger. "You are mine. Do you understand? I don't share."

"I'm sorry. I didn't mean to upset you."

Jack didn't speak on the rest of the way home. When the truck stopped, he came around and helped her out of the car. The house was dark. Johnny and Maria must have already been in bed. Jack led Fallon down the hall to their bedroom, ushering her in and closing the door.

When the door closed, Jack backed Fallon up against it. He took her mouth in a punishing kiss. His hands freely roamed over her body. He whispered to her, "Be my wife."

Fallon pushed him back. "What are you doing?"

Jack responded, "This is not right. This is natural for us, we have chemistry. Stop denying it doesn't exist between us." He pulled her back into his embrace, this time kissing her gently.

Fallon stopped him. "Please, I'm not ready. I'm just getting used to the fact that we're married. Please give me more time. I know it is crazy, but I want to be in love. I don't want to sleep with you because it's tradition or it's expected of me."

"You are killing me, Fallon. I'm going to take a cold shower." Jack stormed off to the bathroom.

Fallon got ready and climbed in bed. She felt guilty and she didn't want Jack to be upset with her. She wanted him to love her. The truth of the matter was she was crushing some on Jack. How could she not? He was a good guy who was extremely hot. He acted like he wanted to be her husband, but she needed to be sure that it was love, not lust.

Jack came out of the bathroom. He looked at Fallon in bed. He walked over and pulled back the covers and climbed in bed. Fallon reached over and turned out the lights. "Night Jack."

"This is ridiculous." Jack scooted over in bed and pulled Fallon against him. "Please don't ever dance with another guy. I almost went to jail tonight. If he had put his hands on you, it would have been over."

Fallon turned over in bed. "I was just dancing. I'm not allowed to be around other men?"

Jack crawled on top of her. He let his full body weight rest on her. "As I said earlier, I don't share." Jack leaned down and kissed Fallon. It was tender at first, but it turned passionate quickly. Jack roamed her body with his hands. He leaned up and tugged up Fallon's shirt. He made a trail of kisses down her throat and neck. Fallon moaned.

Jack took the rest of her shirt off. She was bare skinned next to him. He was continually kissing her. "Say yes. Baby, be mine."

Fallon moaned again as he kissed her. She was unable to resist his touch. His hands were everywhere. Fallon pulled at his shirt and Jack pulled it off in one quick motion. He leaned down and kissed her again. He was in the process of removing the rest of his clothes when a knock on the door sounded.

Jack stopped suddenly. He was laying on top of Fallon. The door creaked open and Johnny peaked his head in. When he saw Jack in bed, he quickly pulled his head out of the door. "Sorry, but I need you to come with me, Jack."

"Now?"

Johnny replied, "Carlos has been shot and I need to have a meeting."

Jack sagged against Fallon. "I'll be there in a minute."

Johnny closed the door. Jack braced himself over Fallon. Fallon looked up him and laughed and said, "Well I'm embarrassed."

Jack replied, "I'm sorry, I've got to go. Family business." He kissed Fallon one more time and got out of bed.

"I hope he is okay."

"Someone is always getting shot around here. You'll get used to it."

Fallon was taken aback by his statement. "If you don't mind, can you avoid getting shot? I'm too young to be a widow."

Jack got dressed. He came back over and gave her kiss. She could tell that he did not want to leave her. "Goodnight, princess." He kissed her on the head and left.

Fallon got back into her clothes. Sleep didn't come easily as she was worried for Jack.

Fallon woke to find that Jack was not in bed. She got ready and walked into the kitchen. Maria was busy making breakfast.

"Have you seen Jack?"

"The boys will be back soon."

"How is Carlos?"

"I think it was bad, but they think he will be okay." Maria replied.

"Thank goodness. Do we need to do anything for him or his family?"

Maria smiled at the question. "The boys have taken care of everything. Sit and I will bring you some breakfast."

Fallon sat at the table as directed. She wondered where Jack had been all night. All of the worst-case scenarios played in her mind. She had little knowledge of what the Valentino family was involved with locally. She was afraid to ask. It couldn't be good if people routinely got shot.

Fallon was finishing her breakfast when she heard the front door open. A few moments later Jack and Johnny walked in followed by two other men. Jack walked over and tipped her chin up and kissed her lightly as he sat. After he broke the kiss, he whispered in her ear, "I thought about you all night."

"Me too," answered Fallon.

Jack pulled out a chair beside Fallon. She couldn't help but stare at him. He had dark stubble on the lower half of his face making him look incredibly sexy. Maria brought the group of men their plates.

Fallon looked at Jack, "Is everyone okay?"

Jack nodded. Fallon took the cue that he didn't want to talk about it now.

"Did you sleep last night?" Fallon reached out and touched the stubble on his face.

"No, I'm going to go to sleep after breakfast."

"I will get my stuff out so you can rest."

After breakfast Fallon walked Jack to the room. "Get in bed with me for a while." Jack requested.

Fallon climbed into bed and Jack followed. He stripped down to his underwear and snuggled in close. In no time, Jack was sound asleep. Fallon managed to escape his hold and slipped quietly out of bed. She stopped and stared at Jack as he slept. He was so handsome. Fallon smiled and took a silent picture of Jack asleep. She wanted a picture to keep while he was away.

Fallon spent the day watching videos and reading. She missed Jack's company. It was strange that she had switched her feelings about him in such a short amount of time. It was simple. She wanted him.

Jack slept the whole day away. Johnny came in at 5:00 and told her to wake Jack up. Fallon crept into the room. Jack was still passed out. He looked so young and at peace that Fallon hated to wake him. She walked over and sat on the edge of the bed.

Fallon didn't know what came over her. She leaned over and gave Jack a kiss on the mouth. He didn't respond. She ran her hand over his face. "Jack it's time to get up." She leaned back over and gave him another kiss.

Jack groaned. She lifted her head but Jack caught her before she could get up. He pulled her down and gave her a big kiss. "That's how a man likes to wake up."

"Your dad wants you to get up."

Jack put a pillow over his face. "It's always something. Hurry up and graduate so I can move you to Cambridge with me."

"I'm working on it." Fallon got up. "Your dad seemed impatient. I wouldn't be surprised if he didn't show up in here in a couple of moments."

"I'm getting in the shower. If he comes, tell him I will meet him in the office."

"I'll let him know."

"Hey, do you want to go out for dinner? I was thinking some pizza again."

Fallon smiled, "Sure, I would love to get out of the house."

Jack went in and took a shower. Fallon was still sitting on the bed as he came into the room. She couldn't help but stare as he got ready.

"Did you enjoy the show, Mrs. Valentino?"

"What are you talking about? I was busy reading my book."

Jack laughed. "Really? Lying is not your strong suit."

Jack got dressed. "I'll meet up with you in a minute. Be ready to go."

Jack kissed her briefly as he was leaving the room.

Fallon spent the next thirty minutes getting ready. She wanted to look perfect for Jack. She waited patiently for the next hour for him to return. Finally, she walked into the kitchen. Maria was cooking dinner. "Do you know what Jack is up to?"

Maria shook her head. "I have found it better not to question them in situations like this. They will let you know when it's appropriate."

"Do you need help?"

"For the millionth time, no." Fallon sensed that she was bothering Maria. It concerned her because Maria was so friendly. What was going on?

Fallon grabbed a banana and headed back to her room. She started watching a show on the internet. Fallon had been back in her room for another hour before Jack showed up. He entered. Fallon could tell that something was wrong when he walked back into the room.

"Jack, what's wrong?"

"Well if you were really my wife, I would tell you. As the situation stands, I can't. I'm leaving."

"Where are you going?"

"Can't say."

Fallon walked over, "Is everything okay?"

Jack walked away. "This is the consequence of our current arrangement.

"Please don't leave this way. I'm worried about you."

Jack stopped at the door. "You need to decide what kind of relationship that you want with me. I don't want to play games."

He turned and walked out the door before Fallon could respond. Fallon wanted to run after him because she was scared that she was going to lose him too. It was all she could do to stay in her room and let him go. After he left, Fallon had a full-on panic attack. She crawled under the covers and curled into a ball.

Fallon woke up early the next morning. The house was quiet. She put on a robe and walked into the kitchen. Maria was drinking coffee as usual. Fallon inquired, "Where are the boys?"

Maria looked puzzled as Fallon sat down. "Did Jack not talk to you?"

"No, he wasn't in a good mood when he left."

Maria stroked her coffee cup. "They left last night to track down the shooter. Johnny had a lead. They probably won't be back for a couple of days."

"Are they in danger?"

Maria shook her head. "I don't think so, but you have to know this is the family way. Someone will pay for Carlos being shot."

"Should I call Jack or leave him alone?"

"I would wait till later in the day to see if he makes contact with you. Take my advice, don't bother them when they are handling business.

"I understand. Will you let me know if you hear anything?"

Maria got up. "Of course, I will tell you. Let me fix you some breakfast."

Fallon was nervous the entire day. She was starting school the next day and she had no idea where Jack was today. She was worried that he was in danger. Most of all, she was worried that he didn't want to be married to her.

It was a terrible day. Today, all Fallon got was loneliness and the constant reminder of their death. Never had she felt so alone and miserable. The pain of abandonment by her family and Jack was almost too much to bear. Trying to help the situation, Fallon waited till nightfall to text Jack. She simply said, "Hi". Jack didn't respond. She didn't matter to him.

Fallon felt sick at her stomach. She knew that she had blown it with him. It seemed like he had run out of patience with her. Everything was fine, but now it seemed broken. The whole day was a big depression fest for Fallon.

Fallon tried to call before she went to bed. No answer. She felt homesick and heartbroken as she got her clothes and materials ready for her first day at school. She set her alarm and tried to sleep. Early in the morning she finally managed to close her eyes.

Fallon's alarm startled her out of sleep. She woke up and rubbed her eyes. It took her a moment to focus and realize that Jack was sitting in a chair across the room staring at her.

"Morning," Fallon said.

Jack remained silent.

"Are you okay? I was so worried about you."

Jack continued to sit without speaking.

Fallon was unsure what to do. She crawled out of bed and walked over to where he sat. His eyes were on her the entire time. Fallon stopped short of sitting on him, silently asking for permission. He nodded.

Fallon sat on his lap. She balled up in his arms and finally Jack wrapped her in a tight hug. They sat there for a long time. This is what she needed, she needed comfort from Jack.

Fallon moved first. "I have to get up and get ready for school." Jack released her. She got up and Jack took off his clothes and crawled into bed.

Fallon came out of the bathroom to find that Jack was asleep. Fallon tried to be quiet and get her stuff out of the room. A gruff voice said, "I'm not asleep. I'm taking you to school."

"I know you're tired, I'll be fine. Stay here and rest."

Jack got out of bed and pulled his clothes back on. "I'm leaving to go back to school after I drop you off. I'll be back next weekend. I would prefer not to find you dancing with some random guy."

"Roger!" Fallon saluted him.

Jack looked at Fallon. "What are you forgetting?"

Fallon checked her appearance. She could not find anything wrong. She looked questioning at Jack.

Jack held out her diamond. Fallon smiled and walked over and took it. "I'm sorry, I am not used to wearing such a big ring."

"Do you want a just a band to wear?"

"Are you going to wear one?"

Jack stared straight at her. "I will wear one when I have a real wife."

The remark cut her to the bone. Fallon turned red but she didn't respond. She gathered her stuff. "Are you ready?"

Jack followed her out of the room. Fallon went to the kitchen. Johnny and Maria wished her a good day at school. While they were in the kitchen, Jack took out his wallet and handed Fallon $1000. Fallon's eyes grew big.

"What is that for?"

"I thought you would need some money for lunch and supplies."

Fallon reached up and kissed Jack on the check. "That is very thoughtful of you."

Jack led Fallon to the garage in the back of the house. He lifted the garage door. There sat an assortment of cars. He had every expensive car on the market.

"Pick one. Which one would you like to ride to school in?"

Fallon smiled. "This is a wonderful collection. I've always wanted an American muscle car, so I choose that one." Fallon pointed to a black racer.

"Nice choice. The car is now yours." Fallon stared at Jack in disbelief. "Really?"

"I'm sorry about yesterday. You need a ride that belongs to you."

It took Fallon a moment to find words. "Thank you, I've always wanted a car of my own."

They walked over and got in the expensive car. The engine roared to life. Jack was quiet as he drove her to school. The security was following closely in the black SUV's. Jack pulled in the parking lot. There was heavy tension in the car. Fallon felt shy. She wanted to talk to Jack, but it was uncomfortable.

"Have a good first day." Jack leaned over and kissed her on the check.

"Be careful going back to school. Try to get some rest." Fallon collected her things and got out of the car. She felt hopeless. He was leaving and he was so distant from her. Fallon started to walk off but stopped. She turned around and walked back to the car. Fallon tapped on the window and Jack rolled it down.

"Really, Jack? That was your goodbye to me? You just give me an incredible gift and then just abruptly leave?"

"What do you want Fallon?"

"I want a proper goodbye kiss. Get out of the car."

Jack looked stunned at her boldness, but he followed her directions. Jack got out of the car and leaned against it. He didn't make a move.

"I guess it's my turn. You know I'm crazy about you?"

Jack replied, "Is that so?"

"Please don't make me beg." Fallon turned a bright shade of red.

Jack pulled her in close to him. "I'm crazy about you." He leaned in and kissed her properly. Jack pulled back. "Bye, Wife."

"Bye, Mr. Valentino."

Chapter 10

Fallon watched as Jack left. She turned around and realized that a group of kids were staring at her. Fallon lifted her chin high and walked to her first class where she found Ellie waiting in the hallway for her.

"Making out with my cousin in the parking lot? Everyone is talking about it."

Fallon couldn't help herself. "If he was your husband, wouldn't you?"

"Well, that's gross."

Ellie kept up the light banter as they walked to their first period, World History. As Fallon walked into the room, everyone stared at her. The teacher was not in the class so there was no one to take the attention away from her. Fallon took the open seat in the front row. The bell for first period rang, and the teacher did not show up. A few minutes later, Mr. Williams walked in with a young female teacher.

Mr. Williams addressed the class. "Students, this is Ms. Jones. She will be the instructor in this class for the rest of the year. Mr. Ebert has experienced some health problems."

The class erupted in talking. Mr. Williams shushed them and briefly spoke to Ms. Jones, and left the room.

Ms. Jones was tall, red headed, and beautiful. She also looked to be in her early twenties. Too young to be teaching. She must have been fresh out of college.

"Good morning, class. I understand you were on page 247. Let's turn there and start."

The class grumbled, but did as they were told. At the end of class, Ms. Jones called attendance. Fallon's name was not on the roll. Fallon walked up as class was ending.

"Excuse me, Ms. Jones. My name was not called this morning. "Oh yes, Ms. Valentino. They told me that your name will appear tomorrow. We are both having our first day here. Good luck with the rest of the day."

Fallon responded, "You too."

Fallon tried to focus in the rest of her classes. The trouble was they were behind where she was at her old school so there was nothing to distract her. Being away from Jack and the house allowed Fallon to think about her sister and the cryptic message. She had to get to Tennessee so Fallon started making her travel plans.

Fallon made it through most of the day with no problems. She was walking in the hallway to her last class by herself when she saw a group of girls staring at her. She heard what they were saying as she walked by. "This is a forced marriage because she is pregnant. My cousin told me that Jack told him he hated her. She is a gold digger."

Fallon turned and stared at them. The lead girl Emily Salvatore walked over to Fallon. "Do you have a problem?"

Fallon responded, "Do you have a problem? Just so you know, I'm not pregnant."

The girl responded, "What does Jack see in you?"

"More than he saw in you." The girls in the group gasped. Emily slapped Fallon hard across the face. The force knocked Fallon down and the girls in the group laughed.

Fallon stayed down for a moment. The rage she felt was almost out of her control. When she started to get up, a teacher and her security ran over to the commotion.

When she stood, Fallon was escorted to the office with the group of girls. To her horror, Johnny was called. Fallon felt so embarrassed. Of course, the girls blamed it on Fallon. Fallon decided not to fight it, it would not serve her.

Fallon's security team escorted her to the house. Johnny was waiting for her in the office. Fallon pushed open the door and Johnny walked over to examine her face. "Are you hurt badly?"

"No, I'm just embarrassed. Please don't tell Jack."

"Jack already knows."

Fallon took a seat and slumped in the chair. "I'm really sorry. They were saying such horrible things about Jack and me."

"I have been informed of the situation. We'll work it out. Why don't you go and get some ice on your face?"

Fallon felt small leaving the room. She was so embarrassed and humiliated. Fallon went to her room and checked the status of her face. A small bruise was appearing on her check. Fallon stared at the mirror. She couldn't help herself. She started to cry, sobbing out loud. She felt sorry for herself. She was alone and in misery.

Fallon heard a knock on the door. It was Johnny. "Fallon, let me in."

"No, I'm fine."

"No, you are not. I can hear you crying in the hallway. Open the door now!"

Johnny had never raised his voice to her before. Fallon walked over and open the door. Johnny took a look at her tear stained face and opened his arms. Fallon walked into them so Johnny could pull her into a hug. "I'm sorry. It was a bad first day. It will be better tomorrow I promise." Fallon cried some more. Her tears wet the front of Johnny's shirt.

Fallon finally stopped crying. "I've ruined your shirt. So sorry."

Johnny lifted her chin, "Don't worry about the shirt or what happened today."

Fallon nodded. She felt exhausted. "I think I'm going to lie down for minute."

Johnny gave her hug and left the room.

Before Fallon got in bed, she walked over and put on Eva's necklace. She wanted to feel close to her sister. Fallon decided then that she was going to Tennessee. It was all she had left of her family. She carefully planned her escape as she needed to go on her own. She was worried about leaving. All she had was her fake driver's license that Ellie had given her. Would it be enough to get her through security?

Fallon checked the flight times into Tennessee and Alabama. This was her stomping ground. Shiloh National Battlefield sat in a remote area in Tennessee. Fallon found a flight that left at 6:30 in the morning that arrived in Huntsville, Alabama. That was the closest airport to Shiloh. She then checked the status of a car rental. If her ID would pass, she would be able to make it to Tennessee easily. Looking at return flights, she concluded she could be back in New Jersey by midnight.

Fallon was scared to upset Jack and Johnny, but she had to go. She needed answers. Fallon booked the flight and car rental. She had to take a chance. Fallon then called the taxi service and arranged for them to meet her down the street at 5:00 a.m. the next morning.

Fallon's phone rang showing a video call from Jack. Fallon reluctantly accepted the call. Jack looked angry as he answered the phone. "How bad is it?"

Fallon showed him her face. "It's fine."

"It's not fine. Tell me what happened."

Fallon replayed the story to Jack. Jack listened and said, "Sorry" when she was finished.

"This will be taken care of," he promised.

"Jack, no. Please leave it alone. I just want to finish school in peace. If you make a big deal out of it, school will be bad for me."

Jack considered her plea. "I'll think about it. I spoke to dad. He will decide how to handle it."

Jack was in a room filled with people. "I have to go, but I'll call you later."

"Okay, thanks."

Jack hung up the phone. Fallon continued her travel search.

After dinner, Fallon was in her room getting ready for her trip. Maria knocked on her door. "Johnny wants you in his office now."

Fallon was nervous. Did he know her plans?

Fallon walked on jelly legs to Johnny's office. She was surprised to find the girl from school and her father in the room. They both cast down their eyes when she came in the room.

Johnny started talking, "Mr. Salvatore and his daughter have something to say to you."

Emily stepped forward, "I'm sorry for what I said and that I hit you."

Mr. Salvatore joined in, "My daughter has embarrassed our family and caused you harm. I'm very sorry." Mr. Salvatore looked at his daughter. He reared back and punched Emily in the face. The force of the blow knocked her backwards.

Fallon let out a cry. She rushed over to Emily. She tried to help her up. Johnny picked Fallon up and held her. Mr. Salvatore walked over and continued to beat Emily. He kicked and punched her a few more times.

Fallon screamed out, "Stop!"

Mr. Salvatore stopped. "Please, no more." Fallon yelled.

Emily was crying and bleeding on the floor. Fallon started towards her, Johnny stopped her again. "Understand Fallon, no one is to ever lay a hand on you. You are Jack's wife."

Fallon stared at the mess in front of her. Mr. Salvatore helped Emily out of the room. As they left, he said again, "I'm sorry."

Fallon just stood there. She was in shock. She knew there was Valentino law, but she didn't realize how far it extended.

"I know it was hard to watch, but it was necessary. Jack will be head of this family when I'm gone. He can't be seen as weak. No one will dare treat you badly from this moment on. She is really lucky, Jack called for a hit on her today."

"A hit, do you mean…"

"Yes, he was angry. I talked him out of it."

"Thank you. I don't know what to say."

Fallon left Johnny's office in bewilderment. She was scared and shocked. Johnny scared her. He had so much power over people here. What would he do when he realized she had left in the morning? Fallon went to her room and weighed her options. After spending some time weighing the positive and negative sides of the argument, Fallon decided Johnny and Jack would be mad whenever she went. She might as well get it over with. Fallon crawled in bed and tried to sleep. She would need it.

Chapter 11

The alarm went off at 4:00, waking Fallon from a light sleep. She got up and got dressed. Then she packed a small carryon to keep from looking suspicious in the airport. She stuffed in a change of clothes and some toiletry items. Time flew. It was time to get out of the house.

Fallon knew the code to the alarm. She typed it in quickly and left out the side door. Everyone was still asleep. There was no movement in the house. She crept silently across the lawn. Fallon had to climb a small fence to get into the neighbor's yard. She was able to scale it with little trouble.

Fallon walked through the yard. There sat a yellow cab. Her plan was working so far. Fallon got in and gave the directions to the driver. She was filled with anxiety and fear as they drove away from the house.

The ride to the airport took close to an hour. Fallon was nervous that she was going to miss her plane. She bypassed the check in as she had printed out her boarding pass the night before. Fallon was shaking as she walked up to the TSA security. With an unsteady hand, she handed her ID to the agent. The agent put it under a scan while Fallon held her breath. A Bing sounded. The guard handed her ID and boarding pass back to her and wished her a good day.

Fallon let out a big breath. She made it through security and on to her gate. They had begun boarding before she got there. She made her way on to the airplane quickly. Fallon took the first available seat. Nothing looked suspicious, so Fallon began to relax. The plane taxied down the runway and Fallon was in the air to Alabama.

Looking out the window at the beautiful Alabama landscape, Fallon felt a sense of relief when the plane touched down. It was good to be home in Alabama. This is what she knew and loved. Fallon made her way through the airport to car rental terminal as her nerves started to kick into full gear. She went to the counter and handed her ticket to the agent. The agent processed her car and made her fill out a bunch of forms before the agent handed her the keys.

Fallon made her way to the designated area to pick up her car. The process had been extremely easy. She wondered if Jack knew that she had left the house.

It took two hours to drive to Shiloh National Battlefield. Fallon felt her excitement grow as though the answers were calling for her to hurry. Eva made it clear for her to go to the Hornet's Nest. Good men had lost their life at the sacred place; Fallon was trying to get her life back. She needed answers.

The Welcome Center looked like a small Antebellum Plantation home with faded red brick and large beige columns. Fallon walked in and saw there were a few people milling around. She was greeted by park rangers who did not seem to recognize her. Fallon walked up to the front desk where the ranger handed her a brochure. Fallon's hand shook as she took it from the Park Ranger. She looked in his eyes for any recognition. There was none.

Fallon anxiously opened the brochure. It just had the park information. Fallon walked lost around the museum. After a while, when no one approached her, she began to feel sick. She had betrayed Jack and Johnny for nothing.

Fallon got in her car and headed to the different monuments and to the Hornet's nest. She pulled up in front up in front of the largest monument in the park. It was a tribute to the lost soldiers in the Shiloh battle. Fallon had always been fascinated with the monuments. Eva would always ramble on about the significance of the symbols. Fallon was lost in thought about Eva when she heard a door close in the background. Turning around, she watched Dr. Smith get out of the car.

Fallon had a moment of fear. *Was she going to be killed by the mysterious Dr. Smith?* She froze in place. He was here for her.

He walked over. "Hi Fallon."

"Hello."

"I know this seems odd, but I need to talk to you. We have about five minutes before your husband and his men arrive."

"Jack is on his way here?" Fallon squeaked out realizing that she was in big trouble.

"He is, and from what I hear he is extremely mad."

Fallon crossed her arms. "Do I have time to leave?"

"No, you need to be with Jack. I don't understand why Eva sent you here. She needs you to get to Gettysburg tomorrow. Not before. Do you understand?"

"What's in Gettysburg?"

"I'm not at liberty to tell you. Go where she told you to go. You are now being protected. Get there tomorrow."

There was too much information for Fallon to process and she had multiple questions. "I don't understand why I'm here. Please tell what is going on."

Dr. Smith shook his head. "I not sure that I understand it all. You must believe in Eva."

Dr. Smith jerked his head around. "Jack is here." He looked at Fallon straight in the eyes. "Tell me what you are to do."

Fallon heard the cars coming. "I'm to go to Gettysburg."

A SUV jerked to a stop in front of them. Two guards jumped out in full black commando gear. They were armed with machine guns. Jack stepped out of the car.

"Get away from her." Jack yelled.

Dr. Smith put up his hands up in the air. "Fallon, get there." Dr. Smith turned towards Jack with his hands in the air. "Mr. Valentino, good afternoon."

Jack looked at Fallon. "Get in the truck, now!"

Jack walked over to Fallon and grabbed her by the arm. He had her arm in a tight, painful grip. Fallon resisted. "Jack, please. I need to talk to him."

Jack handed her over to one of the guards who shoved Fallon in the car. Jack could hear Fallon banging on the window.

Jack walked up to Dr. Smith. "Who are you and what do you want with her?"

Dr. Smith answered, "I know that this looks bad, but you must know I am here to help her. She needs to be in Gettysburg tomorrow. She knows where to go."

"Fallon is going home."

Dr. Smith responded, "Eva told me you would cooperate. Fallon will be there tomorrow. The question is, are you going to help her?"

"Sir, you don't know your place." Jack pulled out his handgun and pointed it at Dr. Smith. "I am taking Fallon home."

"Jack, you are a good guy. This needs to happen tomorrow if she is ever going to be safe again. Put the gun down."

Dr. Smith made a fist and raised it in the air. Jack heard wrestling sound in the woods. They were surrounded. Red dots suddenly appeared on Jack's chest from gun lasers that were pointed at him. "Sorry, I need you to understand. Fallon is now a concern of national interest. If you care about her, get her to Gettysburg." Hands in front of him Dr. Smith walked over to Jack, leaned in, and whispered in Jack's ear.

Fallon saw Jack jerk his head and look at Fallon. Whatever was said made him put his gun down. She could see him questioning Dr. Smith. Dr. Smith slapped him on the back like they had been friends forever.

Jack walked back to the truck. He climbed in beside Fallon and took out his phone. He sighed and then dialed a number. Jack spoke into the phone harshly, "Change of plans, we need to get to Gettysburg, Pennsylvania tomorrow. I need a full team and a safe route for tonight." Jack put down the phone and glared at Fallon. He leaned forward and tapped the driver. "Take us back to the plane."

Fallon tried to speak to Jack but he raised his hand up to indicate that he didn't want her to speak. Fallon sat in silence. Jack took a phone call. He was angry with the person on the other line. "I understand, but what am I do to? I have obligations to my family. Do what you have to do." Jack hung up the phone.

Jack finally spoke, "Well that was my coach, I just lost the starting position for the spring game because I have missed so much practice. There is a high probability I will be kicked off the team, so thanks."

Fallon didn't know how to respond. "I'm sorry. Let me go on my own. Go back to Cambridge. It will be fine."

"No Fallon, it is not fine. You don't understand what is going on here. For some reason, we are being played like pawns in a chess game. I am not letting you go alone. We will go tomorrow and end this. When this is over, you are moving to Cambridge, and we are going to have a normal life."

Fallon stared out the window. What could she say? A tear rolled down her cheek. What she really wanted to do was to go home to Alabama and stay. She wanted to live in her house, go to her school, and live her life. Fallon reached up and wiped a tear away but more tears fell. She couldn't handle this anymore.

Jack watched as Fallon tried to hide her tears. He tapped the driver, "Stop and pull over." The driver did as he was told. Jack got out and walked around the truck. He opened the door and pulled Fallon out. "I really don't know what to do with you. Should I admire your courage, or should I put you over my knees and beat the mess out of you?" He wiped away a tear that fell from her eye.

Jack backed her up until her back was against the truck. "Say you understand my plan and you agree." He put his hands on either side of her head on the truck. "Say it Fallon. Say you agree."

Fallon sniffled and said, "I agree. I'm so sorry."

Jack brushed the hair out of her face. "Baby, you've been through it the last couple of months. I get why you are doing this." He leaned in and kissed her. He could feel Fallon crying against his lips. He pulled his arms around her. "We are okay. Let's go to Pennsylvania and end this." He kissed her again.

Fallon melted against him. He was so safe for her. It felt right when Jack was with her.

Jack helped Fallon back into the truck. Taking her hand, he said, "We are at the airstrip in Corinth, Mississippi. It will take us about an hour to get there. I'm waiting on our route for tonight and tomorrow. I'm sending an advancement team into Pennsylvania tonight. Where are you going at the Battlefield?"

Fallon said through a shaky voice. "It could be two places. One is the Alabama monument. That is where the quote came from. The second is the shop where the necklace was bought. I don't know the name of the shop; I just know where it's located."

Giving her hand a reassuring squeeze, he said in an authoritative tone, "We'll figure it out."

Jack held on to her as they made their way to Corinth. Before arriving, Jack received a call about the plans. "I understand. Tell dad."

Jack looked at Fallon. "We are headed to Washington, D.C. for the night. We will be close to Gettysburg."

Fallon nodded her agreement. It was a relief that Jack was finally taking her to Gettysburg, and she would finally get some answers about her family.

The drive to the plane was quick. Fallon was lost in thought while Jack was talking non-stop on the phone about arrangements. They were ushered out of the car to the plane and they were in the air in a matter of minutes.

Fallon went to the bedroom and climbed on the bed. Exhausted, she closed her eyes and fell asleep. All she needed was a few moments of sleep.

Jack spent the entire trip ensuring their safety. He was taking them to DC to have access to a high-level security hotel.

Jack woke up Fallon as they made their final decent into DC. "Wake up baby, we're here."

Fallon rubbed her eyes. She was disoriented for a few moments. "Where are we?"

"We are going to Washington, D.C. tonight. I've got us ritzy hotel room and plenty of security. Get up and I'll tell you our plans."

Fallon got up and prepared to land. She felt much better after sleeping for a few hours.

She joined Jack in the front seats of the plane where she looked at him and said, "I don't know how to express my thanks other than to say I love you."

Jack was caught off guard but recovered and smiled. "Back at you."

Jack took held her hand until they landed. Walking off the plane, they were greeted by the usual black SUV. The door opened and Johnny stepped out. Fallon felt sick having to face him after her actions.

Jack took Fallon's hand and led her down the stairs to the waiting truck. They walked up to Johnny. Fallon could see the disapproval on his face.

Fallon let go of Jack's hand. "I'm sorry."

Johnny looked at Fallon. "I forgive you, but if you ever pull a stunt like this again, I will kill you myself. You have put us all in danger."

Fallon dropped her head, "I know. I feel terrible about the trouble I've caused."

Johnny pulled her in hug, "I was sick this morning when I didn't know where you were. Please don't do that to me again."

"I won't. I want this to be over so that I can live my life with Jack."

Johnny released her. They climbed in the truck. Fallon was surprised when they pulled in the parking garage of the most expensive hotel in DC. A group of security met them when they parked.

Johnny opened the door. "Mr. Valentino, the building is secure. We have your rooms ready." Johnny nodded in thanks.

Johnny, Jack, and Fallon were led through the back entrance of the hotel. The manager of the hotel greeted them and took them to their rooms.

Fallon's jaw dropped when she saw the hotel room. It was a big, beautiful suite. Everything was luxurious. A knock sounded on the door. One of the security men brought in Fallon's bag and some shopping bags.

"I had your bag removed from your car and I had some clothes bought for you," Jack mentioned.

"Thank you. That was thoughtful."

"Are you hungry? They have great food here."

Fallon's stomach grumbled at the thought of food. She had not eaten all day. "Yes, please, I'm starving. I'm going to get a shower while we wait for the food." Fallon took her bag and went in the bathroom.

Chapter 12

She turned on the shower and got in. It was heaven. The water felt so good against her skin. The door opened and Jack slid in the shower with her. Fallon felt herself turning red. She tried to cover herself from him.

"Stop." Jack whispered in her ear. He pulled her close to him. It was an intimate act.

Fallon relaxed and started shampooing her hair and Jack helped her rinse her hair. When they were both clean, Jack turned her in the shower. He reached up and grabbed her face gently with his hands as he leaned in to kiss her. Fallon responded, causing Jack to tighten his hold on her and pull her close. Jack reached down and pulled up Fallon's legs and wrapped them around his hips. Jack shifted her up so that her back was against the shower wall. Jack was almost out of control; he had to stop before this went too far.

He stopped kissing Fallon, "We need to get out of here before dinner arrives." Fallon laughed and Jack released her legs. Fallon scooted out of the shower and rushed to get a robe on to cover herself. Jack took his time getting out of the shower and covered up with a towel. He stood and watched as Fallon got ready.

Fallon was nervous getting ready in front of him. She hurried as much as she could to get out of the uncomfortable situation. Resisting Jack was useless. He had won.

The knock on the door broke the silence. Jack walked out, his towel hanging from his hips. It was Johnny telling them that dinner had arrived. Fallon hurriedly dressed and walked into the main room. Jack was still sitting in his towel. His dad looked at Fallon and then at Jack, "Son, get some clothes on."

Jack laughed and left the room.

Fallon sat down at the table and Johnny joined her. There was a huge spread of food. They both waited on Jack to return.

Johnny spoke to Fallon, "You and Jack look happy together. I understand from Jack that he wants you to join him in Cambridge. How do you feel about that?"

"I want to be with Jack. I think it is better for us to be together."

"I agree. I will make the arrangements when this is over tomorrow."

Jack walked in and ran his hand through Fallon's hair. "What are you talking about?"

"Future plans," answered Johnny.

The hot food was served and the conversation was light. Johnny was eating when his phone rang. He looked at it and held up his hand for everyone to be quiet.

Johnny answered. He got up and left the room. Fallon looked at Jack.

"Don't worry, happens all the time. Everything is a crisis."

Johnny was gone from the room for a long time. Dinner was finished. Jack and Fallon were sitting on the couch. Fallon leaned against Jack and he put his arm around her.

Johnny walked back in the room. He sat down and took a hard look at Fallon. He looked at her with puzzlement in his eyes.

"Fallon, I need to ask you some personal questions about your parents."

"Okay"

"I don't want to upset you, but I need to know the answers. Did your parents ever say you looked like anyone in your family?"

Jack interceded, "Dad, what are you doing?"

Fallon sat up straight. "No, why?"

Johnny continued, "Did they ever talk to you about being adopted?"

"Dad, stop. You're upsetting her. Why are you asking this?"

Johnny motioned for all the security in the room to leave. "Fallon, we have reason to believe that you are not biologically related to your parents. I just received a call from a contact in Italy. They think the trouble surrounding you has to do with your biological parents. We don't know who they are, but they are important."

Fallon sat in stunned silence. Was she adopted? She felt her stomach do a summersault. Jack started rubbing her back.

She squeaked, "What about Eva?"

Johnny replied, "I don't know. If you can think of any information, please tell me."

Fallon shook her head, "My parents never said anything."

Jack interjected, "Why would Eva go to the trouble of leaving pieces of information for Fallon? Who is she working for?"

"I think she is FBI. They have an interest in this, I just don't know what the connection is yet," Johnny answered.

Fallon felt sick to her stomach. She realized that she was going to lose the food she had just eaten. She put her hand over her mouth and ran from the room. Johnny and Jack could hear her throwing up in the bathroom. Jack got up to follow her but Johnny stopped him.

"I need to know the truth, is she really your wife?"

"Does it matter?"

"Jack, I think she is someone very important. It is important now she is with us. This is no longer about debt. This is about status in the world. If you haven't done your job, do it tonight. We need this."

"Dad, please. I don't need a pep talk about responsibilities. She is my wife. I don't care about status. I care about protecting her."

Johnny nodded his agreement, "Does she know about Eva?"

"No, I was told to keep it quiet. Eva needs time, and I am going to give to her. I think she is trying to protect Fallon the only way she can. By the way, who was your contact in Italy?"

"The boss."

Jack's eyes grew big. "He's involved with this?"

"Yes, whatever this is, it's big."

Jack started to leave the room to go to Fallon. "Take care of her Jack. I will see you in the morning." Johnny got up and left the room.

Jack went into the bathroom and found Fallon laying on the tile of the bathroom floor. "Do you think what he said is true?"

"I don't know."

"I've been thinking about my family, and the only thing that comes to mind is that my family made me learn German and Italian. They didn't make Eva take lessons."

Jack looked surprised at Fallon, "You speak German and Italian?"

Fallon nodded.

Jack pulled Fallon off the floor. "Let's get you cleaned up."

Fallon got up and brushed her teeth. She rinsed her mouth out. Jack took her hand as she finished. "Let's go in the living room."

Fallon went in to the room and sat down on the couch. Jack sat down beside her. He put his arm around her. Jack took the time to explain the routine for the next day.

Fallon leaned back and closed her eyes. "I just want this to be over."

"I know. When this is over and I finish the semester, I would like to take you to Italy."

"I would love to go. I have always wanted to travel."

Jack looked at her and said, "You're so beautiful. I missed you."

Fallon smiled. "You can't leave me again. I felt so alone."

Jack took his arm that was around Fallon and pulled her closer. He brushed his lips across her mouth, "Tell me again you love me."

Fallon closed her eyes and kissed him gently, whispering, "I love you."

Jack moaned against her mouth. He pulled Fallon up to his lap. As she straddled him, Jack reached up and pulled her mouth to his hard kissing.

Fallon responded by running her hands under his shirt before she pulled it over his head. Jack lifted her up, crossing her legs around his back. He walked them to the bedroom where he laid her down on the bed. She slowly removed her clothing. Eyes blazing with passion, Jack stared at her with hungry eyes. Fallon tried to cover up. "Don't," he begged.

He leaned over and kissed her. "Be mine."

Fallon nodded.

Jack continued to kiss her. He trailed kisses all over her body. Fallon was at the breaking point when Jack climbed in bed with her. "Tell me again"

Fallon looked at him, "I love you." Jack made her his in one quick motion. "You're mine, now."

Fallon gasped in pain. Jack whispered, "It's okay, baby," and Jack kissed her hard again.

Jack stilled himself. "Are you okay?" He stroked her face. "Sorry baby."

Fallon moved under him.

"Fallon stop, I won't be able to control myself."

Fallon moved again. Jack moaned out loud. "Say you are mine."

"I'm yours."

Fallon matched Jack in her passion. It was if they couldn't get enough of each other.

Jack collapsed on Fallon. He was paralyzed. He had never had a sexual encounter like that before. He was exhausted.

"Jack, I can't breathe."

"Sorry baby." Jack rolled off Fallon. They both laid in silence for a couple of minutes.

Fallon got up to go the bathroom. "Are you okay?"

"I'm fine." Fallon walked into the bathroom.

Jack followed and found Fallon standing in a robe. She had turned on the shower.

Jack looked at her, "You are amazing."

Fallon smiled, "You're not so bad yourself."

Jack walked over and gave her a small kiss "We are good together, Wife."

Fallon grabbed his hand and pulled up his ring finger. "I believe you are missing something."

Jack smiled, "I will take care of it first thing tomorrow morning."

Fallon smacked him on the butt, "Good, because I don't share."

Jack left the room. New sheets were delivered and Jack had the bed made up when Fallon returned. Jack pulled back the covers, they needed to get some rest.

Fallon climbed in bed with Jack. Jack spooned her, "Tell me again."

"I love you."

Jack tightened his grip around her waist and didn't respond. Jack fell asleep quickly. Fallon thought about her family. She wished they were there so that she could talk to them about Jack. It took some time but Fallon fell asleep in Jack's arms.

Fallon woke up to the sound of a phone alarm. Jack reached over and turned it off. Fallon moaned. Jack snuggled back up to her. "We have to get up."

Fallon covered her head with a pillow. Jack pulled it off, "Wake up."

Fallon took the pillow and hit Jack with it on the head.

Jack reached down and started tickling Fallon's ribs.

Fallon screamed out, "Please stop!"

Jack stopped to pull her under him. "Good morning."

"Good morning, Husband."

Jack kissed her. Fallon pulled him closer and she wrapped her legs around him. Jack groaned. "We are ditching everyone later today. I think I need some alone time with my wife."

Fallon ran her hands up and down his chest. "I agree."

Jack kissed her again. "I think I could get used to waking up to you this way."

Fallon moaned.

Jack got off her, "We need to get up."

"I'm not a morning person."

Jack got out of bed and Fallon burrowed under the covers. He pulled the covers off her, "Come on baby. We need to go."

"Please don't talk."

She looked so beautiful. He walked over to her and kissed her head, "Tomorrow we will stay in bed all day." He held out his hand. Fallon took it and climbed out of bed.

The lovers took a quick shower together. Fallon had trouble focusing on getting ready because Jack was so near. She enjoyed watching him shave and go through his morning routine.

Jack slapped her with a towel. "Get ready."

"I am." Fallon applied light makeup and dried her hair. She looked great.

For the day, Fallon chose a blue casual dress with comfortable shoes to wear. Jack slipped on a dark charcoal suit with a white shirt and dark blue tie. He looked professional and hot.

Fallon asked, "Do we need to pack our things?"

"No, we are coming back here tonight."

Before they left, Fallon grabbed her bag. She was nervous, but ready to go.

There was a knock on the door. Jack opened it to find Johnny in a fancy suit also. Johnny walked into the room. "Are you ready to go?"

"Yes, I'm ready."

Jack took Fallon's hand and led her out into the hallway. There were a group of soldiers in all black waiting for them. Fallon started to question Jack, but he stopped her.

"Don't ask, I'm not taking any chances."

The group was led to the parking garage. Fallon was loaded into a car with Jack, Johnny, and security. They had two SUV's in front of them and two SUV's in the back of them. They exited the building.

"It's going to take a couple of hours to get there, so relax," said Jack.

Fallon watched the buildings pass. She could hear a helicopter overhead. She strained her neck to see what the sound was coming from.

"Is that helicopter following us?"

Jack looked at Johnny who replied, "They are with us. Just an extra level of security. We will also have extra teams when we get to Gettysburg."

Fallon looked surprised.

Jack reassured her. "We are being overprotective. We just don't know all the players yet. Until we are sure, we have to be careful."

"I wish I knew what is in Gettysburg."

Johnny and Jack looked at each other.

Johnny responded, "Today will be a good day."

Jack scooted over and put his arm around Fallon. He whispered in her ear "Are you feeling okay?"

Fallon smiled, "I am fine."

"No, are you physically fine? I'm afraid that I was too rough with you last night. I know you must be sore."

"I'm fine, just focused on what we are about to do."

Jack swept her hair aside and he planted a kiss on her neck. Fallon leaned into him.

"Alright you two. You should know I had quite an interesting night listening to you. I don't want a floor show today."

Fallon turned a bright shade of red while Jack laughed. "Sorry dad, but she is beautiful and we are young." Jack squeezed Fallon and she sat up. They kept a respectful distance for the rest of the trip.

Fallon got increasingly nervous as they got close to Gettysburg. They stopped short of town to prepare for battle. Security piled out of the trucks and Fallon could see the men pulling out weapons. The men had both large and small guns. They attached slings to their bodies and stuffed every pocket with small weapons.

Jack could sense the tension in Fallon. "It's okay; this is normal for our family. You will get used to it."

The men loaded up after the stop and they headed back towards town. Gettysburg appeared and they saw signs for the battlefield. They headed into the downtown area and turned on Carlisle street. This area looked familiar to Fallon. They pulled up in front of a local Civil War shop.

Jack looked at Fallon. "Is this it?"

Chapter 13

"This is it."

The back SUV emptied of men as they surrounded the store. One of the men gave an all clear motion to Jack.

Fallon was shaking as Jack walked around and opened the door to the truck.

Jack gave Fallon a reassuring smile. "Ready?"

Fallon gave him her hand. He could feel her tremble. Johnny joined them. Jack led Fallon on the short walk to the front of the store. Johnny went in first followed by Jack and then Fallon.

The shop was empty. Fallon looked around panicked. "It's okay. Someone wants to meet you." Jack said to Fallon.

The door to an office opened up. A tall, dark olive-skinned man with jet-black hair walked into the room. Both Johnny and Jack dropped their heads. Fallon didn't understand.

The man walked over to Johnny and gave him a kiss on each check while shaking his hand. He did the same routine with Jack. They didn't speak to each other.

The man eyed Fallon. He walked over and dropped to one knee. Both Johnny and Jack dropped to their knees. Jack was delayed in his response. He didn't know what was happening.

The man took Fallon's hand and kissed it. "Princess, it is an honor to meet you."

Fallon pulled back her hand and looked at Jack. "Baby, it's okay."

The man stood.

Fallon went over and tried to stand behind Jack, but he stopped her. He took her hand to reassure her but Jack kept her in front of him.

The man addressed Fallon. "Fallon, I know this is unexpected. I am your cousin. My name is Romano Rossi. I came here to welcome you to the family."

Fallon latched on harder to Jack. Johnny interceded.

"Mr. Rossi, Fallon has been through a rough week and even rougher past few months. She has survived but not without scars."

Romano answered, "I know since my family has been monitoring the situation." He looked at Fallon. "I know you must have many questions."

Fallon spoke up. "Did you kill my parents?"

"No Fallon, we did not. I did not become aware of you until after they were gone. In fact, Eva came to Italy to implore our help to protect you."

"What, why did Eva contact you?"

Romano answered, "I know this is much to take in, but your sister planned this for you. You are Italian mafia royalty in our family. Much like Johnny is a head of a family, you are an important part of my family. We control all the families in Italy and the United States. When we have time, I will explain further."

Jack questioned Romano. "Who is after her? Is she in danger?"

Romano shook his head. "I don't know the answer. We will have to ask Eva."

It took a second to process then Fallon felt her heart stop beating. She rushed to him. "Is she alive?"

Romano looked puzzled at Jack and Johnny. "Does she not know?"

Johnny answered, "No, we were told to keep it secret."

Fallon cut her eyes at Johnny and Jack. She turned and looked at Romano. "Take me to her please."

Romano answered, "She is here somewhere."

Before he could say more, Fallon excitedly announced, "The Alabama Monument."

She started walking towards the door. She left the men staring after her. She stopped and said, "Are we going?"

Romano gave a signal and his men with Johnny and Jack exited the store. Johnny stayed behind with Romano as Jack and Fallon sped off to the monument. Jack tried to talk to Fallon as they got in the car but she ignored him. "Baby, I just found out at Shiloh. Dr. Smith said I wasn't to tell you that it would put you in danger. He said that this had to play out to get you back to her."

Fallon just stared out the window as the truck started, taking them toward the battlefield.

It was a short ride to the hill where the Alabama Monument was located. Fallon could barely contain herself as they approached. Fallon jumped out the door when the truck stopped with Jack quickly following. The security team followed close behind. Fallon ran up to the monument only to find it was empty.

Jack walked up behind her.

"It's beautiful. We came here often. Do you know what it means?"

"No, I don't."

"The symbolism of the monument is you should continue to fight, even when things are bad. It's beautiful."

"Fallon, please know I only wanted what is best for you. I thought if I kept quiet this would turn out right for you. I wanted you to have Eva back. I promise to tell you everything. Please don't be mad at me."

"I don't want to talk about it now. We can talk later." Fallon walked all around the monument. She ran her hand over the inscription, "Your names are inscribed on fames immortal scroll." Nothing was there, it was empty. Fallon went and sat on the bottom of the monument. "I don't understand why Eva would want to meet here." Restless, Fallon got up to look around the monument again.

The first bullet hit Fallon in the left arm. Before Jack could react, she was hit again in the left shoulder. Flinging his body, Jack knocked her down. He lay on top of her as a barrage of bullets hit the monument. He turned his head toward the south, and he could see a group of men advancing. They were trained killers moving in unison as they advanced. They took aim on Fallon.

The security team returned fire. Jack continued to lay on Fallon. Warm sticky blood began to soak into his shirt. The metallic smell was strong. Jack leaned up enough to see the damage. She was bleeding badly.

Jack put his hands over the wound to keep her from bleeding out. He was screaming at his dad, who had arrived, and the security team to get her out of there. The fighting raged around him. His security team made a line in front of Jack but they were taking hits.

Jack heard the resistance before they got to their position. Attack helicopters flooded the sky, firing down on the attacking men. They were slaughtered on the sacred battlefield. The bullets stopped hitting the monument.

Jack tried to pick Fallon up. The blood on his hands caused her to slip out of his grasp. He tried to pick her up again. Jack was frantic to try to help her. "Fallon! Stay with me baby, stay with me! Stay with me!"

Fallon was unresponsive and she was losing blood fast. Jack was still trying to stop the bleeding with his hands.

Soldiers rappelled out of the helicopters. They ran over to Fallon and knocked Jack out of the way. One soldier had to hold him as he tried to get back to her. Jack heard one of them say, "Phoenix One is down." A man jerked off his mask, revealing Dr. Smith. He started frantically working on Fallon. A man jumped in carrying a bag. They started an IV and started administering medications. A black truck pulled up, screeching its tires. A stretcher was pulled out of the truck by soldiers.

One of the men working on Fallon spoke to Jack. "I'm taking Fallon for a while."

"No!" yelled Jack.

The man ripped off his mask. It was Eva.

"Sorry Jack, but she is with me. I will take care of her."

Jack lunged for Fallon. A man knocked him down. They loaded Fallon on a stretcher and started for the truck. Jack got up and tried to stop them.

Jack was yelling for his father to help but Johnny stood still in the background.

Jack tried again to get to Fallon. Eva stepped in his way. "Jack, stop. I will be in contact."

The truck carrying Fallon sped off. The truck was not stopped by Jack's security.

Eva approached Romano, who had just appeared on the scene. "Sorry for the mess. My people will clean it up."

"We were late." Eva said as she shook her head.

Jack walked up. He was visibly upset. Johnny walked over and put his hand on his shoulder. "Son, it's okay."

Romano looked at Eva with questioning eyes. "It's confirmed?"

Eva gave a quick nod yes. "We need to move her to a secure location."

Romano interjected, "Italy will take her."

Jack held up his hand, "What do you mean Italy will take her."

Eva ignored Jack and then responded, "That is a kind offer, but we have a vested interest in her. She is ours for the moment."

Jack couldn't believe that they were talking about his wife like this. "Stop this now, tell me what is going on."

Eva looked at Romano and at Jack. "Jack, listen. Fallon is special. She is now under the protection of the United States Government. I'll leave it to Romano to give you the details."

Eva turned and started to walk off. Jack yelled at her "You can't have her, she is my wife. She goes with me." Running after her, he grabbed her arm.

Jack came face to face with a gun. Eva had it pointed directly to his forehead. "Jack, you are a good guy and Fallon seems happy with you. I will bring her back to you if you want, but I need some time with her."

Jack backed away, looking over the barrel of the gun into Eva's eyes. "When will I see her?"

"I will be in contact." Eva turned and left.

Jack walked back to his father. Johnny motioned for them to enter the truck. Jack got in the truck, but he was furious. He hit the back the seat with a fist and let out a moan. Johnny got in beside him and shook his head.

"It's okay, son."

"It's not okay. She is hurt. I should be with her." Jack's voice was shaky.

"She is with Eva and will be fine. They will take care of her."

Jack sat back hard in his seat, rested his head on the headrest and closed his eyes. He was covered in Fallon's blood. Every time he inhaled, the scent of her blood flooded his nose. It was making him sick. Trying to hold the vomit in was no use, he stumbled out of the truck and threw up in the grass while holding on the side of the vehicle. Johnny got out of the vehicle and walked around and handed Jack a bottled water.

Looking again at his shirt, Jack tore it off quickly. He took the water bottle and rinsed out his mouth.

Johnny handed him a t-shirt to put on. "We can find a hotel here so you can clean up."

"I don't want to clean up, I want to find out where they took Fallon. Dad, please help me." There was desperation in Jack's voice.

"Son, this is out of my hands. I don't like it either, but should put our faith in Eva. She said she will contact us. We must trust her."

"I don't! She put Fallon in danger today. I think she used her as bait today. There was no reason for this to happen. All of this could have easily been dealt with at our house. Why put Fallon out in the open? It doesn't make sense."

"I agree and I will push Romano for answers later. This is serious business and I want to know what is going on. Something isn't right. I think we were all put at risk today."

Jack stared out the window feeling helpless. He could see the teams working on cleaning up the mess as they drove out of the park. Jack vowed to make Eva pay for what happened today. Fallon should not have to suffer.

Chapter 14

In a truck racing toward the local airstrip, Fallon was going in and out of consciousness. Dr. Smith was hovering over her when she began to stir. She could hear Eva's voice, but couldn't see her. "Fallon stop, it's okay. You are safe." She tried to sit up, but was forced back with a bunch of hands holding her down. Fallon screamed as the panic set in. She felt a stinging sensation in her arm. They must have given her something. She remembered the feeling of being lifted out of the truck. Everything went to night after that.

A jet waited on the tarmac of the small local airport. Dr. Smith, Eva, and other men lifted Fallon out of the truck onto a stretcher and then they loaded her up into a private jet. There was a medical team waiting on them in the plane. They all jumped in and the jet screeched down the runway, rising to the sky.

Jack was looking out the window. He saw the small plane takeoff in the distance. The plane was maxed out on power and pushed to the limit to get up in the air quickly, disappearing out of sight. He knew in his heart that Fallon was on that jet. Clenching his hand together was all Jack could do to keep himself together and not allowing violent images of Eva's death to take over in his mind. His family had killed for less. How dare Eva to try to separate him from his wife?

Jack and Johnny followed Romano to a house outside of town. They were escorted inside by security. Jack was given a clean set of clothes and directed to the shower. The hot water of the shower was stained with red as the water cleaned his skin. He couldn't watch as the blood washed down the drain. He needed to get it off his body quickly. It was a reminder of the horrible events earlier.

He needed information so Jack walked into the kitchen to find his dad and Romano in a deep discussion. They stopped when he walked in the room, and Romano pulled out a chair for him.

"Please tell me what you know," Jack demanded.

Romano started talking. "We received information a couple of months ago about a possible missing member of our family."

Jack inquired impatiently, "How did you receive this information and what does this have to do with my wife?"

"Eva came to Italy and requested a meeting with me. That girl has spunk. She walked right up to one of my guys and demanded a meeting."

"What did she tell you exactly?" asked Johnny.

"She said that she thought that her baby sister was a member of my family. I did not believe her. She went on to say that she had reason to believe that Fallon was the granddaughter of Mussolini by his oldest daughter. You can imagine my shock. At first, I thought Eva was not right in the head."

"Wait a minute, did you say Mussolini? How could she be his granddaughter? She is way too young," Jack asked in frustration. This didn't make sense.

Johnny admonished Jack. "Listen and learn. We will get the full story."

Romano continued, "As crazy as this seemed, I allowed Eva to tell the full story. Apparently, Fallon was a test tube baby. At the end of WWII, the specimen was smuggled out of Europe. We think by accident or by grand plan, Fallon's parents had her unknowingly. We can assume they were killed shortly after they found out the truth, unless they were in on the plan. We aren't for sure at this moment."

Johnny muttered, "This is unbelievable."

Romano replied, "Eva was told before her parents were killed. She came to me to seek protection for Fallon. I directed her to you. I did not know the connection she had to you when she first came around."

Abruptly, Jack stood up. "This is crazy! This can't be true."

"Sit, Jack." Johnny said with a firm voice.

"We let Fallon go today because she needs her sister and the protection of the government. I know this not what you want."

"If this crazy story is true, where does that leave us?" Jack looked at his dad.

Johnny answered, "If this is true, you have married probably the most important person in our world. She is a true blood. This is great for our family. You know our roots run deep in Italy to Mussolini. Once you and Fallon get settled, you will have children and take over the family business. On top of everything, you will have a unique opportunity to unite the heads in Italy. While you are not technically royalty, in our world you will rule."

Jack shook his head, "I can't think about this now. I want my wife back. I need to know she is safe."

Romano replied, "Be patient, we have to know who is after her and why."

"Who is the father?" Jack questioned.

"We don't know. We think it was someone in Italy, and we are working on it as we speak. We don't know where the sample came from other than it was Mussolini's oldest daughter. James told Eva where to look. She was then able to confirm through DNA the Mussolini match. It doesn't matter who her father was, she is an Italian mafia princess. She is a direct bloodline."

Johnny smiled at Jack. "Do you understand the importance of this?"

Jack shrugged his shoulders. "Not really."

"You have married a pure bloodline. Fallon could take over as head of the family if she chooses. Your children will be royalty in our world."

Jack sat silently as these two powerful men decided his future. He was angry. He knew this meant his dream of playing football was over. All that he had worked for was done. He had no interest in being mob royalty or the head of the families.

"Excuse me." Jack got up and left the room. He went outside and stared at the sky wondering where Fallon was at this moment.

Johnny watched him leave out the front door "He will be fine, he needs to process. I know that he cares for her. He is just struggling with his own life plans."

Romano asked, "What plans?"

"Jack has plans to play professional football. He has worked hard to get where he is and I'm sure he is struggling with what this means for him."

Romano rubbed his chin. "I would be willing to take Fallon to Italy to give Jack some time to adjust. He could play football and when he is ready, he could come to Italy with us."

"That is a kind offer, but she stays here with us. Fallon Valentino is under my protection." Johnny replied in snarky voice that left no room to argue.

"We will not fight today about this. It was just an offer. I just don't want Fallon caught up in his adolescent tantrum about not playing a game."

"Fallon will not be caught up. Jack knows his place. They both just need some time together. They were happy before all of this happened. I give you my word that Fallon will be taken care of by my family." Johnny extended his hand. Romano shook it hard.

Romano added, "When she is better, I want her to come to Italy to meet the family."

"Of course, she should know her people." Johnny answered in a strained voice.

Chapter 15

Fallon woke up in a sterile room. She was hooked up to multiple machines that were beeping and blinking lights. Her whole left side hurt and felt like it was on fire. She tried to move, but the tubes kept her from getting very far. Trying to talk failed as her throat was extremely dry. It took a moment of concentration but she finally felt around on the bed and found a call button. Pressing it hard, Fallon heard a beep off in the hallway.

A few seconds later, Dr. Smith entered the room. He was in scrubs and a white coat. "Hello Fallon." He walked over and poured her a glass of water. She took the cup and drank greedily from it.

With a scratchy voice Fallon asked, "Where is Jack?"

"Jack is with his father. He was not hurt."

Fallon looked around. "Eva?"

"She is not here. I am here to take care of you."

"Where am I?"

"Walter Reed Medical Center."

"Why?"

"You were hurt badly. We did surgery. That is why your voice sounds scratchy."

"Am I okay?"

"You will be fine. Are you in pain?"

Fallon nodded. "When can I see Jack?"

Dr. Smith didn't answer. He pulled out a syringe and placed it in her IV. "Don't worry Fallon, we are going to take great care of you."

Needing her questions answered, Fallon tried to talk but she felt the medicine enter her system. The drug was pulling her under and she was asleep in a matter of seconds.

Dr. Smith left the room to find that Eva was waiting outside. "She asked for you and Jack."

"I know, I heard."

"What's your plan? She would heal better if he was here."

"That's not an option right now. I'll go in when she wakes. I just don't want to overwhelm her."

"She needs to see you, it would help her heal."

Eva nodded and Dr. Smith left.

Eva went into Fallon's room and watched her sister as she slept. Eva felt bad that she had been shot. There was no other way. They had to use her for bait to see who was after her. The answer that Eva had found shocked her to her core. She sat down beside Fallon and whispered into her ear, "Fallon, it doesn't matter your DNA, you were raised by great people who taught you right from wrong. You have the unique ability to change the world for the better. Use your strength. I'm always with you." Eva leaned over and kissed Fallon on the head. Taking a seat, she propped her feet upon the bed and fell asleep.

Fallon slowly came out of her drug induced haze. It took her eyes a couple of moments to focus. She thought she was dreaming. Eva was asleep on the chair beside the bed. Fallon shook her head to make sure she was awake.

In a raspy voice Fallon said, "Eva?" Eva stirred in her seat. Then she felt her sister take her hand and kiss it. "Hello, baby sister."

Tears rolled down Fallon's face. She couldn't help it. She wasn't alone anymore. Her nightmare was over. Through her tears she asked, "Why did you leave me?"

Eva sat back in her chair. "Things are complicated, Fallon. I had to go to protect you. When the time is right and you're better, I'll tell you everything. It will make sense. Right now, all I want you to focus on is getting better."

"I want Jack." Fallon was barely able to squeak out.

"I know you want him here, but it's not safe for you. I will get him here as soon as I can."

"Can I talk to him? I want to hear his voice."

"Wow sis, looks like Cupid's arrow found its mark. I will see what I can do. How are you feeling?"

Fallon groaned a bit. "I've been better. Can we call Jack, please? I need to talk to him."

Eva squeezed her hand. "Let me go see what I can do about this. In the meantime, let them give you some pain medication. When you wake up again, we'll call."

Eva motioned with her hand and a nurse entered the room. She did a quick check of Fallon. The nurse administered medication and Fallon fell asleep.

Eva left the room to find Dr. Smith was waiting on her. "She looks good considering the amount of blood she lost. She will be back on her feet in a couple of days."

"I hope so, we need her to get better quickly." Eva replied. Eva then looked at Dr. Smith. "What do I do with her, Smith? Do I bring Jack in or do I separate them?"

Dr. Smith scratched his chin. "It's a complication. I think I would get him here and see their interactions. She may need him to go forward. He is a wild card in all of this."

Eva nodded. "I agree. I'll make the arrangements."

Dr. Smith stopped her before she left. "Are you okay?"

"I'm fine. I am just lost in knowing how to handle this."

Dr. Smith pulled her in a hug. "You are not alone in this."

"Thanks, Smith. Now go and save some lives." Eva gave him a kiss on the check and left.

Chapter 16

Jack and Johnny left Romano's house to head back to DC. They had been back at the hotel for an hour when Jack's phone rang. The caller was blocked. Jack answered the phone, "Hello".

"Jack, it's Eva. Fallon is doing fine. The surgeons removed the bullets and got her patched up. She is in recovery now."

"Where is she, Eva?"

"She is fine for now and will call you later. In the meantime, I need for you to go back to your life. Go back to school, I will be in contact regarding bringing you to her."

"You want me to pretend like this didn't happen? You are out of your mind!"

"Please understand, Jack, if I had my way you would be out of the picture. Fallon is desperate to see and talk to you. So for now, you stay. Be warned, don't make trouble for me. Do you understand?"

Jack answered in a defeated tone when he wanted to threaten her, "Yes. When will you call back?"

"Fallon has been given some powerful pain medication. When she wakes, we will call. I give you my word."

"Okay."

"One last thing, don't ask Fallon where she is, Jack. The call will be dropped and I will have to move her. That is the last thing she needs today. Do you agree?"

Jack hesitantly replied angrily, "Yes"

"Good. We will talk when she wakes up. By the way, she asked for you first when she woke up."

"Thanks Eva."

The phone went dead. Jack explained the conversation to his father. Johnny reassured him that he was doing the right thing. Johnny agreed with Eva that Jack should go back to school and get back to his old life. When the time was right, Fallon would be back.

Jack and Johnny left the hotel and headed for the plane. They would drop Johnny off in New Jersey and Jack would head back to Boston. Jack felt so empty getting on the plane without Fallon. It didn't feel right without her here with him. This girl had changed his life so quickly.

The plane landed in New Jersey. Johnny gave Jack a hug. "Let me know when she calls. I don't care what time it is. Love you, son."

"Love you, Dad." Johnny exited the plane and Jack was back in the air headed to Boston. Jack was impatient to land. He wanted to hear from Fallon.

The plane landed in Boston with no word from Fallon. His driver took him back to campus. Jack called his coach and asked for a meeting in the morning. He had to try to smooth over their relationship from the last conversation they had. He didn't want to lose his position on the team.

Jack got back to the apartment. It was so quiet. He went in and took a shower and sat down on the couch. He didn't realize how tired he was. Jack fell into a deep slumber sitting up on the couch.

Chapter 17

Fallon slowly regained consciousness. She was alone in the room. She woke up because her stomach was empty, hurting from being hungry. She pressed the call button. Dr. Smith entered the room. "How are you?"

Fallon replied, "I am starving. Can I have some food?"

"Of course, I will order a tray for you." Dr. Smith came over and checked Fallon's bandages. "You are a lucky girl. Jack saved your life. Do you remember what he did?"

Fallon shook her head no. "I don't remember anything. What did he do?"

Dr. Smith pulled up a chair and sat down. "When we got there, Jack was on top of you, protecting you from the gunfire. Luckily for you, he is a smart guy. He was holding pressure on your wounds. Jack probably saved your life by stopping the bleeding. From what I understand, he tackled you to ensure you were safe."

Fallon sat stunned by this information. Did Jack feel the same about her or was it his natural instinct? The need to be loved by him was overwhelming. Although she confessed her love for him, he did not return the words to Fallon.

Dr. Smith continued, "Eva had to put a gun in his face to let us take you. Jack was ready to take out all of us to get to you. It was touching."

Fallon let the information sink in. "Was he hurt?"

"Not that I am aware of. I think Eva is trying to secure a line for you to be able to talk to him."

Fallon asked, "Do you know why all of this is happening?"

"I think Eva has the details. Let her talk to you; it's not my place."

Dr. Smith got up to leave. Fallon called out, "Thank you for saving me again. Maybe someday, I can return the favor."

Dr. Smith stopped in his tracks. He turned and faced her. "Repay me by keeping America safe."

Fallon didn't know what that meant. Everyone seemed to talk in code. The food tray arrived and Fallon was able to only eat a few bites, enough to make the pain in her stomach stop. Fallon was dozing when Eva walked back in the room.

Eva smiled at Fallon. "You are one tough little scratcher."

Fallon smiled. "I'm not feeling so tough at the moment. Can I call Jack?"

Eva walked over and handed Fallon a different looking phone. "It's a satellite phone. It is very hard to trace. I talked to Jack earlier and he is expecting your call. The rules are simple don't tell him where you are. If he finds out, we will have to move you."

"Why, Eva?"

Eva screwed up her face. "Fallon, we aren't sure who's after you." We are trying to clear the Valentino family. We just don't have enough intel yet. When we clear them, you can go back to Jack. Fair enough?"

Fallon nodded and held out her hand for the phone. The number was on the screen. Fallon pressed send. The phone rang twice before it was picked up. "Fallon, baby is that you?"

"Yes."

"Please tell me you are doing better."

"I'm in some pain, but they tell me I was lucky."

"Baby, I'm so sorry. I shouldn't have let you go."

"Jack, please. It was my choice. They told me what you did to save me. Thank you."

He was quiet. Fallon continued. "I'm hoping to be able to see you in the next couple of days. Eva is trying to arrange it."

Jack replied, "I don't know if I can wait that long. I miss you."

Fallon giggled, "I miss you, Mr. Valentino."

Eva gave Fallon the signal that it was time to hang up. "Jack, I've got to go. I love you."

Jack was hesitant in his answer "I know, Baby. Take care of yourself. Call me when you can, anytime of the day."

Fallon hung up the call. She was hurting again. Eva looked concerned. "I'm going to call for some more pain medication." Fallon nodded.

Eva looked at Fallon with a strange expression on her face. It was a look of anger mixed with curiosity, "You tell him you love him. Does he tell you?"

Fallon shrugged no. "I don't think he's there yet." Fallon grimaced in pain.

Eva pressed the call button and a nurse walked in the room. Eva requested some more pain medication. She then took Fallon's hand. "I know that you have been through a lot the past couple of days. Remain strong. We need you better."

Fallon let out an involuntary grunt of pain. The nurse walked in and gave Fallon more medication.

***

When Jack hung up with Fallon, he called his dad to give him the update. Johnny had questions but Jack was unable to answer them all. He finally hung with his dad after a long conversation and went to bed. He had a busy day tomorrow. Tomorrow was the day to try to right the wrongs in his life. His coach needed to understand and let him have his starting job back on the team.

***

Fallon woke to early morning in pain. She had a rough night. Eva had been beside her the whole time. Fallon tried to sit up but the pain in her left side was unbearable. She moaned.

"Fallon, are you hurting?" Asked Eva in a sleepy voice.

Fallon groaned in pain. Eva hopped up off her cot. She realized that Fallon was trying to sit up. Eva helped Fallon get into a sitting position. Dr. Smith walked in and helped the girls.

"Ladies, did we have a good night?"

"No," Fallon responded.

Dr. Smith came over and checked the wounds. "Well these are looking great. I think we need to get you out of bed today."

Fallon groaned again.

"It is necessary for you to keep your strength. We will start small and work our way up."

"Easy for you to say, you don't have two bullet holes in you."

Both Eva and Dr. Smith laughed out loud. Dr. Smith pulled off his white lab coat and his scrub top. He proceeded to show Fallon a series of scarred bullet holes. Five in total.

"I stand corrected." Fallon conceded then said, "When can I see Jack?" Fallon looked to Eva.

Eva looked at Dr. Smith who nodded his head. "You are clear on my end. You will have to take it easy. I'm fine if he wants to come here."

Eva added, "Fallon, we are working on clearance for Jack. It may take a couple of days. When it's clear, I will go and get him for you. Okay?"

Fallon nodded again. Her side was hurting so bad. She grimaced.

Dr. Smith said, "Let's get some food in you and switch you to oral medications so we can get this IV out."

Dr. Smith left. Eva and Fallon looked at each other. Fallon addressed Eva, "Please tell me what's going on. I have a right to know."

"I know you have a right to know. Just give me some time. I promise that I will tell you everything. I'm going to go and shower and see where we are with Jack.

"Thanks Eva, love you."

"Love you kiddo."

Chapter 18

Jack woke up in Cambridge, exhausted. He made himself get out of bed and into the shower. He had an important meeting with Coach Crandle this morning. Jack had to face the coach after missing practice. It would not be an easy meeting.

Jack left the apartment and headed down to the parking garage to his SUV. He got into his Black SUV and turned on the ignition and started moving out of the parking garage. A car turned behind him and followed him down the lane. Jack took a turn and the car turned with him. The trailing vehicle was a few cars back behind him in traffic. Jack took another turn. It was obvious he was being followed.

Hitting the call button on the steering wheel, Jack dialed his father. His dad answered on the second ring, "Good morning, son."

"Dad, I'm being followed." Jack explained. Johnny listened.

"Do this. Go meet with coach and go to class. Stay in a populated place on campus. I will send a team to you. I think it's Eva, but we need to be careful. Stay very public."

Jack pulled up to the athletic facilities. The car that was following him pulled into a parking spot nearby. Whoever was following him wasn't trying to hide. Jack took his gym bag and walked inside to his coach's office, looking over his shoulder the whole way.

The meeting with the coach went much like Jack expected it to. His coach was mad. Jack couldn't talk about Fallon, so he just spoke in general terms. The meeting ended with him losing his starting place for the spring game. His coach informed him that he would have to earn his spot back. Jack was angry, but he didn't blame the coach.

Doing what he was told, Jack went on to his classes. It was weird to be back after an eventful span of time. He looked at his friends and was envious. They weren't married to a woman who was being hidden by the government. They didn't see her shot, nor did they feel her blood pouring out of her. Jack wanted to be free of Fallon and his responsibilities. He wanted his old life back.

Jack left his last class with a group of friends. They went to the Student Union to get some food. He encouraged them to hang out with him. He started buying food for people to get them to stay. The word got around. Soon the Union was packed with people and Jack continued paying for everyone's food. Someone brought some alcohol and the party started at the Union.

The pressure of this situation was always with him. Jack couldn't enjoy himself. He was the puppet master today. He was using his friends and random people for protection until his security team arrived. Jack kept looking around to see if anything unusual was happening. The party lasted for hours. They were eventually made to leave when his friends started acting crazy and bothering people.

Jack and his friends were on their way out when he saw his protection team enter the room. A group of men from New Jersey in suits located Jack and walked over and surrounded him. He breathed a sigh of relief. They came over and made contact. Jack greeted them with a handshake. He questioned them as to the plan, "Am I headed to New Jersey?"

The answer was no. He was to stay in Boston. They had him covered. Jack was unsure this was the best course of action. It might be better if he was with his father. The team took him out of the room while Jack's friends stared at him. They had no idea of Jack's involvement with the mob life.

His team hustled him to a group of parked black trucks. Jack got in and was heading to his apartment when his phone rang. It was Fallon, "Hello."

"Jack?"

"Hey baby. How are you feeling today?" Even though the pressure of his old life had haunted him all day, he still missed Fallon.

"I'm sore, but I'm better. They took out the IV earlier. I'm working on getting out of bed today. How has your day been?"

"Eventful. I met with my coach. He wasn't happy." Jack continued, "Also I'm being followed. Can you see if Eva is behind that?"

Fallon was irritated. "I'll get it to stop if it's her. I'm sorry about your coach and that you are being followed."

"Don't worry, I can take care of myself. My family won't allow me to be hurt." Jack said with a smile.

"I miss you. Eva said she's working on clearance for you to be able to come and see me."

"I can't wait to see you. I miss my woman."

Fallon replied, "I've been thinking about Italy."

"Italy?"

"I was thinking we could take a real honeymoon there when I get better. I've never been."

"We can go anywhere you want. It will just have to wait till summer."

"Sounds good. I miss you." Fallon said.

"Get better, Baby. Find out if Eva is having me followed. Talk to you later."

"Love you!"

Jack hung up the phone without responding.

Fallon sat the phone down on the bed and narrowed her eyes at Eva. "Are you having Jack followed?"

Eva answered, "Yes. It's a protection detail. We are worried about Jack's safety."

"I think it upset Jack. He sounded stressed."

Eva rolled her eyes and dialed Jack's number. "Hey, they are there to protect you." She hung up the phone without letting Jack talk.

Fallon looked at Eva. "I want answers now."

"Okay, but I want you to know that this doesn't change how I feel about you. You are my sister, always. I love you."

"Love you, Eva. Now, spill the beans."

Eva closed the door to the room. Her voice was shaky when she started talking. "Fallon, this is not easy to tell you. Dad came to me in Missouri right before he was killed. I was shocked when he turned up at my work, but he was saying crazy things about you. He said you were a test tube baby and he told me you were not his child. He asked me to protect you and instructed me that I should go to Italy and talk to Romano Rossi."

Fallon screwed up her face as Eva talked.

"Fallon, Mom and Dad are not your biological parents."

"I know." Fallon replied in a flat voice and looked away from contact with Eva's eyes. "I was told by Johnny. He had gotten some type of information on me."

Relieved that Fallon knew, Eva continued. "Dad kept saying how important you are. He said you were too important, and I couldn't let anything happen to you. He made me promise to protect you at all costs. He said for me to take you to Johnny Hearts if Italy was not an option."

"Eva, who are my parents?"

Eva looked at Fallon. "We only know one."

"Who is it?"

Chapter 19

"We have reason to believe you are the granddaughter of Mussolini. The daughter of Edda Mussolini."

Fallon sat straight up in bed. "Are you kidding? How is that even possible?"

"No, I'm afraid, I'm not kidding. We took DNA samples from Mussolini's grave and that of his daughters. You are a match. We believe you were smuggled out of Europe at the end of World War II as a test tube baby."

"This can't be. I'm a good person and he is..."

"Fallon, your DNA does not determine who you are. Your actions determine who you are."

Fallon immediately thought of Jack. "Do Johnny and Jack know?"

Eva nodded yes. "They knew after the shoot out."

Fallon was relieved they knew but was still afraid of how Jack would think of her. Suddenly, all of these awful thoughts were running through her mind. Her brain felt like it would explode from the horror of being related to Mussolini. He was the Fascist leader of Italy, a monster. He helped Hitler try to destroy the world. Did that make her a monster?

Fallon thought for a moment. "Who is the other DNA supplier?" It was weird to speak about her creators like it was a scientific experiment and not her loving parents.

"We don't know. We are trying to find out. Whoever it is, those people at Gettysburg were afraid of you."

Eva walked over and sat on Fallon's bed. "We had to draw them out. That's why I sent you to Gettysburg. I thought they would make an appearance. We were able to capture two men and we are trying to get information from them. It's a process."

Fallon was lost in thought. "Why can't I see Jack? Be honest."

"I sent you there to be safe. I never dreamed that you would marry him. It's a complication. I think Johnny and Jack are using you for status with the Italian families."

Fallon replied, "Eva, he's my husband. Don't keep him from me."

Irritated, Eva retorted, "Do you know what Jack and his family are into? Do you know the family business?"

"No," answered Fallon.

"They are in some bad business. The usual mob stuff like guns, drugs, and prostitution. That's where your dearly beloved makes his money. He makes money off the suffering of others. So remember that the next time he spends money on you."

Fallon closed her eyes. "This is bad. Everything is bad."

Eva grabbed her hand. "I'm not going to get in the way of you and Jack, but know there is always an escape plan. You don't have to stay married. You can divorce him."

"What? Are you crazy? I will not divorce Jack, and it makes me mad to hear you say it. In fact, don't you have something else to do?"

Eva got up. "Sorry, I don't want you angry at me. I had to lay the cards on the table for you. I will clear Jack. I'll try to get him tonight or tomorrow."

"Thanks," Fallon replied curtly to Eva. She was angry.

The room fell quiet after Eva left. Fallon sat on her bed with her thoughts running through her head. *Was she a monster? Why would someone go to such trouble to make sure she was born? She didn't even know anything about Mussolini other than he was a bad dude who hurt Italy and her people. Was that her family? Her legacy? This had to be wrong. This had to be a bad joke that was being played on her.*

Pulling the covers over her, Fallon tried to close her eyes and wish away this horror. There was no escape, no release from this nightmare. She was stuck with no way out. Could she learn to live with this knowledge? It had to be hidden from the public. No one could ever know about her true parents. She needed a new beginning.

Sara LeMay

***

Jack was back in his apartment after the long day at school and practice. His cousins were taking turns protecting the place. Jack's phone rang. "Hello."

"Jack, it's Eva. I'm downstairs. Tell your mobster family to stand down so I can come and talk to you."

"Come up, they won't bother you." Jack hung up the phone and informed his crew to let her pass.

A knock sounded on the door and Jack went over and opened it. He wanted to open the door and smash her in the face, but she was the only way to Fallon. His revenge would come soon enough. Eva stood there waiting on him to speak. "Hello, Jack."

"Eva, glad to see you don't have a gun in my face this time."

"Sorry about that, Brother-in-law. May I come in?"

Jack opened the door. Eva walked in and looked around. "Nice place."

"My dad bought it for Fallon and me as a wedding gift. Please take a seat."

Eva walked over and sat on the couch. Jack sat across from her, fighting the urge to strangle her with his hands. It would be so easy for him to watch her take her last gasp of air.

"How is she?" He asked impatiently.

"She is doing remarkably well considering the events of the last few days. I have been sent here to collect you and bring you to her."

Jack sat back in his seat. "When do you want to leave?"

"I was hoping to sleep here and we could leave after school tomorrow. I could really use some sleep."

"Does Fallon know where you are?"

"Yes, she sent me."

Jack got up. "I will show you to your room."

"Jack, are you mad?"

Jack turned and stared hard at Eva. He couldn't believe she had the nerve to ask him if he was mad. She had no idea of the rage boiling inside of him.

"You played on my sympathies. I wasn't ready for a wife. Then, she is mine and you put her in danger. I can't even see her without going through you. Yeah, I'm mad. If you were anyone else, you would be dead for messing with my family." He stared at her with menacing eyes as he spoke. His words were dripping with warning.

"Jack, I'm sorry. Everything I've done has been to protect her. I'll tell you the same thing I told Fallon, I will not get in the way of you two. I want her to be happy."

"She was happy with me. You should have left her alone instead of putting her out in the open. You almost killed my wife."

Eva looked sad. "I wish I could leave this alone. It's bigger than all of us. Are you ready to protect her from the whole world? You know she may always be a target. She can't escape her lineage."

"Are you really asking the prince of the New Jersey mob if he's going to protect his wife? You are unbelievable. We marry for life. I would give my life to protect her."

"I meant no offense. I was just trying to see if this is what you want."

"What I want is for this to calm down. I want her with me here at school so we can have a normal life before I have to join my father in our business."

"I agree," answered Eva. "Just love her. She is so lost right now."

"Don't dictate my feelings Eva. I will take care of her."

"I don't want you to take care of her, I want you to love her!" Eva yelled at Jack.

"Don't push me. You have no idea how I feel. Leave it be."

"Leave it be? Let me make myself clear to you. If she is unhappy, I will pull her out."

Jack walked up to Eva and got in her face, his voice menacing. "Don't threaten me. No one is going to stand between me and Fallon. If you or anyone else tries, I will put a bullet in your brain. I don't care who you are. Don't threaten me."

Eva smiled. "Okay, you pass. I just needed to know you cared."

Jack looked at Eva with a frown. "You need mental help."

Eva smiled and pulled him in a hug. "You know you're my brother now, I think we should try to stop threatening to kill each other."

Jack released her. "You first."

Jack showed Eva her room. "Come and get me if you need me."

Eva replied, "Good night, my brother!"

"Night, sociopath."

Jack spent a restless night thinking of Fallon. He called his father to tell him of his plans. Johnny was excited to hear Jack was going to see her. He sent his best wishes to Fallon.

Jack hit his alarm three times the following morning. He felt like he had not slept. He got ready quickly. He went in to peek in on Eva and saw she was dead asleep.

He made it through his classes and football practice without incident. He asked to speak to his coach after practice. Jack informed him that he needed a couple of days off from practice. Coach Crandle lost it. "Valentino, you are a disgrace to the team." He continued to scream at Jack for a good thirty minutes. It ended bad after Jack told him he still needed time off. Coach Crandle kicked him off the team. "Get out of my office. You are off the team. I don't have time for your petty little excuses. Get out!"

Jack didn't argue or fuss. He understood. He stood up and tried to shake Coach Crandle's hand. The coach cussed at him and told him to get out. Jack went to his locker in the athletic building. He filled a bag with his stuff and walked out. He felt so angry and sad. Everything that he had worked for was gone. His life had changed because he had a wife. He flipped between hating her and a desperate need to be by her side. This situation was out of control. Unable to handle his anger and frustration, Jack punched the door to the building. An imprint of his knuckles was left in the wood.

Jack walked into the apartment. His face was taut and his movements were in quick jerks. Eva could tell something was horribly wrong. "What's wrong?"

"I just got kicked off the football team for missing so much practice."

"Oh... Did you tell him what was going on?"

"No."

Eva fell silent. She could see the disappointment on Jack's face. She felt bad for him. Football had been his whole life.

Jack walked out of the room. Eva made a phone call to base. She explained the situation and asked for assistance.

Jack and Eva left the apartment and headed to the airport. They boarded a private jet. Eva turned to Jack: "She is in Walter Reed Medical Center."

"Thanks." Jack was quiet and brooding, still angry from before. His gaze piercing Eva with every look.

Chapter 20

Back in Boston, the Athletic Director, Mr. Kemper, was finishing dinner when his doorbell chimed. He opened the door to find two federal agents flashing badges.

"Mr. Kemper, I am Agent Brown and this is Agent Johnson. May we come in?"

"Sure, what's this about?"

"We have a situation that requires your attention. Due to the sensitive nature of our conversation, understand disclosing any information from this meeting will lead to your arrest."

Surprised, Mr. Kemper asked, "Do I need my attorney?"

Agent Brown addressed the concern. "This issue is regarding Jack Valentino. We just need reassurance the information shared tonight will not leave this room. It involves our national security."

After pondering for a few seconds, Mr. Kemper agreed to the terms.

The two agents spent the next few minutes explaining the situation involving Jack. Mr. Kemper keep quiet and listened intently. The agents asked for Jack to resume playing football. They made it clear that he was helping the United States out of a sticky situation.

As they were leaving, they questioned Mr. Kemper. "Can you help us with our little problem?"

Mr. Kemper responded immediately, "It will be handled tonight."

"Thank you, Mr. Kemper."

The two agents left. Mr. Kemper went to the phone and called Coach Crandle for a meeting at his house immediately.

Coach Crandle arrived thirty minutes later. Mr. Kemper showed him to his office.

Cradle questioned immediately, "What is this about?"

Mr. Kemper sat down at his desk. "Crandle, you know I don't interfere with your job. This will be an exception. Jack Valentino will be reinstated to the team. He will maintain his starting job."

Cradle turned red in the face. "Are you kidding me? What, did daddy call and make a donation?"

"Careful Crandle, I'm not the enemy here. This has nothing to do with his father or donations."

"I won't do it. He has missed way too many practices. I'm trying to build a team."

"I appreciate your effort for your team, but I want you to take it easy on the boy. He is dealing with stuff we don't understand."

"You can't tell me how to run my team. I don't care what he is going through. The team has to come first."

Mr. Kemper started to get angry with the coach. "Please don't put me in an awkward position. You know that your contract extension is coming up. I would consider it a personal favor, if you would do this for me."

Cradle was visibly angry. His face turned a bright red and he started to sweat. "You can take your contract and put it where you wipe. I run my team the way I want."

Mr. Kemper pleaded, "Please don't do this. I need your help with this."

Coach Crandle gave Kemper the middle finger and started to walk out.

Mr. Kemper called out, "If you walk out the door, you are fired."

Cradle gave him the middle finger on the other hand.

Mr. Kemper yelled out, "You're fired. I will have security help you clean out your office in the morning."

Coach Crandle kept walking. Mr. Kemper picked up the phone and called the president of the university and informed him of his decision. Mr. Kemper arranged for the news to be released to the media.

Chapter 21

Jack and Eva's plane touched down in Maryland. Jack received an alert on his phone. "Coach Crandle fired from football." Jack looked at Eva and hoped she wasn't behind this.

"Please tell me you had nothing to do with this." He showed her the alert.

Eva shrugged. "I didn't have him fired. He must have been unreasonable."

Jack ran his hands through his hair. "Eva, this is not appropriate. The team will suffer if we have to have a coaching change."

"I just asked for them to talk to him. To smooth the way for you. I don't know what happened to have him fired. That's on him."

Jack's phone started blowing up with messages regarding the coach's firing. Jack tried to answer some of them. Eva came over and held out her hand for Jack's phone.

"I will give this back when we return to the plane. Sorry, I know it's weird not to have your phone with you."

Jack eyed her suspiciously. He reluctantly held his phone out to her.

Jack and Eva made their way to the hospital. They had to go through three levels of security to get to the right floor. Jack was agitated by the time they got to Fallon's room. Eva knocked on the door. She and Jack walked in to find Fallon asleep. Eva nodded at Jack and left the room.

Finally, he was with his wife. Jack looked at Fallon and felt sick to his stomach. She looked so pale and frail in the bed. It seemed to swallow her and she was deathly white. Jack sat down in a chair beside the bed and watched her sleep.

This girl had wrecked his whole life. He wanted to hate her, but he couldn't find the strength. She was his. His heart hurt to look at her. She was so beautiful. He wanted to grab her up and run far away from this place. He wanted to take her home.

Fallon slowly opened her eyes. Her beautiful husband sat in a chair near the bed. He was eye candy. "Hello, handsome."

"Hello, beautiful." Jack got up and kissed Fallon lightly on the lips and sat back down. "How are you?"

"I'm better now you're here." Fallon reached for Jack's hand.

"How bad are you hurt?"

"It's not too bad."

Jack got up again. He moved over to her wounded side and gently dropped the hospital gown until he could see her wounds. When he saw them, he gasped, "Baby, I'm so sorry. This should not have happened."

"I'm going to be fine, I just need some time to heal. I'm doing better. I'm in less pain than I was."

Jack kissed her again on the forehead.

The night passed quickly. Jack and Fallon spent the night talking. They avoided the topic of her parents. Jack slept on a bed that had been brought in for him.

Eva walked into the room bright and early, waking both Fallon and Jack. "Good morning, you love birds."

Fallon groaned. Jack jumped up and went to her. "Are you okay?"

"No, my neurotic sister just woke me up."

"Jack, you know she is not a morning person." Eva quipped.

Fallon asked Eva, "What are doing in here so early?"

Eva shrugged "I just wanted to say hi and we have a clearance date for you to return to Massachusetts."

Fallon sat up straighter, "When?"

"Dr. Smith wants another couple of days for you to heal. Then we'll send you to Cambridge."

Jack smiled sarcastically: "I'm glad that Dr. Smith gets to determine her future and I have no say in it."

"Be calm, Jack. You should be happy she is going to get out of here so quickly." Eva replied. "I need to take you back to Cambridge today and we need to implement a security detail for Fallon. It will take us that long to make sure everything is in place."

Fallon looked at Jack. "Go. I can't wait to be out of the hospital."

"We will leave around 3:00." Eva said as she was heading out the door.

"Well, Mrs. Valentino, I'm finally going to get you in my bed."

Fallon blushed.

"You are so beautiful. I can't wait to show you Boston and my school. We will have so much fun there!"

"I can't wait." Fallon replied then blushed again. "I need to ask an embarrassing favor of you."

"What is it, Baby?"

"Could you help me take a proper shower?"

Jack smiled his sexy smile. Giving Fallon a wink he asked, "Are you trying to seduce me this early in the morning?"

Fallon turned a brighter shade of red.

"Lady, it would be honor to help you get a shower. Let me go arrange it."

Fallon felt like she was dying of embarrassment.

Jack returned. "After we eat breakfast, they have a large shower stall available for our exclusive use."

"Thank goodness. You have no idea how badly I want a shower."

A few minutes later, a nurse arrived with breakfast and the needed toiletries. She gave Fallon instructions for taking care of her wounds. They wrapped Fallon's bullet holes in plastic, put her in a wheelchair, and took her to the shower area.

Fallon was not stable on her feet. Jack realized how weak Fallon was as he helped her. The nurse stood by. Jack turned to the nurse, "I think it better if I take care of this alone."

The nurse nodded and showed Jack where the call button was located in the shower.

Jack went in and turned the water on. He came out and started undressing. Fallon's mouth went dry. His muscles were sculpted. He was a living piece of art work. Jack caught Fallon staring.

"Do I have something on my face?" He inquired.

"What?" replied Fallon.

"You were staring. Just making sure I didn't have anything on my face."

Fallon was embarrassed. She didn't know what to say.

"Looks are free."

Fallon retorted, "I'm glad, because I'm currently without cash."

Jack walked over to where she sat in her wheelchair. "Ok baby, let's get you in the shower." Jack turned off the charm. He helped Fallon get undressed. He picked her up out of the wheelchair as if she weighed nothing. He held her close and slipped them both under the stream of hot water. Fallon moaned as it ran over her; it felt so wonderful to be clean.

Jack placed Fallon on her feet. She swayed some, but Jack held her tight. He took most of her weight against him. With his other arm, he poured shampoo on her hair. Fallon washed her hair with her good arm. They followed the same procedure with the conditioner and body soap.

Fallon fell deeper in love with Jack in this moment. He was helping her at her most vulnerable moment. It was one of the most intimate acts. When they finished washing, Jack held her against him in the shower. It was a romantic, beautiful moment.

Jack whispered in her ear, "When we get home to Cambridge, we will shower together every day." Fallon nodded.

Jack kissed her neck and said, "We need to get out." He reached around and shut off the water. He grabbed a towel hanging outside the shower and wrapped it around Fallon. He picked her up and took her back to the wheelchair. After he put her down, he covered himself with a towel. He then took another towel and wrapped Fallon's hair.

He helped Fallon up and placed a robe around her. Jack got dressed while Fallon enjoyed the show. He looked super-hot in his tight football shirt and jeans.

Jack pushed Fallon back to her room. Fallon took down the towel holding her hair. She tried to brush to out, but her side was hurting. Jack took the brush and brushed it out. When it was done, he leaned down and said, "Brushing your hair does things to me."

Fallon giggled at his declaration. Jack took the hair dryer and dried her hair. She felt so much better when it was finished. He helped get Fallon back on the bed. She was exhausted and in pain. She didn't want to take any pain medicine because she didn't want to miss out on any time with Jack.

Dr. Smith came into the room later and instantly recognized that she was in pain. Fallon was holding her side and had a pained expression on her face. He checked her wounds. She grimaced when he touched her side.

"Fallon, are you in pain?"

Fallon didn't want to answer. She shook her head no.

Jack looked at Fallon. He could see it on her face.

"Doc, give her some meds."

"No, I don't want them. It will make me go to sleep."

Jack looked at Dr. Smith. "Don't listen to her, get the meds."

Dr. Smith nodded and left the room.

"I'm not taking them. I don't want to sleep while you are here."

"Fallon, be reasonable. I will be back as soon as I can, I know where to find you now. Take the medication. He assured her, "I need you well when we get to Cambridge. We have a life to live."

Fallon responded, "I know, but I miss you when you're not here. I don't want to waste this time together being in a drugged stupor."

The nurse walked in and handed Fallon a small paper cup with two white pills. Jack walked over and took them out of her hand. He leaned over and gave her a kiss on the lips, deepening it slowly. Fallon moaned. The nurse cleared her throat.

Jack pulled back, "Take the medicine."

Fallon reluctantly puts the pills in her mouth and swallowed. The nurse left the room.

"Scoot over. I need a nap."

Fallon moved over and Jack joined her on the bed. He snuggled her the best he could. Ironically, Jack fell asleep before Fallon. She could hear his steady breathing. Fallon felt the medication slowly kick in. She placed her hand over Jack's and fell into a deep sleep.

Dr. Smith walked into the room. He was shocked at the scene before him. Fallon was draped over Jack. They were both sound asleep. Dr. Smith shook his head and left the room.

Eva was walking down the hall. Dr. Smith stopped her. "I wouldn't go in there."

"Why not?"

"Those two are disgusting. He is sleeping in the bed with her. I'm not crazy about it, but they seem to be resting."

Eva rolled her eyes, "Yuck!"

Dr. Smith added, "Let them rest."

Eva rolled her eyes and walked away.

In the afternoon, a nurse came in the room to take Fallon's vitals. She woke both of them up. Jack was angry because he was finally resting next to his wife. He climbed off the bed and sat in a nearby chair.

Fallon yawned, "I think I could have stayed asleep all day."

Jack replied, "Wife, when we get home, I'm going to dare someone to bother us. I'm going to shoot first and then ask questions."

Fallon giggled. "That would be awkward."

Time passed quickly. Eva came in to the room looking grim at 3:00. "Are you ready?" She looked at Jack.

Jack nodded. He went over and gave Fallon a passionate kiss. "Bye, Wife."

"Bye, Husband."

Eva seemed out of joint. "We need to go."

"Eva, are you okay?" Fallon asked.

"I'm fine, just tired. Let's go, Jack."

Jack kissed Fallon on the head. "I'll be back as soon as I can to take you to Cambridge."

"Love you." Fallon whispered.

Jack smiled. "See you later."

Eva addressed Fallon, "I'll be back tomorrow after I get things set in Cambridge. Try to get some rest. Love you."

"Thank you, Eva. Love you."

Both Eva and Jack left the room. Eva led Jack down to the waiting car. They loaded up. Instead of heading for the airport they headed in a different direction.

"Where are we going Eva?"

"We need to make a pit stop."

They drove for a couple of minutes then stopped in front of an office building. Eva looked at Jack, "My boss would like a word with you."

Chapter 22

"Who do you work for Eva?"

Eva didn't answer. "Take the meeting."

Eva got out of the car and Jack followed her into the building that appeared to be a normal office building. Eva stopped in front of the secretary. The secretary motioned them to an office door. Eva stepped in followed by Jack. They stayed there for a few moments, then another door opened.

Jack walked into a hallway. It looked like it was straight out of the movies. It was a secret office for the FBI. Agents were busy working all around. Eva stopped in front of a conference room. She led Jack in and told him to take a seat.

Eva left Jack and returned with an older looking black man. He held out his hand. "I'm Agent Daniels."

Jack shook his hand. He knew that this was bad.

Agent Daniels spoke, "Mr. Valentino, we find ourselves in a unique situation. You have married probably the most important news story in recent history. We need your help."

"What kind of help?"

"We want you to keep her happy. Your wife is an asset and a threat to the United States."

"A threat?"

Agent Daniels glanced at Eva. Eva shook her head.

Agent Daniels looked at Jack. "We have reason to believe that Fallon's other biological parent was an important person in history."

"Who?" Jack was impatient.

Eva stepped in. "Jack I had no idea. Please understand I just found out today myself."

"Who is it, Eva? Tell me now."

Eva said in a voice with no emotion. "Nothing has been confirmed yet, but we think there is a possibility that..." Eva couldn't finish. She couldn't find the words to say that her sister was a byproduct of one of the most evil humans that had ever lived. Eva started to tear up. Her voice became shaky. "Jack, I'm so sorry." She sniffled back a cry with the back of her hand over her mouth.

Jack looked at agent Daniels. "Tell me, I can take it."

Agent Daniels started the story, "We received intel last year that there was possibly a child had been born out of a crazy experiment during WWII. We dismissed the intel because our scientist deemed it was impossible. We had worked with Eva before, in our special operation divisions. She contacted us and asked for our help after her dad told her the situation. We gave protection of Eva and Fallon over to the Italians as we thought this was their issue."

He continued, "We received more details after the Gettysburg event. We were able to question one of the survivors. They wanted Fallon dead and they wanted to stop her from being out in public. They are afraid of her."

"Why would they be afraid?" Jack quizzed.

"They told us that Fallon was a result of a scientific experiment in WWII between Germany and Italy."

"What are you trying to say? That Fallon is the daughter of Hitler and Mussolini?" Jack asked in a snarky voice.

Agent Daniels replied in a cold stone voice, "We think she is the daughter of Hitler and the oldest of Mussolini's daughter, Edda."

Jack's mouth flew open. He sat in stunned silence. Eva had tears running down her face. It took Jack a few moments to gain his composure. He asked, "How would you verify this? It can't be true."

"We have run several DNA tests on Fallon. We have also hunted down all the relatives of Hitler that are still in existence. Our scientists are working on it. We will have proof soon."

Jack felt sick. "What do you want from me? I'm not going to be married to a monster."

Agent Daniels added, "That was what we were afraid of. The world needs to see a united front here. It would leave her vulnerable, if you divorced her."

"That is not my problem," Jack snipped.

"Well, it is your problem now." Agent Daniels hit a button on the phone. A few agents entered the room. They had folders in their hands. They placed them in front of Jack.

"What is this?" Jack was turning red in the face. He was getting angry.

"That is your dad's criminal file. We have enough now to stop your organization, take away all of your money, and send your dad to jail for the rest of his life."

Agent Daniels continued, "The US government will gladly look the other way if Fallon is being protected by you and your family. We think it is the best way to keep her safe. We feel she needs more protection than we can offer her at this time. Wouldn't it be wonderful, if these files just came up missing permanently?"

Jack looked at Eva. "I hate you so much right now. You have destroyed my family."

Eva looked away. She knew that he was right.

Jack looked at Agent Daniels. "I want this in writing. I am seeking immunity for all of my family."

Agent Daniels nodded his head, "I will get it to you as soon as I can. I understand this is overwhelming. We will stop and let you get back to your family. Where would you like to go?"

Jack answered abruptly, "I want to go home to New Jersey."

Agent Daniels signaled to an agent and then he walked over and shook Jack's hand. "We will be able to do great things together."

Jack didn't answer as he shook the agents hand. They got up to leave. Eva was following Jack. He stopped and looked at her, "Leave me alone Eva, I don't want to see you again."

Jack left the room and walked out of the building. He got into the waiting car and made his way to New Jersey to see his father.

Eva stayed at the office. She decided not to go back to the hospital. She needed some time to process what she had learned this morning about Fallon.

Jack landed in New Jersey a few hours later. He made his way to his father's house with the protection team. He hadn't notified his father that he was on his way. He pulled up at the house and finally called his dad. "I'm here, let me in."

The lights came on in the house and the gate opened to let Jack through. He dad opened the front door. Jack nodded to his dad, "We need to talk." Johnny followed Jack into his office.

Johnny sat down behind his desk. "I'm surprised to see you. Things must be really bad if you are here and not with Fallon."

Jack looked straight into his father's eyes, "Did you know?"

"Know what, son?"

"Tell me the truth, did you know?"

"Jack, tell me what's going on."

"I'll tell you what is going on. You made me marry a monster. How could you?"

Johnny leaned forward and rested his chin on his palms. "You know all I know about her. Start from the beginning and let me know what happened."

Jack told Johnny the whole story including the file that they had against him. Johnny sat back in his chair stunned. He shook his head "I had no idea. Believe me, I didn't know. I'm sorry."

"What I am going to do? If I don't keep her happy, we are all going to be in jail. If I accept the immunity plan, we are safe. I just don't know if I can tolerate the sight of her."

Johnny got out of his chair. He laid a hand on Jack. "I'll go to jail. I'm surprised they have let me operate this long without coming after me. I won't press you to stay married to her. You are my son and all I've wanted was for you is to be happy. I thought you two would be happy."

"Dad, no."

"You have paid for my debt once already. I would not let you pay again."

"It's my decision to make. Let me have some time. Can you arrange for me to get to Cambridge tomorrow morning? I'm exhausted. I want to go to bed and sleep."

"I'll make the arrangements. Before you go, you should know I've prepared for this day for a long time. Give me some time if you decide not to accept the immunity deal. I want to ensure that you and Maria are taken care of if I go to jail."

Jack got up and gave his dad a hug. He had made his decision. He would accept the immunity deal. He couldn't stand by and let his dad go to jail. Jack walked to his old bedroom but it didn't seem right. He stayed there for a couple of minutes and then went to the bedroom he and Fallon shared. He was sitting on the bed staring at the floor when Maria walked in. She went and sat down by him on the bed. "Your dad just told me." Jack stared at the floor.

"Let me ask you something? Did you love her before you knew?"

"Maria, I'm not in the mood. Let it be."

"No. Did you love her?"

"Maria, please. I don't want to be disrespectful to you. I want to be left alone."

Maria got up. "It was a good thing you married her. I thought you were happy. I never took you for the type of man that would go against his vows before God and his family. Don't disappoint me, son. I raised you to be a man your mother would be proud of. I gave her my word."

Jack felt a tear roll down his face. "Did my mother tell you how to deal with this?"

"Yes Jack, she did. She taught me to fight, not to ever give up." Maria kissed Jack on the head. "I love you."

Jack felt more tears rolling. He wiped at his face. "Please don't talk about this to anyone. It could be dangerous for you."

Maria laughed, "My whole life has been dangerous." Maria left the room.

Jack crawled into bed and went into a deep sleep. He dreamed that he was trying to find Fallon with no luck.

Chapter 23

The following morning found Fallon bored in her hospital room. She had completed physical therapy and was waiting for Eva. She was getting stronger and her pain had decreased. She was on the mend.

Fallon was sitting in a chair when Eva walked in. "Eva, is everything ok?"

Eva smiled. "Jack went to New Jersey to see Johnny Hearts. I decided to come back. I have a team in place taking care of the arrangements."

"How was Jack?"

"He was fine. He is heading back to school today. We can call him later."

Eva pulled up a chair next to the bed. "I want to ask you some questions. We are still trying to find out why someone is after you."

Fallon nodded her agreement.

"Fallon, did our parents ever to talk to you about being born? The actual birth?"

Fallon scrunched her face and responded. "Mom always joked that I broke her from wanting kids. She said when they lost my twin, they did emergency surgery to get me out quickly."

Eva raised her hand to make Fallon stop talking. "What do you mean the twin?"

Frustrated, Fallon responded, "Eva, come on. They told that story a million times. I was a twin, remember? They lost the other baby first, and they made Dad leave the room? It was very dramatic and sad. Mom almost died. The hospital took the baby away before either of them could see it."

Eva shook her head. "I don't remember. They didn't tell me. I have never heard this before."

Fallon rolled her eyes. "You have heard this story before. You have just forgotten it."

Eva got up abruptly. "I forgot I had an appointment. I'll be by later."

Eva rushed out the room in a hurry. When she got outside the door, she leaned against the wall. It all made sense now. If she was right, there was another baby that lived. A baby who now is calling the shots. The person who was trying to hurt Fallon. Someone who had sent the killers to Gettysburg and killed her parents. The pieces to the puzzle were coming together. Eva felt sick to her stomach. She ran to the nearest bathroom and emptied the contents of her stomach into the toilet. She heaved multiple times until nothing came up and sat on the floor. She had to get to Alabama. Hopefully, there was some information in her house.

Eva washed out her mouth and pulled out her phone and relayed the information to Agent Daniels. She stepped out find to Dr. Smith leaning against the wall. "Feel better?"

Eva smiled. She wiped at her mouth again. "I'm going to have to leave. I need her taken care of."

Dr. Smith said, "She will be fine, I will take good care of her."

Eva continued, "Call Jack for me. He will need to keep in contact with her. He was not in a good place when I left him yesterday. Press him, make him take the call."

"Will do. Where are you headed?"

"Home. I don't want to bring anyone else in on this."

Dr. Smith looked at Eva and raised a brow. "I think it's late for that. I'm in deep."

Eva whispered in his ear. "Fallon has a twin, I think. I need to go home to Alabama and see if I can find any proof. I think it's the twin that wants to hurt her."

Dr. Smith nodded and said, "Godspeed my friend. When you get back, you owe me a date."

Eva gave Dr. Smith a sad smile and went back into Fallon's room. "Hey, I've got to head out for a spell. Dr. Smith will take care of you. When I get back, I will take you to Cambridge."

"Where are you going?"

"I'm headed back to Alabama. I'm taking a team to see what we can find out. We have to know who is after you."

"Please don't go. Stay here with me and forget all of this. I'll go with Jack. He will keep me safe. I want this to end. You need a break, please stay with me."

"Fallon, this is bigger than the both if us. I need to go to try to find out information. I will be safe. I've got to go. Dr. Smith has a phone that you can use to get in touch with Jack. I'll call in and check on you. Love you."

Fallon teared up. "Love you, sister."

Eva turned and walked out the door. Fallon sat in her bed and cried. She felt abandoned again. She had a sinking feeling something was terribly wrong. She could feel it deep in her soul. Eva was headed to Alabama for a reason. Fallon desperately wanted this to be over so her life could be normal again.

Dr. Smith came in later in the afternoon. He pulled out the phone. "Want to call your lover boy?" He winked at Fallon.

"Well thank you, Sir. I believe I do." Fallon returned with a smile.

He handed the phone to Fallon and she dialed Jack's number. He picked up after the fifth ring.

"What?" He answered, sounding agitated.

"Hello, Husband."

"Fallon, are you okay?"

"Yes, I'm fine. How are you?"

"Busy, I'm at practice. I've got to go."

"Umm...sorry to bother you."

Jack hung up without responding. Fallon held the phone back to Dr. Smith. "I think he was busy."

"Don't fret, we'll call him later tonight."

"Thanks."

Dr. Smith left and Fallon went to physical therapy. She came back to her room. All she could think about was that something was wrong. Fallon had a powerful feeling things were off. It was time for her to leave the hospital, she needed to be with Jack to make sure he wanted their relationship. She tried to take her mind off it by watching TV. It was no use. She was restless by the time Dr. Smith came back into the room two hours later.

"What's up, Doc?" She smiled and said.

"Do we want round two with your man?"

"Yes, please."

Nervously taking the phone, Fallon called Jack again. This time he didn't answer. Fallon's fears were confirmed. Something had happened. She looked at Dr. Smith for answers.

"I know you know what's going on. I'm not stupid, so talk to me."

Dr. Smith looked at her bewildered. I'm afraid I don't know what you're talking about."

"Stop the games. I want to know. Tell me now." Fallon yelled at him.

"Fallon, please. There are things that I'm obligated to keep secret. I'm sorry but Eva will be back soon, I'm sure that she will share with you what she knows."

"Wrong answer, Sir. Tell me now."

"I can't talk to you about anything I know. You need to stay here and get better. You are making great progress. Focus on that." Dr. Smith moved forward to check her wounds.

Fallon backed up on the bed. "Don't touch me. You talk or I'm leaving."

Dr. Smith stopped. "I'm sorry you are upset. You can't leave. You are on a secure floor. If you leave, we can't protect you. Please give Eva some time. She is working hard to find out who is threatening you so please be patient."

"What if I don't want to be patient or a patient?"

Dr. Smith rubbed his chin. "I would hate for things to go that way. We would secure you to the bed and medicate you."

Fallon got off the bed. "I don't think so." She backed away from him.

Dr. Smith sat down and said, "Such a fighter." He checked his watch, looking bored. He started talking, "I would never want to keep you in a place where you don't want to be. I have fought alongside your sister to keep you safe. So please don't turn me into the bad guy. Understand I will take whatever measures are necessary to keep you safe. Please get into bed. I don't want to fight with you tonight."

"I hate all of you. My life is destroyed and you act like I should just stay in bed. Why won't you talk to me? Please give me some information, I'm going crazy!"

"You know I can't."

Fallon walked over and checked the window. It was secure. The only exit was the door behind where Dr. Smith was sitting. She could possibly get past him if she tried. The problem was she didn't know what was waiting on the other side. Fallon decided to test the waters. She calmly walked toward the door. Dr. Smith didn't make a move to stop her. She walked out the door into the hallway. She had only seen the hallway briefly when she went to physical therapy.

There were double doors at the end of the hallway. She started walking toward them. Two security guards stepped in front of the doors. "Ma'am, please return to your room."

Fallon stopped in front of them. She didn't speak. She just looked at the guards with an evil stare. She turned and looked around. There were no other people on the hallway, except for Dr. Smith and a couple of nurses.

Fallon walked back down the hallway. She stopped in front of the nurse's station. She looked at the desk. She tried to see if there was a button that controlled the door. There was nothing visible to the eye. She was stuck.

Fallon walked back to her room. Dr. Smith walked in behind her. "I'm sorry. This will be over soon and you can go to Boston. I'll take you there myself."

Fallon felt the tears start. "Please leave." She turned away from him so he could not see her cry.

Dr. Smith saw her tears, but decided to leave her alone. He walked out of the room. Fallon walked over to the window looking out as the tears continued to fall. She was heartsick over Jack. She knew he was upset. She just didn't know what it was about. If only he would talk to her.

Chapter 24

In Cambridge, Jack had just attempted to work out his frustrations with a brutal exercise session. He completed his training and was headed out the door when he was met by Agent Daniels and his crew in the parking lot.

"Mr. Valentino, I wanted to come and personally see how things were for you in Massachusetts."

"Agent Daniels." Jack replied curtly.

"Have you decided?"

"I will take the immunity for my family."

"Good, Mr. Valentino. I was worried when I reviewed a report that your wife was having a hard time in the hospital and she hadn't had any support from you."

"What goes on between me and my wife is my business. Stay out of it."

"With all due respect, Mr. Valentino, what goes on between you and your wife is the business of the American government."

Jack shook his head. "When can I expect the paperwork?"

"We will have it to you in the morning for you and your dad to sign."

Jack dropped his head. "Okay."

"As soon as we get the paperwork taken care of, we will move Fallon here. I understand she gave the staff some trouble today."

"Is she okay?"

"She is fine, just tired of being locked up in the hospital."

"Is that all, Agent Daniels? I have dinner plans."

"Call your dad and get him here tomorrow so we can lock this down."

Jack nodded. The agents left and Jack got in his SUV. He dialed his dad.

Johnny answered "Son, how are you?"

Not replying with the normal pleasantries, Jack said, "I'm taking the immunity deal. I need you in Cambridge tomorrow morning to sign."

Johnny responded, "I've decided that this is a bad deal for you. Tell the Feds to forget it."

"Dad, be here in the morning to sign. Don't make me come after you." Jack hung up the phone. Johnny tried to call Jack back but Jack didn't answer. With nothing else to use on his frustrations, Jack punched the steering wheel in his car. He was so angry.

Blowing off his dinner plans, Jack went back to the apartment because he felt bad. It bothered him that Fallon had had a rough day. He wanted to comfort her, but he couldn't get past who she was and what her heritage stood for in the past. After worrying and resisting the temptation to be on a plane to get her, Jack fell asleep on the couch watching TV.

The phone ringing woke up Jack. The number was blocked, "Hello?"

"Hey Jack, this is Dr. Smith. We met in Shiloh at the Battlefield."

"Is everything fine with Fallon?"

"She is fine. I was wondering if you wanted to talk to her tonight? She has had a rough day."

"Not tonight, I'm in bed."

"What would you like for me to tell her?"

"Tell her I'll see her tomorrow."

"Good night, Mr. Valentino."

Jack hung up the phone and went back to sleep. He couldn't deal with Fallon tonight. He wanted and needed a break.

Dr. Smith walked into Fallon's room. "I just talked to Jack. He was asleep so he wanted me to tell you he will see you tomorrow." She sat up in bed.

"Wait, am I leaving tomorrow?"

Doctor Smith smiled and nodded, "I hope to get you out of here late tomorrow. So be cool and don't start any trouble."

Fallon saluted. "You will have no trouble from me."

"Good night, Fallon. See you in the morning."

Fallon leaned back against the bed. She dismissed the worry she had about Jack as nerves. She was so excited to get out of here. All she needed now was for Eva to show up and give her some good news. Being separated from her sister was hard and added to her stress.

Jack was still asleep on the couch the next morning when he heard the front door opening. He grabbed a gun out from under the cushion.

"Easy, its me." Jack lowered the gun. It was his father. He was followed in by his team of lawyers.

Jack rubbed his eyes. He had not slept well. "Good morning."

"Son, I brought a team of lawyers to make sure that we are covered in the immunity deal. Do you know what time they will call?

Jack shook his head no. "I'm expecting a call at any time." He handed his dad the phone. "I'm going to get a shower."

Johnny took the phone and caught Jack in a hug, "Love you!"

Jack kissed his dad on the check. "Love you, Dad." Jack went into the bathroom. He got in the shower with his emotions all over the place. He was excited, angry, and nervous to see Fallon today. One truth remained. He missed her. Leaning against the shower wall with hot water dripping over him, he fought a constant battle of whether to walk away from Fallon or should he stay. She was his wife. Could he learn to live with the fact that her parents were two of the worst figures in world history?

Jack's phone rang while he was in the shower. Johnny answered. "Hello, Mr. Valentino." "This is agent Daniels with the FBI. I am the contact for your son and Fallon. I see you brought your group of lawyers with you. I am sending over the immunity deal. Check it over. When your team is ready, call this number and we will sign."

Johnny responded. "Send it over."

Jack walked into the room as Johnny was hanging up the phone. "Was it them?"

"Yes, they are sending over the deal for us to review."

"Good, I'll go to class. Be ready when I get back. I want this over as soon as possible."

Johnny nodded and said, "Be careful."

Jack grabbed his backpack and left the room. He was angry. He didn't want to look at his father. He wanted this to be over with quickly.

The immunity deal paperwork arrived at the apartment soon after Jack left. The team of lawyers dissected the pages that promised to get the Valentino family off the hook. Johnny was impressed with how much the government would allow in this deal. Jack had secured a great deal for the family. With a few minor adjustments, the contract was approved by the team.

Jack returned home after his classes. He wasn't in a better mood. Johnny was waiting for him on the couch. "You secured a good deal for us. Thank you, son."

Jack nodded, "Make the call and set the time." Jack went to his room to get ready. He went into his closet and pulled out a suit. He would look professional as he went to sign the contract. His phone rang as he was getting dressed. He knew it was Fallon so he acted like he didn't hear it ring. He didn't want to talk to her this morning. He would deal with her later tonight.

The morning passed in a blur for Jack. The contract was signed by everyone within the hour. His dad seemed relieved. The agents made arrangements to have Fallon in Cambridge around 10:00 p.m. tonight.

Fallon received word through Dr. Smith she would leave tonight for Massachusetts. She was nervous but excited to see Jack. She got up and took a shower by herself. She made herself as presentable as possible.

Eva walked into her room. "Hello sunshine!"

Fallon jumped up and gave her a hug. "I missed you. I was worried."

"I'm fine. No luck in Alabama. Are you ready to go?"

"Yes!" Fallon answered. "Have you talked to Jack?"

"No, I think he's been busy."

"Oh, I was just wondering."

Eva sat in the chair. She debated telling Fallon the truth. Weighing her options, she decided to leave it alone. Fallon deserved a chance to be happy. She didn't need to worry about this.

"So you know, I'm the crazy sister. I want you to be open minded about what I'm going to show you. Okay?"

"What is it?"

Eva looked down at the floor. "I want to make sure that you always have a way out. A way to get away from Jack and his family. An extraction plan."

"An extraction plan? Really, Eva?"

"I know it sounds crazy, but I think it is important. Be open-minded."

Eva got up and opened the door. A group of people walked in. There were two females and two males. Surprised, Fallon looked directly at Ms. Jones, the teacher from the Academy. Eva introduced each one of them. "Fallon, pay close attention. They are here for you. No one in Jack's family knows them. They will always be around you. Only make contact if you want an extraction. Do not identify them to anyone. They are in deep cover. Understood?"

Fallon nodded yes. Each of the people came over and greeted her. Eva spoke again. "These people are your life line. We can have you out of Cambridge quickly. We don't expect problems, but we want to be prepared if things go bad."

"Everything will be ok, Eva. I know Jack isn't perfect, but he's good to me. We will be fine."

"I hope so, sister. Also, we have arranged for you to go to school in Boston to finish your high school courses. Johnny arranged yesterday to have your clothing and items from New Jersey sent over to the apartment in Cambridge. They should be there when you arrive."

"Thanks, I can't wait to be back in my own clothes."

"Last thing, you will have a security team with you at all times. It must be this way until we know who is after you. We feel confident you will be safe in Cambridge. It might seem weird at first, but you will get used to it."

Fallon was desperate to go, so she agreed to the security detail. She had to get to Jack to figure out what was wrong. "What time will I leave?"

"We'll leave around 8:00 tonight. I'll go and get you some of my clothes to wear."

Eva and the team left the room. Fallon was alone with her thoughts. Her desire to leave was strong. She couldn't wait to be back in Jack's arms. He would keep her safe. She could have a life with him.

The day passed slowly for Fallon. By the time Eva returned around 7:30, Fallon was irritated and ready to leave. She had been bored out of her mind all day. Eva came in carrying a clothing bag. "Get dressed, we need to leave in a couple of minutes."

Fallon pulled the clothing out of the bag. It was jeans, t-shirt, and some running shoes. Fallon was disappointed. She had hoped to dress up to see Jack. She reluctantly got dressed doing the best with what she had. Fallon came out of the bathroom. Eva was sitting on her bed. "Sorry for the clothing, I was in hurry."

"No worries, are we ready?" Fallon inquired.

"Fallon, I…"

"What is it?" Fallon went over and sat down by Eva.

Eva couldn't do it, she couldn't tell her today. She looked excited and happy. Eva covered quickly, "I will miss you, that's all."

Fallon took her hand, "I'll miss you too. Move to Massachusetts and be near me."

Eva chuckled, "Can't do, I am staying here. Cambridge and Boston are not ready for me."

Fallon laid her head on Eva's shoulder. "We will be fine."

"Sisters forever, no matter what."

"No matter what happens," Fallon echoed.

"Let's go before we end up crying and looking ugly when we leave."

Fallon laughed. "Please, let's go."

Eva got up and Fallon followed. They left the hallway. Fallon said goodbye to the nurses. Dr. Smith was waiting at the end of the hallway. He held out some papers for Fallon, "These are your discharge papers. I put my number on them, so if you are having any trouble, call me."

Fallon gave him a kiss on the check. "You've saved me twice. Maybe someday, I can return the favor."

"Goodbye, Fallon. Take care." He walked off.

Fallon looked at Eva, "That was weird."

Eva giggled. "Big men don't handle emotions well. He's fine."

Fallon and Eva left the floor. Fallon didn't realize how big the hospital complex was until she was off her hallway. It was massive. They reached the ground floor. A group of men in suits were waiting for them, and an older Asian man stepped forward, "Mrs. Valentino, I'm Mr. Li, head of your security."

Fallon shook his hand. She was surrounded by the group. They escorted her to the waiting car. There were two agents in the car with her and Eva.

Night was falling as Fallon and Eva boarded the private jet. The security team was onboard. The jet took off into the black of night.

Chapter 25

Jack managed to make it to practice after the crazy morning he had. He was dreading seeing Fallon. He wasn't sure he would be able to resist her. He dreamed of her every night, and he could feel her next to him in bed. Every time he gave into his desires and was ready to forget she was the daughter of evil, images of the Holocaust would fill his mind. That was her legacy. She was the daughter of a monster, and now she was bound to him in marriage.

Getting ready, Jack put on his best suit and checked his appearance in the mirror. He walked out of the room. His dad was waiting for him in the living room, "Are you ready for this?"

"I'm ready."

"How are you going to handle her?"

"I think that I'm going to tell her we need to slow down our relationship. We moved so fast, I wasn't ready. I just need some time to work through all of this."

Johnny nodded, "That might be best. She needs to graduate high school and start college in the fall. She is so young."

Jack wanted to reassure his father, "We will be okay. I just need some time to figure this all out."

A knock sounded even though they weren't expecting company. Jack walked over and grabbed his gun out from under the couch. He put it in his belt. He walked over and opened the door. It was Agent Daniel.

"Mr. Valentino, may I have a word before we leave for the airport?"

Jack opened the door. Agent Daniels acknowledged Johnny. He sat down on the couch.

"How may I help you?" Jack asked in a sarcastic tone.

Clearing his throat, Agent Daniels said, "Fallon doesn't know about her father. Eva felt Fallon was not in a good place emotionally. We want to keep this from her until we have more evidence. We need you to cooperation in keeping this a secret for now."

"Fallon should know. It is what it is," Jack replied.

"We would like to control the information that is given. Eva is working hard to find some evidence. We just haven't had any luck."

"We won't tell her," Johnny said.

Jack gave his dad a look.

Agent Daniel continued, "As soon as we have the information we need, we will tell Fallon. All we have now are theories, and we think it better to keep this close. No leaks."

Jack nodded and abruptly said, "We need to go. It'll take us some time to get to the airport."

Jack, Johnny, and the security team left for the airport. Jack was nervous to be around Fallon. He was shaking his leg in a nervous twitch. He just wasn't ready to face her. They arrived at the airport and waited for the plane to land. Everyone was quiet in the car.

Finally, they saw the approaching lights of the airplane. Jack turned to his dad. "I'd like to go and greet her by myself if is okay."

Johnny nodded. "I'll wait in the car. Give me a signal when you want me to get out. She is my daughter. I don't care about her heritage."

Rolling his eyes, Jack gave his dad a frustrated look. The agents came around and opened the door as the plane was gliding to a stop. The stairs to the plane unfolded. Jack stepped out of the car. Gone was the boy from before. Here was a man prepared to greet his wife.

The security team came off the plane first. Fallon followed Eva out of the door, spotting Jack immediately. Her heart thumped. He was devastatingly handsome, dressed in a sleek suit leaned against the car waiting on her. Fallon waved. He gave a quick nod back.

Fallon descended the stairs with shaky legs and assistance from her security team. Jack walked over and gave her a quick hug. "Glad to have you back."

Fallon looked around. Something was wrong. Jack was acting weird. He was acting like she was his sister, not his wife. Jack took Fallon's bag from Eva.

He was distant to Eva, not even acknowledging her. Fallon caught on there were problems between the two of them.

Fallon started walking toward the car. Eva did not follow. Fallon turned around. "Eva, are you coming?"

"No baby sis, I have to head back."

Fallon felt her tears starting to develop. She tried to hold them back as she walked back to Eva to give her a hug. "Thank you Eva, you saved my life."

Eva returned her hug and whispered in her ear, "Remember your people from today, use them if you need to get out."

Fallon nodded and said, "Love you."

"Love you." Eva turned and walked back to the plane.

Jack walked over to Fallon as she watched Eva climb the stairs to the plane. "Are you ready to go home? Someone is waiting for you in the car." Jack motioned to the car and Johnny Hearts stepped out.

Fallon gave Johnny a big smile and a wave. He walked over to where they were. Johnny pulled her into a big hug, mindful of her injuries. "Daughter, I have been so worried."

Fallon felt relief because she didn't get any weirdness from Johnny. He treated her like he always had. Johnny kissed her head. "How are you feeling?"

"I'm doing much better now I am out of the hospital. I hated being there."

Johnny replied, "You are home now. You can heal and get ready to start school in the fall."

Jack opened the car door and looked at Fallon, "Are you ready to go? I have class early tomorrow morning and a full day of practice, so I need to go."

Fallon was shocked. Jack had never been so rude to her. She cut him a look, "My apologies, of course we can go." Fallon climbed in the car with Johnny.

Johnny kept up the conversation throughout the trip home. Jack was silent. Fallon could feel the tension in the car. Fallon looked out the window. She had never been to Boston before. Johnny could see the wonderment in her eyes.

"When you feel better, I will come back and give you the grand tour of Boston."

Fallon smiled, "I would love that. I've never been here before."

"You'll love it. Great food and great people."

It took about thirty minutes before they pulled up at the apartment. The security exited their vehicles first. Jack got out and held out his hand for Fallon. She took his hand to help her out of the vehicle. As soon as they got out, Jack dropped her hand.

Johnny got out of the vehicle and walked over and to give Jack a hug. He whispered something in Jack's ear. Jack nodded. Johnny took out an envelope and gave it to Fallon. "This is for you and Jack. Love you both."

Fallon gave Johnny a hug and said, "Love you, Johnny Hearts. Thank you."

Johnny nodded. He got into a waiting SUV.

Fallon was alone with Jack, except for security. Jack got her bag out of the car and headed for the elevator. He didn't speak as they rode up. Fallon felt nervous as they got out. Jack opened the door to the apartment. Fallon followed him in. It was gorgeous. It looked like it came straight out of an interior design magazine with modern furniture and decor.

"What do you think?"

"It's wonderful."

Jack led her to a bedroom and dropped her bag on the bed. He gave her a tour of the room. Jack opened the closet. It was full of Fallon's clothing and shoes.

Fallon couldn't help herself. "Why are we not sharing a room?"

Jack sat down on the bed. He had been dreading this moment all day. "I think it's better if we slow down some."

"What does that mean, slow down?"

Jack ran his hand through his hair in a nervous gesture. "I need some time to adjust to our relationship. We need some time to get to know each other."

Fallon felt herself start to panic. She was right with her weird feelings. This confirmed Jack didn't want to be married to her.

"If you didn't want me here, then why didn't you let me stay with Eva?" Fallon yelled at him.

Jack turned red in the face. "We're married, you belong here with me."

Fallon went over to the closet. She looked at her clothing and shoes. "I will call Eva and I will arrange to be out of here tomorrow."

"I don't think so. You are staying here with me."

Fallon looked him directly in the eye, "You are not my boss. I don't have to do what you say."

Jack got up. "Don't make me lock you up in here."

"Get out!" Fallon walked over to where he was standing. "I said to get out of here. Now!"

Jack got off the bed. "Try not to act like a child."

Fallon became enraged, pushing weakly at Jack to get him out of the door. Fallon felt a stitch rip in her arm and groaned in pain. She whimpered.

Jack saw her react in pain. "Are you okay?"

Fallon held her arm in place. "Get out, I don't need you."

Jack walked back to where she was, "Let me see your arm."

"No, get out."

"Fallon, please. I don't want you to be hurt."

"I'm fine, get out."

Jack looked at her. She was beautiful with her angry face and piercing eyes. He decided to let her cool down before she really hurt herself. "I'm close by if you need me."

"Leave!"

Jack left the room. Fallon was so angry. She went into the bathroom to check her injuries but found it didn't look bad. It had hurt initially, but it seemed to stop after a few minutes. Fallon decided to get in the shower. She wanted to wash off the hospital stay.

Jack heard her turn on the shower. It took all his willpower to stay out of her bathroom. He wanted to go and check on her, but he was afraid that being close to her would be bad for his resistance. Jack listened closely to hear her get out of the shower.

Fallon was out of the shower and brushing her hair when Jack walked in. "Do you need help?"

"No."

"Fallon, I don't want you to go. I've been under some pressure and I need some time to get my head on straight."

Fallon ignored him and continued to brush her hair. Jack was talking. Fallon pulled out the blow dryer and started drying her hair as he spoke. Jack wanted to smash the hair dryer into a million pieces. Jack walked up behind her and pulled the dryer out of her hand and turned it off. "I need your word you will stay here and give us a chance."

"You need to be honest with me. What happened while I was gone? I know something went on. Both you and Eva are acting strange."

"Nothing happened, it's me. Stay with me. Give me some time, things will get better, I promise."

"Things have to be better with us. I can't be here if I am not wanted."

Fumbling over his words, Jack said, "You are wanted here, I am just under some stress. Stay with me. I have classes and practice tomorrow. You have your team if you need to go anywhere I will be back home as soon as I can."

Trying to be an adult, Fallon responded, "Okay, I'll stay." Trying to change the subject, Fallon said, "You need to open the envelope from your dad. It's on the dresser."

Jack walked over and opened the envelope. It simply said, "With love". Enclosed was a statement from the bank to show that Johnny had transferred ten million dollars into Jack's numerous accounts. Jack walked over and handed it to Fallon. "This is from dad."

Fallon took the statement. Her eyes went wide. "What is this for?"

"Dad likes to share his money. It's a gift. We have to accept it or risk hurting his feelings. "We'll go tomorrow and set up a joint bank account so you can access our money."

"I don't feel right accepting this money. It is yours. I don't want any of it."

Jack sighed. "I understand how you feel, but that is not how things are done in my family. We'll take the money. Please don't argue with me over this."

"Goodnight Jack." Fallon dismissed Jack out of the room.

Jack stared at her. She had a way of getting under his skin. Jack turned and left the room.

Fallon got ready for bed. Her arm was really beginning to hurt. She tried to lay down with no success. Every time she moved it hurt. She tried to sleep for over an hour. She tossed and turned trying to get it comfortable. It was no use. She had to get up and get some of her pain medication.

Turning on the light, Fallon got out of bed. She opened the door to her bedroom. The apartment was dark and quiet. Fallon made her way to the kitchen. She turned on the light and tried to find her bag from earlier that had her medication in it. She finally located it. She reached up in the cabinet and grabbed a glass. Jack scared her, "Everything okay?"

Startled, Fallon dropped the glass, which shattered onto the floor. "Jack, you scared me."

Jack walked over to where she was and picked her up to keep her feet off the glass. He could tell that she had lost some weight over the past few days. "I'll clean this up." He placed her gently on the couch. He walked over, got a glass and filled it with water and handed it to her.

Fallon dug out her medication and took it with the water. Jack watched her. He could tell that she was hurting. "How bad is it?"

"I'm fine. I think I popped a stitch earlier."

Jack walked over to where she was sitting. "Let me see."

Fallon shook her head no. "I'm fine."

She got up to go and pick up glass off the floor.

"Sit down. I got this." Jack went into the closet and took a broom. He swept the area clean.

Fallon started to feel the effects of her medication. She should have gone straight to bed but she wanted to watch the great Jack Valentino being domestic. Even though she was mad at him, she still had a crush on him. She enjoyed the show.

It took him several minutes to get the floor clean. Fallon sat on the couch with a dopey grin on her face. She decided it was time to go to bed. She could feel her eyes closing. She stood up, but was unsteady on her feet.

Jack dropped the broom and went over to her. He lifted her up and cradled her against his chest as he walked her to the bedroom and placed her down on the bed. He was able to maneuver her to get her under the covers. Fallon was out of it. He heard her whisper, "Love you, Husband."

Jack sat on the bed beside her for a few minutes. He brushed her hair out of her face. When she was completely asleep, he pulled back the cover and her clothing to look at her arm. The wound was red and agitated. He felt bad. He knew he shouldn't have angered her. Jack took out his phone and took a picture.

Jack left and went back into the living room. He sat on the couch. He took out his phone and called his dad. He explained the situation. Johnny listened. After Jack was through talking, Johnny spoke up, "I'll have a doctor over there first thing in the morning. I know someone in Boston who can help us."

"Thanks for your help."

Jack hung up the phone. He felt better knowing she would have someone to look at her arm in the morning. Jack went in his room and tried to lay down to go to sleep. He was restless, and worried she would need him in the night. Jack got up and went into Fallon's room. She looked so peaceful.

Jack pulled back the covers and climbed in bed with her. She instantly snuggled up to him. He wrapped an arm around her and went to sleep.

Early in the morning, Fallon started whimpering in her sleep. It woke Jack up. Jack sat up. He gently tried to wake Fallon up. "Fallon, wake up. You need to take your medication."

Jack got up and went and got Fallon's medication and water. He gently shook her. Fallon opened her eyes to see Jack standing beside her with a glass of water and medication. "Take these, you are moaning in your sleep."

Fallon didn't argue and she took the medication without complaint. Her arm was killing her. She got up and went to the bathroom. She was surprised to see Jack in the bed when she returned. "Sorry I woke you up."

"Just try to go back to sleep." Jack folded back the covers and Fallon climbed in. She was on the far edge of the bed on her side. Jack sighed and turned over. He waited for Fallon's breathing to even out. He snuggled close to her side and put his arm around her. He was out in an instant.

It took a while to register that there was a knock at the door. Jack slowly came awake. He jumped out of bed, dressed only in his underwear, and went and answered the door. An older Hispanic man stood there. "Hi, I'm Doctor Luis. I'm here to check out your wife."

Jack apologized and showed the doctor to the living room. "Sorry, we had a rough night. Let me get Fallon up."

Jack walked into the bedroom. He gently shook Fallon awake. "Fallon, I brought a Doctor here to check your arm. I need you to wake up and see him."

Fallon stared at him with one eye opened.

"Are you awake? He's waiting on you. Do you want to see him in here or the living room?"

Mumbling, Fallon said, "The living room."

Fallon slowly sat up. She could feel the effects of the pain medication. Jack brought her a robe to put on. Fallon got of bed. She went to the bathroom to brush her teeth and put up her hair.

Fallon walked in the room and Dr. Luis stood up, "Good morning, Mrs. Valentino. I understand that you may have ripped a stitch yesterday, and it is giving you some pain."

Fallon nodded and spoke, "I'm sorry. I am still feeling the effects of the pain medication I took last night."

Jack came back in the room, dressed in workout pants and a t-shirt. He looked hot so early in the morning, Fallon thought.

The doctor examined Fallon's arm. "The good news is I think it's okay. I'm worried you're still able to get an infection easily so I am going to put you back on antibiotics. I'm also going to give you some more pain medication. This one is not as strong, so you can take it during the day if you need to."

Dr. Luis left. It was just Fallon and Jack. Fallon looked at Jack "Thank you for arranging for him to come and see me."

"It wasn't me, it was dad. Thank him."

Fallon had hoped after last night that Jack would be warmer to her. He was back to being cold. Fallon rolled her eyes and got up to go back to bed. She climbed back in and fell back to sleep quickly.

Jack got ready for the day even though it was still early. He decided to go workout, so he left Fallon asleep. Jack worked out hard. He needed to release some of his frustration.

Jack stayed gone for over an hour and returned to find Fallon sitting on the couch watching TV.

Jack walked in and grabbed a water from the refrigerator before he started cooking breakfast. He made eggs and bacon and brought Fallon a plate. They ate in silence. Jack got up and deposited his dish in the sink. "I've got to get ready for class." He left the room.

Jack left without a goodbye. Fallon sat on the couch for two hours. She finally went and got a shower. She got dressed in her own clothing. Her clothes were loose.

Fallon's phone rang. It was Eva. "I leave you with him for a day and you've already had to go to the doctor. What's up with that?"

"I guess I have no secrets."

"None!" Eva joked.

"Jack took good care of me last night."

"Is he emotionally being good to you?"

"Umm... He wants some time to adjust is what he told me."

Eva thought before she answered. "Give him some time. He'll come around."

"I will."

Eva replied, "I'm sending a teacher with some work for you to get caught up. You can start whenever you feel ready."

"I'm ready now."

"I think you need some more time to get better. Get caught up, and we will get you back in time to graduate. I can send her today, if you wish."

"Send her over, Red Rover. I want to finish high school."

As promised, Mrs. O'Brien, a short, red-headed, older woman appeared a few hours later. She was all business. Fallon instantly liked her. They worked for several hours. Jack walked in and found Fallon working with Mrs. O'Brien.

"Who is this?" Jack asked as he walked in the door.

"Jack, this is Mrs. O'Brien, my teacher. She is helping me catch up with school."

Jack walked over and shook her hand. "I'm Jack, the husband."

Fallon rolled her eyes. Jack just said that to state his importance. Fallon looked at him, biting back remarks that would remind him that he wasn't much of a husband.

Fallon and her teacher finished. Fallon showed her out. Jack heard the door close and came out in to the living room. "Are you ready to go to the bank?"

"I am, but I don't have an ID that shows my married name." Fallon responded.

"Check your wallet, I think Eva took care of it for you."

Fallon got her wallet. Jack was right. Her license and social security card listed her last name as Valentino. She was surprised. She didn't know that Eva had done this. Fallon stared at it for a couple of minutes. It made all this seem real when she saw her new name in print.

Fallon put it back in her wallet. "I'm ready."

They spent two hours at the bank setting up various accounts with the money. Fallon had a joint checking account with $100,000 dollars in it for her use. She felt weird having so much money. Jack put most of the money in savings. They had been civil to each other throughout the process. Jack was distant when he talked to Fallon. She just couldn't understand what had gone wrong.

Fallon was ready to return home. Her left arm and side were aching. She had done too much today. The medicine that she had taken earlier was wearing off. "Can we head home?" She asked Jack.

"Sure. Are you hurting again?"

"I just want to be at home."

Jack studied her. "If you are doing alright, I need to meet up with some friends tonight for a study session."

Fallon looked at him and pursed her lips. "I'm not your mother, do what you need to do."

Jack wanted to fire back at her but he didn't. He instructed the team to head home.

Fallon entered the apartment in a hurry. She found her medication and gulped down one without water. Jack came in behind her. He stood there watching her.

"Why didn't you tell me you were hurting?"

"Why don't you tell me what's going on with you?"

"Leave it alone, Fallon. I'll forgive your outburst because you're in pain."

Fallon stuck out her middle finger.

"Real mature. I'm leaving."

Fallon couldn't help herself, "Don't let the door hit you where the good Lord split you."

Jack stopped and turned around. "Grow up." He didn't give her time to respond. He slammed the door close. Fallon was sure every neighbor in the building heard the slam. The security team would know they were squabbling. It was embarrassing.

Fallon put her head down on the arm of the couch. She needed the pain medication to kick in because she had homework she needed to work on. Instead, she felt dizzy from the medication and was asleep in a matter of minutes.

Jack had lied to Fallon about studying. He was meeting his friends at a bar to blow off some steam. His friends had no idea he had gotten married and that he had a wife at home. He would tell them about his wife when the time was right, he dreaded their reactions. He had married a teenager. They would mock him. He was embarrassed he was married to her.

Jack entered the bar and found his friends. The bar was loud and filled with smoke. They started out with beer but changed to hard liquor. Jack had done so many shots he could barely tell what time it was on his watch. He wanted to go home.

Jack said goodbye to his friends. He started to the car but was stopped by security. They took his keys and drove him home. He was having trouble staying on his feet. He had to lean on security to get through the front door.

Chapter 26

Fallon sat up on the couch when she heard them come through the door. She had been asleep since he left. Jack looked funny relying on the security guard to get into the apartment. He looked at Fallon, "It's my beautiful wife, the spawn of the devil. Come give me a kiss."

"Jack, you need to go to bed." She motioned for the security guard to help him to his room.

"No, I need you to come kiss me. I want to see if you taste like evil."

The security guard rolled his eyes. Fallon giggled.

"You think it's funny? You should try being married to Satan's spawn."

Fallon walked up to Jack. "What are you talking about?"

Jack rolled his head around. He was slurring his words slightly. "Can't tell, Dad will go to jail."

The security guard deposited Jack on the bed, and he promptly closed his eyes and started snoring. Fallon looked at the security guard, "Sorry you had to hear that. He is normally not like this."

The security guard smiled and left the room. Fallon stood and looked at Jack. Even in his crazy drunken state, he was still handsome.

Fallon knew there was a reason that Jack had spoken to her like that. She needed to talk to Eva. It was time for the truth to come out. Jack looked at her differently. She felt his anger every time he was around.

Fallon went to her room and found her phone. She dialed the number that Eva had given her. Eva answered, "Hello sister, how are you?"

Fallon squeaked out, "Who are my parents?"

"Why do you ask?"

"It doesn't matter. I have the right to know. I have ways to find out, but it would be easier if it came from you. I need to hear it from someone I trust."

"I'll be at your house tomorrow morning after Jack leaves. Don't tell him I'm coming."

The phone clicked off. Eva had hung up on her.

Fallon felt sick at her stomach. Fallon took her meds and crawled into bed. She fell into a deep sleep. She woke up to find Jack snuggling her in bed. She was confused. He acted like he hated her, and then he was asleep in her bed. Fallon relaxed and fell back asleep.

Fallon woke up to Jack snoring lightly in her ear. He had her in a tight hug. She tried to get free. She had to talk to him. "Jack, you're hurting me. Jack, wake up!"

Jack moaned. He realized that he had snuggled up to her. "Sorry." He let her go and turned over and went back to sleep.

Fallon was exasperated. He hated her one moment, the next he had her in a death grip. She couldn't keep up with his moods. Fallon got up and went into the living room. She made breakfast and was working on homework when Jack strolled in the kitchen. He looked rough. He went to the refrigerator, grabbed a gallon of orange juice, and drank from the carton. He went over to the cabinets and pulled out some headache medicine and swallowed them down.

He stood by Fallon "I don't remember last night. I didn't hurt you in bed?"

"I'm fine." Fallon answered.

"I've got class and practice today. Is your teacher coming over?"

"Yes."

"Good. I'll be back later and we can go to dinner. I'd like to show you Boston at night."

"Sounds fun. Have a good day at class."

Jack nodded and walked out the door. He was gone less than five minutes when Eva walked in. She looked miserable.

She led Fallon over to the couch and they sat down. Eva gave her a quick hug. Eva started crying. In a shaky voice she said, "I wanted to never tell you. Nothing I'm about to say will change how I feel about you. I love you."

"Tell me please," Fallon begged.

"Fallon, we think that your parents are…"

Before Eva could continue, Jack stormed back into the apartment.

Eva stood up. "What are you doing here?"

"You are not the only one with security. Leave her alone."

"Don't tell me what to do, Jack. It's you and your big mouth that brought me here today. Way to go."

Jack looked at Fallon. "What did I say last night?"

Fallon looked down.

"Tell me Fallon, what did I say?"

"You said I was Satan's spawn. You wanted to kiss me to see if I tasted like evil."

Eva walked over and got in Jack's face. "Never speak to her that way again, or I will personally see you rot in a jail cell for the rest of your miserable life. You don't deserve her."

Fallon jumped up and got in between the two of them. She yelled, "Stop! Both of you sit down."

Fallon could see the steam coming off Jack, he was so angry. Fallon pushed on him. He sat down.

Eva sat down also. Fallon looked at the both of them. "I'm done with both of you. I want to know what has happened. Tell me now, or I'm leaving."

Eva looked at Jack. He nodded. Eva looked at Fallon with a sad expression. "We have credible evidence you are the daughter of Hitler and the older daughter of Mussolini."

The silence that followed was deafening. Jack couldn't look at Fallon. Eva was looking at Fallon with a wounded expression on her face. Fallon started pacing the floor.

For Fallon, this was a new level of torture. If this was true, Jack was right. She was Satan's spawn. A weight settled over her soul. She felt lost again.

"You both knew but didn't tell me, why?"

Eva looked at Jack and said, "We didn't want to upset you. You've been under a tremendous amount of stress. We thought it better to give you some time. Blabber mouth over here couldn't keep his trap shut."

Fallon looked at Jack. "What did you mean last night when you were talking about jail?"

Eva gasped. Fallon looked at her. "I know there is more. Tell me."

Eva said in a snarky voice, "Jack, why don't you explain it to Fallon."

Jack shifted uncomfortably in his chair. "It's complicated."

Fallon gave him the death stare. "I'm sure I can follow."

Eva interrupted, "The government gave him and his father immunity if they agreed to keep you happy and Jack not to divorce you."

Fallon started pacing again. The family business was now a pawn in this game. She looked at Jack. "Is it all inclusive? You will not be charged for anything?"

"No," Jack answered in a small voice.

"Good," was all Fallon responded. She continued to pace the floor. Her mind was whirling. Jack was right. She was a monster. She wanted to be alone so she stopped pacing and looked at the both of them.

"I want you to leave. Both of you. I want to be alone, so leave."

Jack started to argue. Fallon held up her hand. "I just need some time alone to process."

Eva got up and tried to hug Fallon. Fallon backed away. "Don't."

Eva nodded her head that she understood. "Love you, Fallon." Eva gave Jack a stare then turned and left out of the apartment.

Jack continued to sit in the chair. "I asked you to leave."

"Fallon, please. I know it seems bad, but we can work this out." Jack got up to give her a hug. She looked so desolate, he wanted to comfort her.

"Don't touch me. I want you to go. Go to class and practice. I need some time to myself."

Jack looked at her with sad eyes. He knew that she was hurting. Jack reached up to touch her face. She blocked his motion. "Go away, I want to be alone."

"Fallon, please."

"Leave."

Jack shrugged his shoulders and left. Fallon felt a sense of relief when they were both gone. She sat back on the couch and started to cry. She cried huge tears and wracking sobs. If what Eva said was true, then she was evil. No wonder Jack had been acting so strange; he felt trapped in a marriage to a monster.

The implications of what she had been told weighed a million pounds on her soul. Hitler? Fallon could not even process the information. It just didn't make sense. There was no way this was true. It had to be a mistake.

Fallon felt sick to her stomach. She texted Mrs. O'Brien and told her not to come. Fallon couldn't deal with school work today. Instead she crawled in bed and cried herself to sleep. Fallon slept the whole day away. When she woke, she stayed in bed and considered her options. Maybe it was time to go to Italy. She knew that she could contact Mr. Rossi and meet her family. He had made his offer very clear. It was tempting to leave all of this behind. Jack would be relieved to get her out of his life. Fallon got up and took a shower. She weighed the pros and cons. It just made sense to go to Italy. She wanted to go where she was wanted and Cambridge wasn't that place for her.

She felt determined. Maybe she needed to separate from Jack and Eva for a while. Fallon went into the kitchen and made herself a sandwich and then ate it alone. She then went to her room and pulled out the suitcase.

She heard the front door open. Jack was back. Fallon didn't care. She knew what she needed to do. Jack deserved to be free from her. Now she understood. She started putting clothes into the suitcase. She wanted to get finished and get out of here. She pulled out her phone and called Eva.

Eva answered, "Fallon?"

"I want to go to Italy tonight so I can meet my family. I need to get out of here."

"Fallon, please. Give this some time."

"Make the arrangements. I will need to stay in a hotel until I can get a flight. Help me, or I will go on my own. I can't stay here another moment."

Eva knew that she was serious. "I'll alert the team. They'll find a safe place for you until I can contact Romano Rossi"

Fallon hung up the phone. She looked up to see Jack leaning in the doorway. "What are you doing?"

"I'm leaving. I'm going to Italy to meet my family. Don't worry, I will ensure your arrangement stays in place. That's the least that I can do for the trouble I have caused."

Fallon continued to pack. She went in the bathroom and grabbed her stuff out of there. She walked back in the room. "I've arranged to stay in a hotel in the city until I can get a flight out."

She found her purse and handed Jack her credit and bankcards.

He held them in his hands for a moment. "I don't want these. They're yours."

"I have money of my own from my parents. I wouldn't feel right taking money from you or your father."

Jack walked out of the room. Fallon could hear him on the phone. He was tense with whomever he was talking with. Fallon finished packing. She pulled her suitcase to the living room.

Jack was standing by the couch. "Where does this leave us?"

Fallon surprised him and said, "There is no us. You were forced, like me, into this relationship. I release you from the obligation. You shouldn't remain married to me. I am what you said. I am evil."

Jack responded quickly, "Valentino's don't divorce."

Fallon laughed an evil laugh. "Valentino's might not, but Hitler, with a mix of Mussolini, does. I'll have the paperwork completed as soon as I can. This will be over quickly for you, and you can go back to your life pre-Fallon. I'm just sorry you got caught up in this."

Fallon grabbed her medication out of the cabinet.

Jack stared at her as she was packing to leave. He didn't know what he was feeling. Was he really going to let her divorce him? He felt suddenly scared that he would lose her. He couldn't speak from fear. He wanted to tell her to stay and be his wife, but he knew this was complicated.

Fallon gathered the last of her clothing and supplies. She looked at Jack and said, "I'm sorry for all this." He could see tears forming in her eyes. Jack wasn't immune to the harsh realities of this situation. He felt tears forming behind his own eyes.

Fallon grabbed her suitcase and started pulling it toward the door. Jack was frozen in place. He knew he couldn't let her go. She made it to the door and was turning the knob when Jack took off running. He hit the door with his hand as she was opening it. He had her caged in with his body. Her back was to him. He was breathing hard.

Fallon pulled on the knob and opened the door
slightly. Jack pushed it closed with his hand.

"I'm not letting you go."

"It's not up to you. I can't stay here. I need to be with my
people who don't think I am a monster."

Jack nuzzled her neck with his lips. "Please stay. I'm
sorry. You are not a monster. I don't want to live without
you. Please stay. I love you."

Fallon turned and faced him. She looked him in the eye.
"If you love me, what was the past couple of days?"

Jack leaned in and placed his lips on hers. He kissed her
gently. She didn't respond. Jack increased the pressure on her
mouth. He let go of the door and cradled her face in in his
hands. He continued to work her mouth with his lips. He
whispered against her lips, "Stay with me and be my wife. Don't
leave me."

Fallon gave in and kissed him back. Jack moved his hand
down from her face to her body. He pulled her against
him. Fallon dropped the handle to the suitcase and pulled him
closer to her. They kissed for what seemed like forever.

Jack broke the kiss. He leaned his forehead against hers.
"Please stay, don't go. We will work this out."

Fallon leaned against him. "I will only stay if I am wanted
here. I don't want you to feel obligated to me or to my family.
Your debt is paid."

"This isn't about debt. I wasn't going to let you go. I had
my team on standby; you weren't going to leave me."

Fallon looked up at him. "What do you want?"

Jack looked at her and smiled his sexy smile. "I want
you." Jack cradled her into a hug. "We have issues, I know.
Leaving me won't solve them. We need each other."

Fallon pushed away. "If I stay, I need you to be honest
with me at all times."

Jack took her hand and led her to the couch. He pulled
her into his lap. "I give you my word I will be honest."

"Do you think that I'm evil?" Fallon asked with
determination.

"Listen, I know I haven't handled this well over the past
couple of days. I know in my heart you are not him. You are
good and kind." Jack looked into her eyes for understanding.

Fallon then said, "I will stay and I want this to work. I recently discovered that I actually like having a husband."

Jack turned Fallon around on his lap. Her legs were straddling him. He cupped her face and kissed her again. He stopped and pulled her phone out of her pocket. "Call off your people. I'll call mine."

They both made the calls. Eva seemed relieved. The call was tense, but both sisters declared their love for each other.

Jack picked up Fallon with one arm, threw down their phones on the couch, and took her to his bed. Jack laid Fallon on the bed, leaned down, and kissed her hard. He crawled over her. He was lying on top of her kissing her when he heard her gasp with pain. Jack immediately rolled off.

Fallon sat and grabbed her side. She winced in pain. Jack realized that he had lain on her injury. He felt awful. "I'm so sorry, I forgot. Are you hurt badly?"

"I don't think so. Could you get my pain medication and some water?"

Jack ran into the living room and pulled her medication out of her suitcase. He brought it back to Fallon. "Baby, I'm so sorry."

"It's okay, I forgot also." Fallon swallowed the medication.

Jack helped her get undressed. She started to leave the room. Jack caught her hand and said, "Where are you going?"

"To my room."

"This is our room. Please get in bed."

Fallon smiled. He could tell the pain medication had started to kick in. Jack pulled back the cover and Fallon climbed in. Jack took off his clothes and climbed in beside her. She turned toward him. He caressed her face. "Don't leave me." Jack gently kissed Fallon. She smiled at him.

Fallon was soon asleep. Jack got out of bed. Careful not to disturb her, he went into the living room and called his dad to update him on the events of the day.

Jack had to finish some class work before he could call it a night. He sat for a couple of hours doing work until he looked up to find Fallon walking into the room. She came and sat beside him on the couch and put her head in his lap. Jack gave into his need for her. Life without her seemed impossible now. He needed her. The horror that he felt about her parentage was muted.

Jack put down his book to play with her hair. She went back to sleep and soon Jack laid his head back on the couch and he closed his eyes.

Jack woke up early in the morning. Fallon was draped over him. Jack managed to get out from under her. He gently picked her up and placed her in bed. Jack crawled in and snuggled up to her. He felt content. This is where he belonged.

Fallon woke up to find Jack staring at her. "You are so beautiful. Are you hurt?"

Fallon moved her side and grimaced. "I think it will be fine. I'm just sore."

"You are under strict order to stay in bed today. You need to heal; I feel terrible about last night. I forgot you had taken two bullets."

"I'm fine. I want to work on schoolwork today so I can begin school next week. I will take care of myself today."

Jack leaned in and gave her a quick kiss. "I've got to go to class and practice. I won't be back until later." He gave Fallon another kiss and got out of bed.

Jack left and Fallon got out of bed. She had some work to do before her teacher arrived. She was determined to get back to school. Fallon's day passed quickly. Mrs. O'Brien stayed until late. They had made progress throughout the day and were working on a math problem when Jack walked in.

Jack gave Fallon a devastating smile. He acknowledged Mrs. O'Brien. He went over to Fallon and gave her a quick kiss on the lips. "Did you follow my orders?"

Fallon laughed. "No."

Mrs. O'Brien got up. She was clearly uncomfortable. She gave Fallon and Jack a goodbye and left the apartment.

Jack produced a couple of menus. "Let's order in."

Fallon looked over the menus and they ordered Chinese. They had fun eating in and making out on the couch. Jack ended up lying in Fallon's lap. He was exhausted. Fallon started rubbing his head. Jack groaned out loud. Fallon continued and Jack closed his eyes and the tension eased from his face. Fallon couldn't help but be in love with him when he acted this way. He made her feel like she was the center of his world.

Fallon thought he was asleep so she stopped moving her hand. Jack caught her hand, "Please don't stop." Fallon leaned over and kissed his head. "Let's go to bed."

Jack smiled, "I'm a lucky man to have you in my bed." Fallon blushed.

Jack stood up and held out his hand for Fallon; he was having trouble controlling himself physically. He wanted to be with Fallon again but he didn't want to push her emotionally or physically.

They got undressed and got in bed. Fallon made the first move. Jack responded "Baby, you have no idea how bad I want this, but I think we should wait until you are healed."

Fallon gave him a look of disappointment.

"Don't look at me that way. You know that I'm telling the truth."

Fallon looked at Jack. "Unbelievable, I have the hottest husband in the world and we can't."

"Can't what?"

Fallon blushed. "Don't make me say it."

"I want to hear it from you."

Fallon whispered, "Make love."

Jack groaned. "You are killing me. I'm putting you on strict bed rest until you are healed." He joked.

Fallon snuggled up to him. "I missed you."

Jack put his arm around her. "I missed you too." They fell asleep in each other's arms.

The next few days fell into the same pattern. Fallon caught up on schoolwork while Jack went to classes and to football practice. They spent the night in each other's arms. They were in their own world. It was easy for Fallon to forget who her biological parents were and their impact on the world.

Life changed the next week as Fallon started school. Fallon was up early Monday morning getting ready as Jack laid in bed watching her. He didn't want her to go back to school. He liked the idea of her waiting at home for him.

When Fallon finished getting ready, she headed to the kitchen for breakfast. Jack got up and followed her. Fallon was fixing toast when Jack put a ring box on the table in front of her.

"What's this?"

"I thought you might be more comfortable with this at school."

Fallon opened the box. Inside she found a plain gold band. She smiled as she slipped it on her finger. "I love it!"

Jack picked up her ring finger and kissed it. "I want those high school toddlers to know you are taken."

Fallon giggled, "Toddlers?"

Jack pulled her into a hug. "I was once one of them. Believe me, they are going to be all over you."

Fallon pulled back out of his embrace. "Where is your wedding band?"

Jack smiled "I thought we could go this weekend and pick out some better options for both of us. Let's go spend some of dad's money."

Fallon giggled. "That sounds like a fun weekend!"

Chapter 27

Jack was gone and Fallon left with her security team. She was a bundle of nerves as she pulled up to the Westmore Day School, an elite private school in downtown Boston. She was happy to be here so she could finish her International Baccalaureate diploma on time.

It didn't take long for Fallon to realize that she was an outsider. Only a few people had said hello to her throughout the first half of her day and the rest openly stared at her. Fallon was uncomfortable, and she wanted to go home. This was a worst-case scenario for her. She didn't need the stress of the social pressure of school to add to her crazy life.

Thankfully, her classes went by smoothly. They were ahead of where she was in her studies, but she would be able to catch up quickly. Fallon had to keep reminding herself that it was only for a short time.

Fallon went to the lunchroom where she grabbed a tray and went to sit outside. She could feel people staring as she sat down. They were curious and rude. She could hear them whispering around her. It didn't help she had her own security team even though they stayed back a good distance.

Fallon put in her ear buds and listened to some music while she ate her lunch. It was miserable. As lunch was finally coming to a close, Fallon looked up to see a guy standing beside her with a big smile on his face. She took out her ear buds and smiled at him.

He was a couple of inches taller than she was. He had short brown hair and dark brown eyes with pale white skin. He stuck out his hand and said, "Welcome."

Fallon shook his hand. "Thanks, I'm Fallon."

He laughed. "I know. Everyone here knows who you are. You're famous. I'm Falk."

Fallon could detect an accent, maybe German or eastern European.

Falk continued, "I'm new here also. They are so rude. They could at least talk to us."

Fallon laughed again. "I think it would kill them if they had to be nice."

Smiling, Falk said, "I think we've had all of our classes together. What's your schedule for the rest of the day?"

Fallon showed her schedule to him. He was right, they had all the same classes. Falk got up to leave. "Sit by me in the classes, we will make fun of the plastic people here."

Fallon thanked him. He walked off to class so Fallon gathered her stuff and followed him. Fallon took a seat next to him for the rest of the day, and he kept her in stitches in all of her classes. He was funny and mean to the people around him. By end of the day, Fallon had determined that he was from Germany. He was here because of his parents' job.

Fallon noticed that the girls went out of their way to get his attention but he ignored them. He didn't seem interested.

Fallon thanked him at the end of the day. "Falk, you are awesome. I was ready to quit at lunch, but you made it bearable."

Falk smiled. "I'll see you tomorrow. There are more jokes to be made about this place."

Fallon waved and left school. She was actually looking forward to tomorrow. Maybe she could handle it if she had a friend.

Jack was waiting for her as she opened the door to the apartment. "Hello, Wife."

"Hello, Husband."

"Well, how did it go?"

Fallon gave him a synopsis of the day, including meeting Falk.

Jack felt a small pang of jealously hearing about her new friend, Falk. He didn't like the feeling so he decided to turn on the charm, "Can I take you out for dinner to celebrate?"

"I would love to go, but I have a ton of work to catch up on. Could we eat in?"

"Of course." Jack answered. He didn't like the idea of Fallon not being able to be with him. He was jealous of school and her new friend. This feeling was new to him. Jack had never had to work to be with a girl. Women had always thrown themselves at him.

Jack pulled out his phone and ordered dinner while Fallon took out her books and sat at the kitchen table. She put on her music and started her homework. Following her lead, Jack went and got his schoolwork. They sat at the table working until the food arrived. Fallon worked while she ate. Jack just sat and watched Fallon realizing she was amazing. He didn't know that she was such a dedicated student. Jack finished dinner and sat on the couch to watch TV. He would periodically look at Fallon to find she was still engrossed in her assignments.

Enough was enough. Jack realized she was going to wear herself out. He walked over and pulled her ear buds out. "Enough for today." He pressed the stop button on her phone.

"Jack, I need to finish this."

"It can wait. Your husband needs some attention." He pulled her up out of her chair. Fallon was smiling. He leaned in and gave her a hot kiss. Fallon melted. She wrapped her arms around him as he pulled her in close. He rained small kisses down her face and on her neck. "I am jealous of school and your new friend."

Fallon pulled back with a surprised look on her face. "What?"

Jack pulled her back close to him. "I like it when you give me all of your attention. I don't share well with others."

Fallon rolled her eyes at him. "Don't you want me to graduate high school?"

"At the moment, no."

"I need to graduate so I can go to college and get a job."

Laughing out loud, Jack asked, "A job? You must be joking. You will never have to work a day in your life."

Fallon looked at him questioningly.

"We are rich, baby."

"How rich are we?" Fallon asked trying not to be hurt that he thought she didn't need to work. She had ambitions and dreams, none of which included being a housewife.

Jack kissed her again. "If you must know, Dad is getting close to that billion dollar mark. If I cashed in today, I would be worth in the neighborhood of 200 million."

Fallon's mouth fell open. "I had no idea." She giggled and said, "You should have gotten a prenuptial agreement. I'm poor."

Jack pulled her up till she was sitting on the table. She opened her legs and he wrapped her legs around him. He pulled

her close. "Valentino's don't divorce." He inched his face close
to her and whispered, "Kiss me."

Fallon grabbed his face and pulled him in for a kiss. He
wrapped his arms around her and locked her legs around his
waist. He picked her up, and took her to the bedroom. Jack was
desperate to be with her again. He undressed her and himself in
record time. Fallon reached out for him and brought him down
to her. She had to be his. Fallon reached and pulled him in for a
kiss. They made passionate love.

Fallon rested her head on Jack's chest. He gently caressed
her back as they lay there. Fallon propped her chin up on Jack's
chest to look at him. "I've got to go finish my homework." She
kissed him on his chest and got up. She put on a robe and went
into the kitchen. Fallon worked for two hours before she went to
bed where Jack was already asleep when she crawled into bed.

The next morning the alarm sounded, sending both
Fallon and Jack scrambling to shut it off. Fallon was exhausted;
she felt like she had just gone to bed. She lay quietly until Jack
gathered her into his arms. He knew she was tired. Fallon fell
back asleep and Jack decided not to wake her.

Fallon woke to find herself late for school. She jumped
out of bed. Jack sat up and laughed. "Oops"

Fallon ran into the bathroom. She took the quickest
shower in the history of mankind. Jack had her breakfast ready
for her to eat on the run. Fallon gave Jack a quick kiss and
stormed out the door.

Fallon made it to her second period class and was stressed
by the time she got there. Falk had saved her a seat. He gave her
the glance over. "Rough night last night?"

"You could say that."

Falk looked at her, "Are you married?"

Fallon smiled and said, "Yes."

Falk stared at her ring. "How did that happen?"

"It's a long story. I won't bore you with the details."

"Are you happy?" Falk asked with a serious expression.

"I'm very happy with Jack."

Falk looked relieved. He turned in his seat and tapped the
girl next to him on the shoulder. She was beautiful with long
blond hair, big blue eyes, and pouty pink lips.

"Fallon, this is my sister Jane."

Fallon held out her hand. "I'm Fallon, nice to meet you."

Jane acknowledged her and turned around to continue talking to her friends next to her.

Falk shook his head. "Sorry, she is a spoiled brat."

The teacher walked in and started the class.

Fallon and Falk talked all day long. It was like they were long lost friends. Fallon was very comfortable with him. He was intelligent and kind to her, and he didn't seem to care if people thought it was weird to have a security detail with you at all times. At the end of the day, they exchanged phone numbers. Falk texted her immediately and he included Jane on the conversation. Fallon responded and they started to talk constantly over text.

Fallon returned home to find Jack passed out on the couch. Apparently, she wasn't the only one recovering from last night. She walked over and stared at him for a couple of minutes. He was so beautiful. She felt lucky he was hers.

Fallon and Jack fell into a pattern. They both went to school and at night they spent their time in each other's arms. Fallon felt content, but Jack began to feel restless. Jack started to go out with his friends at night. He would come home and make passionate love to her.

A few weeks after school started, Fallon brought Falk and Jane back to the apartment to work on homework. As always, Falk was entertaining Fallon. Jack opened the door to find them at the kitchen table laughing. Fallon gave him a big smile. He nodded. He walked over to Fallon and gave her a quick kiss. Falk stood up and introduced himself. "Hello Jack, I'm Falk and this is my sister Jane."

Jack took his hand. "I'm the husband." Jack could see Fallon rolling her eyes at him. Jack looked at Fallon. "I didn't realize we were having company tonight."

Falk and Jane took the hint. They started gathering their stuff. Fallon gave Jack a look of disgust. "Falk and Jane, please don't go."

Falk stood up, "We have to go anyway, our parents will be expecting us. See you tomorrow at school." They left quickly.

Fallon was furious. Jack was angry also. He didn't want a male in his house with Fallon. They screamed at each other for over an hour. Jack stormed out of the apartment. Fallon felt the slamming of the door vibrate through her bones.

Irritated, Jack left and went to the local bar. He knew his friends were there. They still didn't know he was married, mostly because he was still embarrassed to tell them. They met up with Jack and proceeded to get very drunk. Jack started talking. He accidentally told them that he was married to a high school senior.

Jack's friends were in disbelief. Jack made hurtful remarks about having to be married to Fallon and continued to drink. The girls swarmed around their group. One of Jack's former girlfriends, Bonnie, took advantage of the situation. Jack had dumped Bonnie a few months ago after dating her for over a year. She heard the whole conversation. She made her way to Jack and tried to put the moves on him. She kissed him on the mouth. He pushed her away but not before a friend caught the moment with her phone.

The group got so drunk and rowdy that the bar kicked them out. Jack's friends managed to get him to his security detail. Jack was slurring his words and stumbling as he walked.

Fallon heard the front door open. There was a lot of commotion. She got out of bed and slipped on a robe. She walked into the living room to find some of security helping Jack walk in. They deposited him on the couch. Jack was so drunk, nothing he said made any sense.

He reached out and tried to grab Fallon but she moved away. Jack fell face first on the floor. He straightened himself out and passed out. The security guards looked at Fallon.

"I'm sorry for the trouble," Fallon said to the men.

"It's no problem, let us know if you need help." They left Fallon alone with Jack. He was snoring loudly. Fallon reached down to try to wake him up to get him in bed. She noticed a red mark on his collar. She bent down and felt it; it smudged. The smudge felt like it burned her skin. That smudge represented all that was wrong in their relationship. It burned a hole in her heart. Fallon knew that it was lipstick. She was furious. She wanted to kick Jack in the head and cut off his man parts. She left Jack on the floor and went to bed.

Chapter 28

Getting up the next morning was terrible for Fallon. Her heart was broken. Jack had been with another woman last night. She got ready and went into the kitchen to find Jack still laid out on the floor. Frowning at him, she got her stuff and left. The closing of the door woke Jack up. He was so hung over that he could barely walk to get into bed.

Fallon was grumpy at school. Falk could tell that something was not right. He invited her over after to school to work with him and Jane at their house. Fallon accepted without hesitation, and she didn't tell Jack.

After school, Fallon followed Falk and Jane home to a beautiful mansion. Falk had shared his parents were in telecommunications. Her security did a sweep of the home before they would let her inside. Fallon was greeted at the door by Falk's parents. They were both tall and blond and they seemed very interested in meeting her. Fallon caught Falk giving them a signal to leave. It was strange.

Falk showed her around the house. It was professionally decorated, but strange because there were no pictures of the family in the house.

Falk showed Fallon into a private office. "This is my personal space. This is where I take care of business."

Fallon smiled, "What kind of business do you take care of?"

Falk said seriously, "I run my empire from here."

Fallon laughed. "You are so funny."

Jane walked in to the room, "He's serious." She sat on his lap and gave him a kiss. They smiled at Fallon. They seemed to enjoy her shock.

Fallon got up to leave. She couldn't believe that Jane had kissed him. "I think I need to go."

"Have a seat sister, we need to talk." Fallon was confused. Was he talking to her or Jane?

Fallon looked at him and then at Jane. Jane got off his lap and pointed at Fallon. "Have a seat, he's talking to you." Jane pointed at a seat then said, "Don't worry, I'm not really his sister."

Fallon felt fear rising up. She needed her security. She took out her phone and started to dial. Falk walked over and took it out of her hand. "Give me a moment to explain. You are not in danger here." Falk walked back and sat behind her desk. He pulled out pictures of Fallon and Eva and started throwing them casually on the desktop.

"Eva's a pretty smart girl. Just not smart enough to find me."

"Leave Eva out of this. Who are you?"

Falk laughed, "They didn't tell you, did they? Well, I'm Falk and I'm your twin."

Fallon jumped out of her chair. "I'm leaving."

Falk stepped in front of her. "If you want your lover to be kept alive, you'll sit and listen. I could have taken him out last night, but you seem happy with him so I let him live."

Fallon started shaking. "Leave him alone. This has nothing to do with him."

Falk pulled Fallon into a hug. "Don't worry, he is fine and so are you. We are going to be a happy family." Falk took her hand and led her to a couch to sit next to him.

"Are you going to hurt me?" Fallon asked with a shaky voice.

"No, I'm not. You think I planned the Gettysburg thing? That wasn't me. That was some people who aren't happy with our existence. Don't worry, I killed them all." His voice was cheery.

He's a psychopath, Fallon thought. She looked for escape routes.

"You're safe now. We can be together and do what we were designed for."

"What's that?" Fallon asked with a high-pitched voice.

Falk patted her hand. "We are the Fourth Reich. We will raise Germany up to be the leader of the world again, like our father." He knew her secret.

Fallon sat still, trying to figure a way out of this mess. She had to get out of here. He was completely crazy and she was at his mercy.

Falk continued talking. "Of course, we had to remove all the people involved with our births. We had to control the information."

"Did you kill my parents?"

"No, the United States of America and Russia killed our parents. We will avenge their deaths."

Fallon loved history. She got his meaning that the USA and Russia fought against Germany in WWII.

Fallon stopped him, "Did you kill my other parents?"

Falk stopped talking and looked at her, "Your other dad was in on this. He went rogue and messed up the plans. Both your adopted parents had to be silenced."

Fallon sat trembling on the chair. "What do you want from me?"

"I told you. I want us to lead Germany to greatness again. Your presence will ignite my followers. You are the only family I have. I want us to be together."

Fallon's thoughts were moving quickly through her mind. She asked the question that was nagging her, "How will you lead Germany to greatness?"

"War, dear sister. I will follow our father's path." Enjoying her discomfort, Falk could see her shaking.

Falk added, "Our father knew that the world would be better if Germany was in charge. We must rid ourselves of the human parasites that roam this earth. This must be done to follow his example. There should only be a pure race with me and you ruling over all."

The horror that Fallon felt was indescribable. Fallon immediately thought of Rebecca and her whole Jewish Family. The family that had sheltered her when she lost everything. Falk meant to destroy them and others in her father's name. Fallon tried to scoot away from him. He was Lucifer. The evil was pouring off Falk in droves. Fallon had to get away from him. She was visibly shaking while sitting.

Falk looked at Fallon and recognized her distress, "We have discussed enough today. Go home and be happy. We have some time until this is put in play." Falk seemed resolute in speech and actions. He was on a determined path.

Fallon spoke up, "I want no part in this. Are you going to kill all the Jews in the world again? You can't believe that Hitler was right. He was a murderer and pure evil. This is crazy."

Falk slapped Fallon across the face. "Don't ever question our father again!" She fell over on the couch.

Falk stood up and leaned over and got in Fallon's face. "Never tell me I'm crazy again, sister. You live because I deem you important to the cause. Don't get on my bad side."

Fallon held her hand to her cheek where he hit her. She was backed as far as she could go into the couch.

"Do you understand, sister? You need to keep this quiet. I'm monitoring your conversations. I will know if you talk and Eva and Jack will pay the price for your loose lips."

Standing over her now Falk stated, "Nod if you understand me." Fallon slowly nodded. She still had her hand to her face. Falk took her hand down and entwined his fingers with hers. "Come and be properly greeted by my family. They are anxious to make your acquaintance." He pulled her off the couch and steadied her on her feet.

Falk led her down a hallway to the opening for the living room. They walked through and his family went down to one knee as he walked over to them. Each one of them kissed Fallon's hand.

After they greeted everyone, Falk turned to Fallon, "See baby sister, you are German royalty." Fallon nodded. She would agree with anything. She had to get out of here and away from Falk.

Falk walked her to the door as Fallon started to leave. "Your life must go on as it has. No one should be suspicious of me or my family." He leaned in and gave her a kiss on the cheek. "We will finish school and go to Germany. I know that this is important to you. This is my gift to you. We must set an example of education for the German people."

Falk leaned over her. "Give me a kiss back." Shaking, Fallon leaned up on her toes and planted a quick kiss on his cheek.

Falk motioned and Fallon's security team pulled up. Fallon got in the truck. Her face was hurting. She was still shaking. It was too much to process. The ride back was short to the apartment.

Fallon entered the apartment to find Jack sitting at the table waiting on her. He stood up when she entered the room. Her thoughts betrayed her. Even though she was mad at him for last night, she wanted to run into his arms and seek his comfort.

"Where have you been?" He asked in an irritated tone.

"I went over to my friend's house."

"You can't call and let me know you are going to be late?"

Fallon snapped, "You have some nerve. You come in drunk from being with your friends with lipstick on your shirt and you are fussing at me?"

"Nothing happened, I promise."

Fallon didn't have the energy to fight. "I'm going to take a shower." She abruptly left the room. Fallon climbed into the hot water. She turned it on to her face. It was stinging where Falk had slapped her. She stood in the shower shaking. This was a mess.

Jack opened the door and stepped in. Fallon didn't protest. He didn't speak, he just held her for a couple of minutes. The water started to turn cold. Fallon turned it off. She stepped out of the shower first followed by Jack. When she turned her face towards him he saw a small bruise forming on her face.

Jack dropped the towel he was holding and reached for her. "What happened to your face?"

Fallon put a hand up to where she got hit. She stumbled over her words. He could tell she was covering up something when she said, "I fell today walking to class, I hit my face on my backpack." Jack inspected the bruise. Warning bells sounded in his head. He dismissed any concern because she had her security team with her all day.

Fallon got dressed and walked back to the kitchen. She pulled out her homework for the day. Jack sat beside her. "I'm sorry for last night. I was in the wrong."

Fallon looked at him. "I want to go out and meet your friends." She wanted to know what attracted him to the club scene. "I want to go clubbing with you."

Jack sat for a moment. This was not the response that he thought that he would get. "Okay, we can go out Friday night if you like."

Fallon nodded, "Let's do that, I need to blow off some steam." She went back to working. Jack left her alone until bedtime because she seemed to be in a strange mood. She had worked through dinner.

It was time to make things right with his wife. Jack turned on some music. He walked over and pulled her out of the chair, "Dance with me." They slow danced to a couple of songs. Fallon was all over him. He picked her up and took her to the bedroom.

Fallon was exhausted the next morning. It took all of her energy to force herself out of bed. She wanted to miss, but was she afraid of Falk so she went to school. Falk was waiting for her at the door to the classroom. She walked up to him. He said to her, "As firstborn, I'm the leader." He held his hand for her to kiss. She didn't know what to do so he had to tell her. "Kiss my hand and bow to me." She did as she was told.

Falk looked at her and repeated the action to her. "You are the only person in the world I will bow to." He looked at her face. "Good job hiding the mark. I felt bad I hit you last night."

Fallon shrugged and was slow to answer, "It's alright." She looked around for help. Could no one see that she was in distress? Her security was watching. Falk caught on. "Don't worry, they are on my payroll. You are safe with me. Your husband will not know." Fallon felt sick at her stomach. There was no escape.

Falk led her to class. Jane bowed her head to Fallon. Falk leaned over. "She will not speak to you unless you speak to her first. There are the rules about royalty." Fallon nodded her understanding. "You bow to no one except me. We are pure bloods. Everyone else is tainted blood."

Falk spent the entire day filling Fallon's head with information about his plan and her role in ruling the world. Fallon was exhausted at the end of the day. Falk kissed her cheek before he sent her home. Fallon was sure of a couple of things about her brother. He was on power trip and Jack and Eva were not safe.

Fallon returned to the apartment. She was relieved that Jack was not there. She undressed and got into bed. She was sound asleep when Jack got home later. He let her sleep as she looked exhausted.

Fallon didn't wake for dinner. Jack eventually crawled in bed with her and went to sleep. The alarm sounded waking Fallon up. She was sprawled across Jack. Jack hit the alarm to shut it off. Fallon moaned against him and snuggled closer. Jack made his move. He kissed her neck and then made passionate love to her.

Chapter 29

She had dreamed all night about Jack and Falk. She didn't know what to do. She didn't want to go to school. Jack was snuggling her close to him.

"Can you come and get me from school today?"

"Why?"

"I just thought it would be nice to go to lunch and maybe some shopping?" The truth was she needed a way to get away from Falk and for him not to be suspicious.

"You want me to go shopping with you?"

"Yes, please." Fallon could tell that Jack was not pleased.

"Okay, I can be there around 1:00."

"Great." Fallon gave him a kiss and got out of bed. She got ready and made her way to school.

Falk could sense her good mood. "Why so happy today, sister?"

"I have a lunch date with Jack. We're going shopping."

Falk looked irritated. "Are you leaving school early?"

"Yes, is that not alright?"

Fallon couldn't believe that she had to ask permission from Falk.

Falk rubbed his chin with his hand. "I would prefer that you are here with me, but I understand. What are you shopping for?"

Fallon didn't want to be honest about the reason. She decided to be somewhat truthful. "I'm meeting some of Jack's friends tonight and I need something to wear."

Falk thought for a moment. He reached in his pocket and took out his wallet. He handed her a black credit card. "My treat."

"What's this?"

Falk showed her the card. "This is yours. Spend what you like."

Fallon pushed it back at him. "I have one already, but thanks."

She could tell she had irritated Falk. "You don't have to rely on him ever again. I have set up some accounts in your name. This is your card, take it."

"What if Jack sees it?"

Falk shook his head from side to side. "When the time is right, I will introduce myself properly to your husband and father in-law."

Fallon took the card. She knew it would only cause trouble.

Fallon made it through the morning. She was nervous as she wanted to get away from Falk who never seemed to stop hovering over her. It felt like she had a parent with her at all times. The call finally came from the office that Jack was there to get her. She practically ran out of the room to get to him.

Jack felt awkward sitting in the front office. It was embarrassing to tell everyone that he was here for his wife. He got some curious stares as he explained that he was checking her out. He was dreading tonight because he didn't want to introduce Fallon to his friends. They wouldn't understand.

Fallon walked into the office with a big smile. Jack felt his stomach contract. She was so beautiful it hurt. He wanted Fallon to be at home. His little secret. Jack wanted to maintain his life at school and have his life at home.

Jack took Fallon's backpack off her shoulders and put it on his back. They walked out to the car and headed to the local mall. They spent a few hours shopping until Fallon found a short black dress and shoes.

They returned to the apartment to get ready. Jack looked smoking hot in his preppy clothes. Fallon walked out in her short dress. Jack had a moment of panic. He didn't want his friends gawking at her. He certainly didn't want his friends to look at her in the short dress and heels. She was his.

Getting over his anxiety, Jack took Fallon's hand and led her out the door. He took her to a Sushi restaurant first. He was quiet throughout the meal. Fallon could sense that something was bothering him. She tried to question him, but he didn't respond.

They left the restaurant with security in tow and headed to the local night club. Jack handed Fallon a fake ID. She looked at it with surprise. "Thanks"

"I would be a terrible mobster if I couldn't produce one fake ID for my wife." Fallon leaned over and gave him a quick kiss on the mouth.

After security gave the all clear, Jack led Fallon into the club. It was loud and crowded. Jack led Fallon to a table at the back of the club occupied by a group of Jack's male friends. Fallon could see the looks of shock on their faces when they walked up. They were openly staring at her again. It must be a Boston thing. Jack let go of her hand as they neared the group. A few stepped forward and introduced themselves to Fallon. Jack started doing shots. Fallon was standing beside him but was not included in his conversations. She was beginning to feel left out when she felt a tap on the shoulder.

Fallon turned around to see Falk and Jane standing there. Fallon was taken by surprise. She didn't know what to do so she tugged on Jack's arm. He turned towards Falk and Jane. He was tipsy. "Hello little high school friends. How did you get in here?" He laughed out loud.

Fallon could tell that Falk was mad. He took Fallon's hand and kissed her knuckles. "Come see me at my table." Jack missed the exchange as he was talking to his friends.

"I'll be over in a minute. We just got here."

Falk leaned in, "I know, Sister."

Fallon pulled back from Falk. She tried to take Jack's hand but he pulled away from her. Falk saw the exchange and shook his head in anger. Falk nodded at her and turned and walked over to his table, which was close by. He could see everything that was going on with Fallon.

Standing by Jack was awkward as he was obviously ignoring her. He continued to drink shots of whiskey. Jack hadn't even offered to buy her a drink. She was standing there feeling like an idiot in the middle of the group.

Fallon tapped Jack's shoulder. He looked at her with irritation. "I'm going to Falk's table." Jack nodded.

Fallon left and went over to Falk's table. She needed to make an appearance so that she could leave without offending him. He stood up when she came near the table. He motioned and the table cleared. Jane gave Fallon a wave. Fallon took a seat near Falk. Falk leaned in so she could hear him, "He doesn't deserve you. I could kill him for ignoring you."

Fallon giggled. "I don't think it's necessary. He just seems like he doesn't want to have a wife tonight. It's hard for him. He didn't have a choice in this."

Falk replied, "From what I understand, neither did you. You are not out there ignoring him. He is a boy. You need a man for a husband. I don't even know if you are technically married. You could leave him, I would handle the situation and end this problem for you."

Fallon gave him a look of panic and then shook her head. "He's my husband."

Falk motioned and a server brought over some drinks. Fallon refused. "I don't want any alcohol."

"Tell me what you want."

"Could I get a coke?"

Smiling, Falk made another signal and the server came over. Falk ordered for her. Fallon sat back. She was tired and wanted to go home. This evening had not worked out like she planned.

Her drink arrived. She played with it. Falk took her hand. "I see what you are wrestling with in your mind. He is not worth your trouble."

Fallon looked at Falk, "I love him."

"Of course, you do. He is your first lover and boyfriend. It might be time for you to consider taking a break. Come to Germany with me. We can be happy together, a real family at last."

"What would happen to Jack?"

"Nothing would happen. We could give him some time to mature. He is your plaything to do with as you like. I keep Jane around for fun."

Fallon put her elbows on the table and rested her head in both of her palms. She shook her head no. "I just need some time to think. I'm overwhelmed."

Falk patted her on the back. "I know. This decision doesn't need to be made tonight."

She exhaled deeply then looked over at Jack to see a blond girl was hanging all over him. Fallon could tell he was drunk by the way he was leaning against the wall. Fallon sighed.

Falk tensed up next to her. "Say the word, and I will personally take him out."

Fallon looked at him with angry eyes. "Stop talking to me like that. He and Johnny Valentino are to be protected at all costs. Give me your word."

"Finally, you act like the warrior leader that you were designed to be. I give you my word that they will not be hurt."

Fallon looked at Falk and sighed. "This is too much. Let me out, I'm going to the bathroom."

Following her command, Falk stood. He could tell she was angry. "I understand. I won't threaten your quarterback anymore." He held up his hands like he was surrendering.

Fallon glanced over to Jack. The girl was still there. She had backed away. Fallon looked around and finally found the entrance to the bathroom. It took her some time to navigate the crowd.

She was in line to the bathroom when the door to the men's bathroom opened up. A tall, muscular, black-headed man walked out. He was incredibly built with a sexy haircut and muscles that bulged under his tight black t-shirt. He screamed trouble.

By chance, Fallon looked at his face. He made brief eye contact with her. His eyes were beautiful. They were both green and dark brown at the same time. She did a double take. She felt her mouth open up. She quickly closed it. He was one of Eva's men. Her escape. Her extraction if needed. Fallon almost reached out and grabbed his arm for help. She did her best to ignore him.

He walked by without acknowledging her. She looked away as he walked by. Fallon had to control herself not to run after him. She needed to get out. Fallon walked into the bathroom and took the first available stall. She was just standing in the stall in front of the toilet trying to compose herself.

She heard two girls talking. "What a mistake. Can you believe that she's in high school? He looks miserable." Fallon stopped moving around and got very silent. They continued talking. "Jack told Tom that he didn't have a choice. His dad pulled a gun on him and forced him to marry her and that she is an embarrassment to him."

The other girl piped in, "He told Robert that she was terrible in bed and that he couldn't stand to touch her." Both girls giggled. One of the girls said, "I'll wait until he is done with her, and then I'll make him mine, finally. I'll make a good football wife."

Having enough, Fallon walked out of the stall. Both girls stopped talking and looked at her. It was the blond that had been draped over Jack. They looked at each other for a moment. The blond spoke, "Sorry, not sorry, you heard all of that. It's the truth." The other girl giggled at her comment. Pulling out her phone, the friend flashed her a picture of the blond kissing Jack.

Fallon held her head high and walked out the door. She knew what she had to do. She found her muscle man at the bar. She walked over to where he was sitting drinking a beer and squeezed into the seat next to him then called over the bartender. "May I have a coke please?" The bartender made her drink. She tried to pay for it but the bartender waived her off.

She turned to him looking at him with wild eyes. "Hi, my name is Fallon."

He winked at her and held out his hand. "I'm Matt."

"Nice to meet you Matt."

He leaned in. He smelled like cologne and leather. He whispered in her ear, "What are you doing? Go back to your husband. You are being watched."

Fallon smiled at what he said. She playfully hit him on the arm. She leaned in. She acted like she was telling him something funny. "Please help me, I need out now. I'm in big trouble." He laughed at what she said. She knew that he was covering for her.

He took her hand and kissed her knuckles. "My lady, I'm at your service." Fallon nodded at him. He winked at her. Fallon took her drink and walked back over to where Jack's group was still gathered. She had enough for one night and was leaving. She walked up to Jack as he was getting sloppy drunk again.

"Here's my teenage wife." He laughed as he said it. Fallon walked over to him. She grabbed his face and pulled him in for a kiss. In response, he put his arms around her and pulled her close deepening the kiss. He tasted like whiskey. The members in the group started whistling at the two of them. Fallon broke the kiss. She looked at him. "I'm going home. Stay and have fun with your friends." Jack pulled her to his side. "I can go home with you."

Fallon looked at him. It was hard for her say but she meant it, "You belong here." She gave him a quick kiss and started to leave. She walked over to Falk's table. He had been drinking also. "I'm headed home. Goodbye."

He stood up and kissed her on the check. "I'll call tomorrow and we can get some dinner." Fallon took his hand and kissed it, "Sounds fun, I'll see you tomorrow."

Knowing what she had to do, Fallon left the bar. Stopping where she stood, she stole one more glance at Jack as she left. *Would this be the last time she would see him?* She was surrounded by security and felt relieved to be out of the club headed home. When she arrived at the apartment she took a couple of minutes to look around. She knew that she was leaving.

Fallon was broken. She wanted to be fair to Jack. He wasn't ready for this. Tonight had proven that point. Falk was right, he needed some time to mature and Fallon needed to feel safe. She wasn't ready to go to Germany and fight against Falk. She didn't want any part of Falk's diabolical plan to rule the world. She just wanted to be normal so her only option was to escape.

Making her decision to go, Fallon went in her room and packed a small bag. It looked like a purse, so she could take it with her. She didn't know when or where the extraction would happen. She just wanted to be ready. She stowed the purse in her closet. She got ready and climbed into bed. The quietness of the room made her thoughts loud. Fallon cried herself to sleep.

Chapter 30

Fallon felt like she was being smothered. She woke to find a hand over her mouth. The dark figure leaned down and said, "Don't scream, it's Matt. We've got to go."

Fallon sat up. She went over to turn on the light but he stopped her. "No lights, we have to be careful. Grab some clothes and let's move."

Fallon felt where she had left a pair and jeans and a shirt. She slipped them on in the darkness. Matt took her hand and sat her on the bed holding a small flashlight between his lips. He pulled on her arm that was shot. He ran a wand device over her arm and it beeped. He reached into the pockets of his combat pants and pulled out a kit. Quickly, he unraveled the kit. It held a knife and some bandages.

Fallon started backing away from him, "What are you doing?"

Matt caught her arm. "The FBI put a tracking device in your arm. It has to come out, or they will find us wherever we go. Hold still."

Fallon tried to move away. Matt held her steady. "Listen, if you want to go this has to come out."

Fallon bit her lip and said okay. Matt took the knife and made a small incision. Fallon winced and tried to stifle her cry with her other hand. Matt was rough with his exploration. He finally found the tracker device. He pulled it out roughly and then cleaned it and put it under Fallon's pillow. He sprayed her arm with some kind of cleaner that stung. Then he wrapped her arm in a bandage. "Let's go. We have only a couple of minutes to get out of here."

Matt took Fallon's hand and led her through the apartment. He stopped at the door as if he was waiting on something. They stood there for a couple of minutes. Suddenly, the power went out. The building was completely black. Matt took some night goggles out of his pocket and placed them on his face. He opened the door and pulled Fallon through. He checked to make sure the door was locked. He led her through the hallway to the staircase.

Her security team was scattered on the floor. "Are they dead?" Fallon asked with a strained voice.

Chuckling, Matt responded. "They aren't dead, just taking a quick nap. They will be fine in about three hours."

Matt picked her up like she was nothing. He cradled her to his chest and walked down the steps calmly in the pitch black. Finally, they reached parking garage. He walked over to a small luxury car parked near the stairs. He opened the back door and pushed her in telling her to stay down. Matt walked around to the driver's seat and started the car. He didn't turn on the headlights. They exited the garage and turned on the street. He finally spoke to her. "You can sit up now."

"Where are we going?"

"To a safe house for the night."

Fallon sat back in the car. Tears of sadness rolled down her face. She was really leaving Jack. Matt didn't acknowledge her crying. They drove for an hour before pulling onto an unpaved driveway. They drove for a couple of miles on the unpaved driveway before stopping in front of an old house. The lights were on.

"Where are we?"

"We're off the grid now. You're safe here."

Matt came around and opened the door for her. She got out of the car and followed him into the house. She closed the door behind her. Eva stepped into the room. "Fallon."

Fallon looked at Eva and started sobbing. She ran into Eva's arms. Eva held her tight. "I'm sorry Fallon. It's okay now. We're going to keep you safe." Eva kept repeating herself until Fallon stopped crying.

Matt had left the room. Fallon dried her tears. "Who is he?" She was talking about Matt.

Eva looked at her. "He is the best in the business. Ex-Navy Seal, he has done about every dangerous mission you can imagine. He is the best money can buy."

Fallon looked confused, "Buy?"

"He's in business for himself."

"He's a mercenary?"

Eva shrugged her shoulders, "You could say that."

Fallon stroked her head. She had a headache coming on. "What now?"

Eva looked at Fallon. "We have a major leak in our security team. Someone is feeding information out about you to the enemy. We don't know who it is. Until we can patch the hole, Matt is taking you away."

"Away to where?"

Eva responded, "I don't know, it's part of the deal. He needs to control the situation. You will be safe."

Fallon remembered Falk. "Do you know about my brother?"

Eva nodded yes. "Tell me what you know."

Fallon spent the next two hours giving Eva all of the details. Matt listened in on the conversation. When they finished, he spoke up. "We need to get some rest, the next few days may be tough."

Eva led Fallon to a bedroom with twin beds. They got in bed and tried to sleep. Fallon asked Eva, "When will I see you again?"

Eva answered, "When it's safe. Don't try to contact me. You need to be safe. If what you say is true about Falk, this is worse than I thought. Stay hidden."

"Eva, I need a favor."

"What is it?"

"Call Johnny Hearts and tell him to protect Jack. He is not safe from Falk. Give me your word."

Eva responded, "I will try."

"Don't try Eva, give me your word. Call Johnny Hearts tomorrow morning. Jack shouldn't have to suffer because of me. I can't leave if he's in danger."

"I will call."

"Love you, Eva bear."

"Love you Fallon, you little phoenix. I had the FBI gave you the code name Phoenix to you because you are strong. You will survive this." Eva gave her a wink of encouragement.

After some time, Fallon was finally able to sleep.

Eva got up after she knew that Fallon was asleep. She stared at her sister for some time. She felt bad for her because she had lost everything again.

Eva left the room and closed the door. Matt was sitting on the couch. He looked at Eva. "Got what you needed?"

"Yes"

"Take care of her for me."

"You know the drill. No contact."

"I understand." Eva's voice broke.

Matt nodded at her. "She will be safe with me."

Eva nodded. Matt handed her the keys to the car. "Goodbye then."

Matt responded, "Take care."

Eva left the house. Tears ran down her face as she climbed into the car. She knew that this was for the best. It just hurt to say goodbye another time.

Matt slept for a couple of hours. Waking fully alert he walked into the room and found himself staring at Fallon for a moment. She was so young and beautiful. It was hard to comprehend how someone could not take care of her. He had wanted to punch out her husband last night in the bar. She looked so lost and alone there and so desperate to escape. He didn't blame her. He would have wanted out too.

Matt had to get his head on straight. She was the sister of the man who was actively trying to destroy the world. She seemed so innocent. He wondered if that evil existed inside of her also.

Matt shook her awake. He told her to get a shower and be ready to leave in thirty minutes as they had a long day ahead of them. In a daze, Fallon got up and got ready. She was just going through the motions because she felt dead inside.

She left the room. Matt was sitting on the couch waiting for her. He handed her an envelope. "You need to memorize the contents." Fallon opened it and a simple gold band fell out.

Matt got up and picked it off the floor. He took her hand and slipped it on her fourth finger on her left hand. "Congratulations, we're married."

Fallon looked at the ring with horror. She started to speak but he silenced her. "It's easier this way. I'm taking you to the only place where I can keep you really safe. I'm taking you home to my family."

"Where?"

"You'll see. Read the information. We need to go." Matt led her out to the garage. He opened the garage door. Inside was another luxury vehicle. This time it was an SUV. He opened the door for Fallon and she climbed in. He walked around and checked the house to ensure that it was locked. He then climbed in and looked at Fallon. "Ready?"

A tear slid down her face. "I'm ready." Matt reached over and took her hand and said, "It's okay. You are doing the right thing for everyone involved." It was the first time he had shown her any kindness. Matt backed the car out of the garage and started down the lane.

Fallon looked at Matt, "May I know where we are headed today?"

"Florida, we are headed to Jacksonville, Florida."

Chapter 31

Back in Cambridge, the brightness of the sun, combined with the constant ringing of the phone, woke Jack up from a deep sleep. His head was swimming. It took him a second to realize he was not home. He looked over to find his old girlfriend Bonnie asleep on the bed beside him.

Jack had a moment of panic as he looked at Bonnie. She was completely dressed, so was he. He looked for his phone to shut it off as his head was throbbing. It was probably Fallon looking for him. He felt all around the bed but finally found his phone on the floor. He picked it up. It was his dad calling so he hit the end button. He didn't need a lecture from him. It ticked him off Fallon had called his dad to tell on him. He would deal with that later with her.

Jack looked at his missed calls and saw there were 20 missed calls. Jack started to worry. His dad called again. Jack answered. "Hello?"

"Where are you?"

"I'm at home."

"Stop lying, I'm at your house. Where is Fallon?"

Jack sat up straight. "She's not there?"

"No." Johnny answered. "I received a cryptic call from Eva early this morning. She told me to protect you, that you are in danger."

Jack gave his dad the address. He hung up the call and nudged Bonnie awake. "What happened last night?"

Bonnie gave him a seductive smile. "We had fun."

Jack looked at her. He could see her ugly showing through. "What happened with Fallon?"

"She left. You stayed and partied."

Jack jumped out of bed and tried to call her phone. It was disconnected. A voice on the phone stated that it was no longer in service. Jack threw his phone across the room. Bonnie watched him pitch a temper tantrum. A knock on the door sounded. Jack answered assuming it was his dad.

Jack threw open the door. Instead it being his dad, he was met with a gun in his face. Five commandoes dressed in black had the door surrounded. Jack put up his hands and they directed him back into the apartment. One went in the bedroom and dragged Bonnie by the hair into the living room. She was screaming. Jack tried to talk to her to calm her down. She wouldn't listen. One of the men finally hit her on the head with his gun and she went limp.

The door opened and in walked more soldiers all dressed in black. They had his father. His father had his hands over his head in the surrender pose.

"What do you want?" Jack asked in a calm voice.

They didn't answer.

Jack asked again. This time he yelled.

Falk walked into the room. "What do I want? What I want is my sister. Where is she?"

Jack looked at him, "Your sister?"

Falk laughed out loud. "What a good girl she is. Of course, I did tell her I would kill you if she talked. I'm glad she is trustworthy. Now, where is she?"

"I don't know." Jack answered.

Falk made a clucking sound with his mouth. "A real husband would know where his wife is at all times. He wouldn't be in the bed of another woman."

Falk walked over and looked at Bonnie. "This woman is trash. You should have seen Fallon watching you two last night. It was disgusting. So, my question again? Where is she?"

Jack tried to change the subject. "Who are you?"

Falk laughed a diabolic laugh. "I'm the Fourth Reich. The great German leader to carry on the work of the Third Reich. When we find Fallon, I will explain my plan better. But for now, I need my twin with me as she is important to my cause. My little sister Fallon is a Phoenix Rising out of the ashes of despair. When she learns of her power to lead, she will rise to greatness and we will be unstoppable, like our father."

Jack looked at Johnny. Johnny shrugged his shoulders and responded. "We don't know. I was on my way here to get Jack to find her."

"Well this isn't good." Falk started rubbing his chin. "So, she's missing while you are in the bed of this whore? You would dare disrespect the daughter of a German pure blood? The daughter of the greatest man to ever walk this earth?"

Jack looked down. He didn't know what to say.

Falk walked over to one of the soldiers. He motioned. The soldier handed over a military grade black handgun.

Falk started talking. "I think someone here needs to pay up for this sin against Fallon. So, which one of you is dying?"

Johnny immediately stepped forward. "Me."

Jack started to struggle. "No dad, no. Me! This is my responsibility, not his."

Falk laughed an evil laugh. "Such honor between the two of you. How very touching. It's a shame that you don't show the same respect to my sister."

Falk walked over and put the gun to Johnny's head. "Any last words?"

Johnny spoke strong and clear "I love you son, take care of her."

Jack cried out. "Me, shoot me, not him."

Falk lowered his gun. He walked over to Jack. "You are lucky, even though you treated her like trash, she made me promise I wouldn't hurt either of you. She loves you."

Before Jack could react, Falk turned and shot Bonnie in the head. Blood and brain matter splattered all over the walls.

Jack and Johnny stood still. Falk walked back over to Jack. "I'll give you some time to find her. Now leave and get started. As you can see, I'm not patient."

Jack was rooted to his spot. He couldn't stop staring at Bonnie. The blood and gore was everywhere. Johnny pulled on his arm to snap Jack out of his trance. He wasn't sad about Bonnie. He was worried about Fallon. Jack followed his dad out of the apartment where they found their security downstairs. They were all tied up and gagged. Johnny freed them and then they got in the car and headed straight to the airport.

The sleek jet sat on the tarmac. Jack boarded the plane in a state of panic over Fallon. He took his seat feeling sick and worried. This was bad. He stared out the window feeling hopeless and lost. Fallon needed to be found so he could protect her. She had brought uninvited trouble into his life, but now he couldn't live without her. Falk was right, Fallon was a Phoenix Rising from the ashes.

Falk had to be stopped and Fallon was probably the only one who could take him down. The whole world needed her, but Jack needed her more. Nothing was going to stop him from finding his wife. The impact of his treachery was more than he could bear. What had he done? His wife, the Phoenix Rising, was now a Phoenix Falling — and it was all his fault.

Will Jack find Fallon while there is still time? The story continues...

Fourth Reich: Phoenix Falling

Coming Soon

Sara LeMay

Fourth Reich: Phoenix Falling

Fallon

Staring out the window at the passing brown and green landscape, Fallon's heart broke. Jack was in Massachusetts and she was with a stranger, trying to escape her destiny. The day was grueling as they pushed south down the coast on I-95. They barely stopped for food and bathroom breaks. The SUV was becoming more uncomfortable as the day grew longer. Her legs ached from sitting in the same position for too long. There was not relief to be found. Each mile took her away from her home and vaulted her on a lonely path of heartache. It felt as if this vehicle had become her cage. Her own prison where she held the key but couldn't free herself.

Matt was a tyrant. He pushed them both to the brink of exhaustion. Fallon tried to sleep most of the day with no luck. She was miserable, both mentally and physically. There had been limited conversation due to Matt being visibly irritated with her. He scowled when she spoke and would frown at her, making Fallon feel small and stupid. As more miles were put between her and Jack, she felt herself falling into a state of depression. Hot and salty tears streamed down her face. She had lost everyone again, this time by choice.

Fallon reflected over the past couple of days, specifically marrying Jack. Even though she was hurting, she knew she had to leave him. He wasn't ready for marriage and her presence put him in danger. In their private world, they were happy. In the outside world, she was a hindrance to him. Jack would always be Falk's target and leverage over her. She loved Jack enough to let him be free. She didn't want to stand in his way, so she made the only sensible choice and left. Maybe with her gone, he would be safe.

Looking up, Fallon finally saw signs for Florida. Relief filled her. She had to get out of the SUV before she lost her mind. Matt promised they would stop when they got to Florida. Fallon looked out the window again. All she could see was dense greenery and a few scattered palm trees. Stealing a quick look at Matt, she couldn't decide if she liked him or not. He was quiet and he seemed annoyed by her emotional outbursts and her talking. As Fallon cried throughout the day, he would glance over at her and give her a scowl.

"How far till we stop?" Fallon asked.

"We are close to Jacksonville. I have a friend there expecting us. We will be safe there till we can make our plans."

Fallon stared out the window and asked, "Will I be able to talk to Eva tonight?"

Matt let out a long breath. "You have to know you are cut off from her. We can't risk them tracking a phone call. I'm sure she is monitored."

Fallon grunted at him. She knew he was right, but didn't want to give up hope she could talk to her sister again. She questioned herself so many times over the past few hours. *Was she making the right choice? Would this keep Eva and Jack safe?* In her heart, her greatest fear was Jack would be relieved she was out of his life.

Finally, they crossed over the line into Florida. A brightly lit sign welcomed them to Florida. Matt sarcastically said, "Welcome to the Sunshine State. Land of the mosquitos, the big movie mouse, and gators. Everything you could ever want is here."

Looking away from him, she stared out the window and mumbled, "I doubt what I want is here." Fallon yearned to be free from the misery caused by her genetic imprint. In this green, dense land all she felt was anger, resentment, and fear. Her situation was the same as the wildlife in Florida. She was prey just waiting to be attacked. Falk had made her his mark and clipped her wings. Instead of being a Phoenix Rising, Fallon was now a Phoenix Falling.

ABOUT THE AUTHOR

Sara LeMay is the pen name for the original Mad Tiger, Rachael Wilson. A self-proclaimed bibliophile, it wouldn't be unusual to find her in a bookstore with an arm full of romance novels. In her spare time, she is a lover of all things NASA and has a small problem with her love of college football. Her real job is teaching, but hopes one day to be a professional storm chaser. After all, she is the Mad Tiger and should live up to her name.

Please follow the Mad Tiger at www.madtigerink.com.

A Mad Tiger Ink Publication